MID-CONTINENT PUBLIC LIBRARY
15616 E. 24 HWY
INDEPENDENCE, MO 64050

3 0 0 0 4 0 0 6 4 5 1 6 4 1

D0827127

When he reached for her hand, she gave it to him without thinking. He pressed a kiss upon her fingers and let her go. A friendly gesture, she told herself. Nothing more.

"Good night, M...

"Mr. Shaw...

Oh, how sh... ...ing protested a... ...and her spine tingle... ...ge that he was watching her. He would not object, she was sure, if she remained to drink another glass of wine with him, but then what? There was only one way the evening would end if she showed such a preference for his company. And though her body might cry out for relief from the longing that disturbed her nights, Gabriel Shaw was too charming, too attractive, and she feared she might grow too attached to him. She would not risk her heart for a moment's pleasure.

She walked out, closing the door quietly behind her, and kept walking until she had reached the safety of her bedchamber, where she resolutely turned the key in the lock.

WITHDRAWN
FROM THE RECORDS OF THE
MID-CONTINENT PUBLIC LIBRARY

Author Note

The heroine of this novel may be familiar to you—she first appeared in *The Ton's Most Notorious Rake* as the bighearted cook at Prospect House and she masquerades as a rich widow in *Beauty and the Brooding Lord*. I thought she deserved her own story, and here it is.

Nancy's talent for cooking is quite important in this love story (and don't they say food is one way to a man's heart?). This meant a fascinating troll through recipe books of the period, which made for fascinating reading.

Some of the cooks among you might want to try an eighteenth-century recipe. Nancy makes very good Bath cakes, but that requires a spoonful of "barm" (the soupy yeast mixture skimmed from the top of a fresh batch of ale) and I doubt many of you have that to hand! Instead, here is Nancy's recipe for Shrewsbury cakes. Warning: the measurements are in pounds and ounces, the instructions sparse and the cooking times nonexistent, so try this at your own risk!

Nancy's Shrewsbury Cakes:

Take half a pound of butter, beat to a cream. Add half a pound of flour, one egg and six ounces of sifted sugar, plus half an ounce of caraway seed.

On a floured board, roll pastry out thinly and cut out with biscuit cutters. Lay the biscuits on a lightly greased baking sheet, prick with a fork and bake in a low oven until cooked.

Bon appétit!

SARAH MALLORY

—

The Highborn Housekeeper

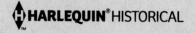

If you purchased this book without a cover you should be aware that this book is stolen property. It was reported as "unsold and destroyed" to the publisher, and neither the author nor the publisher has received any payment for this "stripped book."

Recycling programs
for this product may
not exist in your area.

ISBN-13: 978-1-335-63523-5

The Highborn Housekeeper

Copyright © 2019 by Sarah Mallory

All rights reserved. Except for use in any review, the reproduction or utilization of this work in whole or in part in any form by any electronic, mechanical or other means, now known or hereafter invented, including xerography, photocopying and recording, or in any information storage or retrieval system, is forbidden without the written permission of the publisher, Harlequin Enterprises Limited, 22 Adelaide St. West, 40th Floor, Toronto, Ontario M5H 4E3, Canada.

This is a work of fiction. Names, characters, places and incidents are either the product of the author's imagination or are used fictitiously, and any resemblance to actual persons, living or dead, business establishments, events or locales is entirely coincidental.

This edition published by arrangement with Harlequin Books S.A.

For questions and comments about the quality of this book, please contact us at CustomerService@Harlequin.com.

® and TM are trademarks of Harlequin Enterprises Limited or its corporate affiliates. Trademarks indicated with ® are registered in the United States Patent and Trademark Office, the Canadian Intellectual Property Office and in other countries.

Printed in U.S.A.

Sarah Mallory was born in the West Country, UK, but now lives on the beautiful Yorkshire moors. She has been writing for more than three decades, mainly historicals set in the Georgian and Regency period. She has won several awards for her writing, most recently the Romantic Novelists' Association RoNA Rose Award in 2012 (*The Dangerous Lord Darrington*) and 2013 (*Beneath the Major's Scars*).

Books by Sarah Mallory

Harlequin Historical

The Scarlet Gown
Never Trust a Rebel
The Duke's Secret Heir
Pursued for the Viscount's Vengeance

Saved from Disgrace

The Ton's Most Notorious Rake
Beauty and the Brooding Lord
The Highborn Housekeeper

The Infamous Arrandales

The Chaperon's Seduction
Temptation of a Governess
Return of the Runaway
The Outcast's Redemption

Brides of Waterloo

A Lady for Lord Randall

Visit the Author Profile page
at Harlequin.com for more titles.

To my four-legged companion, Willow, who keeps me company when I write and keeps me fit with regular walks!

Chapter One

The snow started at dusk. Only a few flakes at first, but soon it was falling steadily and coating the icy ground.

Nancy was warm enough, dressed in her riding habit of plum-coloured velvet with its matching curly-brimmed hat and wrapped in a voluminous cloak. Her companion, too, looked snug in a heavy wool redin-gote and shawl and they both had their feet resting on warm bricks and snuggled into sheepskin, but she felt some sympathy for the servants sitting up on the box.

However, when they stopped to change horses at the Crown in Tuxford and her driver suggested that she might put up there for the night, she was adamant that they should continue. William, who had come to the chaise door to issue his advice, pushed back his hat and stared at her, perplexed. His breath formed small icy clouds as he spoke with all the confidence of an old and trusted retainer.

'I don't like it, madam, and that's a fact. The snow don't show no signs of easing. We should stop here.'

'It is but very fine snow,' she responded. 'There is nothing much to accumulate and no wind to cause any drifting, so we shall go on.' She noted his frown and conceded one point. 'You may order yourselves something hot to drink, if you wish, and have them bring coffee out for Mrs Yelland and me. And perhaps you will ask them to provide fresh hot bricks for our feet.'

'You won't step inside, ma'am, just for a few minutes?' The woman sitting beside her spoke for the first time. 'We might warm ourselves by a fire.'

'No, Hester, we will push on.' Nancy shook her head. It was not only the memories this place conjured for her, she dared not risk being recognised.

Her companion read the determination in Nancy's face and sighed as she settled herself back into her corner. 'Very well, ma'am, you know best.'

Nancy heard the disappointment in Hester Yelland's voice, but would not change her mind. She was unusually tall for a woman and that would attract attention. Someone might recognise her. After all, *she* had immediately known the landlord as he stood in the doorway, hands on his hips, watching the travelling chaise as it came into the yard. He had been assessing whether it was worth his while to step out into the cold and she was relieved that his experienced eye noted that it was a rather shabby vehicle. Instead he had sent a servant out to speak to William Coachman, who was calling to the ostlers for fresh horses and be quick about it.

The landlord had barely changed in the twelve years since she had last seen him, save to grow a little rounder, and while Nancy felt very different *inside*, outwardly she knew that with her height and abundance of dark hair she looked much the same as she had done all those years ago, when she had slipped away on the common stage with nothing but a hastily packed portmanteau and the little money she had managed to save. Looking back, it was a wonder she had survived the past dozen years relatively unscathed. But she *had* survived and with very few regrets.

Within minutes they were travelling again. The snow had ceased, at least for the moment, and the waning crescent moon shone down intermittently between ragged clouds. However, it was noticeably colder. Nancy pulled her cloak more tightly about her and tried to sleep, but it was impossible in the lurching carriage. Very soon she became aware that they were slowing again and sat up. When they came to a complete stop she let down the window.

'What is it?' she called. 'What has occurred?'

The coachman had jumped down and was now standing beside the team.

'One of the wheelers has cast a shoe, ma'am,' he called to her, beating his hands together to warm them. 'We'll have to go back now—'

'No.' Nancy looked out at the moonlit landscape. 'No, it makes more sense to go forward rather than back. Let us push on to the Black Bull.'

'But we have come barely two miles from Tuxford—'

'Then we are closer to the Bull,' Nancy told him. 'It has a smithy next door.' *Or at least there used to be.* 'Come, now, let us press on.'

They continued at a much-reduced pace and Nancy

breathed a sigh of relief when at last they reached the cluster of cottages that comprised the village of Little Markham. The Black Bull was a much smaller hostelry than the Crown at Tuxford and it was patronised mainly by local gentry and farmers. Nancy had passed this way frequently in her youth, but she had never stopped here before. Nevertheless, she kept her hood up, shadowing her face as the landlord escorted her and her companion into a small private parlour.

'Thank heaven they have a good fire,' muttered Hester, moving to the hearth. 'I hope to goodness the smith won't be too long about his business.'

'I hope so, too,' Nancy responded, drawing off her gloves. 'But it is not so very bad. We shall take up the landlady's offer of dinner and we can then travel through the night and make up the time. There is some moonlight, after all.'

The older woman turned to look at Nancy. 'You wouldn't stop at Tuxford and now you are very anxious to move on. Why would that be, madam? Do you know this area?'

'I know it very well. I grew up near here.'

Nancy was grateful that she did not press her to say more, but she was not surprised, for they understood one another. Hester Yelland was a widow whom Nancy had hired to be her companion while she was in London. They had become firm friends and when Nancy had invited her to travel north with her, Hester had jumped at the chance.

'After all,' she had said, giving one of her rare smiles, 'there's no one here to care whether I go or stay.'

Now she merely shrugged, accepting Nancy's reticence and saying gruffly, 'Very well, you make yourself comfortable, madam, and I'll go and chivvy the landlady to bring us our dinner as soon as possible!'

When they had finished their meal, the two women moved to the chairs by the fire. Hester was soon dozing, but Nancy was far too restless. She was impatient to be gone, but the coachman had not long returned from the smithy and would not yet have started his dinner. She knew she could insist that they set off immediately—after all, the men were being paid handsomely for their services—but she would not. She knew only too well what it was like to be at the beck and call of a selfish and demanding employer.

She went over to the window and looked out. The sky had cleared and the snow-blanketed fields gleamed bluish-silver in the pale moonlight. An icy frost glittered on the roof tiles of the buildings and all at once Nancy felt stifled by the little parlour. She glanced at Hester, who was snoring gently, then she quietly left the room, picking up her cloak and swinging it about her shoulders as she went.

The night air was so clear and cold it caught in her throat. Nancy paused for a moment, deciding which way to go. The majority of the cottages hugged the roadside to the south of the inn, but to the north the road wound its way through an expanse of heath, the open vista broken only by a small copse in the distance. Nancy put up her hood and set off northwards, striding out purposefully, glad to be active after so many hours cooped up in the carriage. It was very still and nothing was moving—soon even the sounds of the inn were left behind. Fleetingly, Nancy wished she had remembered her gloves, but to go back now might disturb Hester and she was loath to do that, for her companion was clearly exhausted by the journey. She might also try to dissuade Nancy from walking out alone at night, although there was nothing to fear: she had a clear view across the snowy heath and nothing was stirring. There was no sound save the crunch of her boots on the thin layer of snow that covered the iron-hard ground.

She glanced at the eastern horizon, where black clouds were massing, threatening more snow. That might well delay even further her return to Compton Parva and all her friends at Prospect House. She had been away for several months and wondered how they had managed without her to fuss and cosset them. Almost immediately she scolded herself for such conceit. No one was indispensable and she had no doubt they had coped exceedingly well. She hoped they had missed her, then was shocked to realise how little she had missed *them* while she had been in town.

Her only excuse was that she had been very busy and it had not been a trip of pleasure. Nancy had gone to London, masquerading as the rich widow of a tradesman, to help a good friend, but she could not deny she had enjoyed herself, wearing fine clothes and shopping in Bond Street, visiting the theatre, attending parties. Dancing. Flirting. It had all been pretence, of course. A charade, necessary for the character she was playing, but it had given her a glimpse of what her life might have been, if she had not cut herself off from the polite world. She might even be happily married by now. Perhaps with children.

Nancy gave herself a little shake. She had made her choice and it was too late to change now. And she did not regret her decision to remain single and independent. Not at all. Yet the little worm of doubt gnawed away at her, the vague feeling of dissatisfaction, as if something was missing from her life. Not something, she realised now. Someone.

'Bah. You are becoming sentimental,' she scolded herself, her breath misting in the cold air. 'Just because you are passing so close to your old home. That is all in the past now, you have a good life with your friends at Prospect House. And you are not totally bereft of family.'

She had her sister, Lady Aspern, but they only ever communicated by letter, and in secret. Mary's husband disapproved of undutiful daughters who disobeyed their fathers and ran away. Thinking of Aspern, Nancy's lip curled. He was just the sort of gentleman she most despised. She would much rather keep her independence than be wed to such a man.

But the feeling of discontent still gnawed at her and she was forced to admit that she was not as keen to return to her old life as she had thought she would be. The future stretched ahead of her, safe, predictable. Dull.

She was so lost in her own thoughts that it was something of a shock to find herself beside the little wood, the thin, straight trunks and bare branches forming a black latticework against the night sky. Heavens, had she walked so far? She was about to turn back when something in the copse caught her eye. There was no more than a dusting of snow on the ground between the trees and a faint shaft of moonlight sliced between the straight trunks and rested on a more solid block of white, something that almost gleamed in the shadowy copse. Curiosity got the better of Nancy. She stepped into the little wood. Leaves crunched beneath her feet as she moved closer. Then, when she was almost upon it, she realised it was a man's shirt of fine linen. And the owner was still wearing it.

Her heart began to pound heavily. The man was lying face down on the ground and dressed only in his shirt, breeches and top boots. She dropped to her knees beside him and put her fingers against his neck. The skin was cold, but she could feel a faint pulse. Nancy became aware of the smell of spirits and spotted an empty bottle on the ground nearby. Her lip curled. A drunkard, then, who had wandered out half-dressed. Even so, he was someone's son. He might be a husband and father. She could not bring herself to leave him here to perish. She shook him roughly by the shoulder.

'Come along, man, you must get up. If you stay here, you will be dead of cold by the morning.'

There was no response. She took hold of him and tried to turn him over. Nancy was not a small woman and she considered herself no weakling, but he was a tall man and heavy. It took her a great deal of effort to turn him on to his back. His damp shirt front was covered with twigs and leaf mould. Her eyes moved to his face. She expected to see a haggard countenance, blotched and ravaged by drink, but even in the near dark of the trees she could see he was a handsome man, despite an ugly bruise on his cheek. He was clean-shaven, his dark hair tousled and falling over his brow. Absently she put out a hand to smooth it back and felt the warm stickiness of blood on her fingers. Her first thought was that he had been attacked and she snatched her hand away in alarm. She glanced fearfully around her. There was no movement, no sound. She breathed slowly, trying to settle her jangled nerves. She was surely being fanciful, for who would be abroad on a night like this? It was most likely the man had cut his head when he had fallen in a drunken stupor.

'And serves him right,' she muttered, wiping her fingers on her handkerchief. 'Wake up!' She slapped his cheeks. 'Wake up, damn you, or I will leave you here to die.'

A response, at last. No more than a faint groan, but Nancy exhaled with relief. She patted his face again and this time he grimaced and moved his head.

'Confound it, woman, stop hitting me!'

His voice was deep, no trace of a local accent. He was most likely a gentleman, then, and educated, thought Nancy. Someone who should know better than to indulge in a drunken spree. The fact did nothing for her temper.

'I am trying to save your life, you idiot.' She tugged insistently at his shoulder and helped him as he struggled to sit up. 'You may be damnably drunk, but you cannot stay out much longer in this icy cold.'

'I am not *damnably drunk*,' he growled. 'I am not drunk at all.'

'No, of course not.' She sat back on her heels. 'Only a sober man would go abroad without his coat.' He was shivering and she untied the strings of her cloak. 'Here.' He did not object as she wrapped the thick woollen mantle about him. 'Now, can you stand?'

He breathed out, clutching his ribs as he did so.

'Madam, I do not know where you have come from, but I think you should go. Now.'

Nancy gasped. 'Well, of all the ungrateful—'

He interrupted her. 'Being anywhere near me puts you in danger. Someone intended to kill me tonight.'

Chapter Two

Nancy stared at the man.

'If you are not drunk, you are clearly mad.'

'I am neither, you hen-witted woman.' He put a tentative hand to his head. 'I was attacked as I left a tavern in Darlton—'

'Darlton! But that is nearly five miles away.'

'What?' He winced as the exclamation shook him and moved his head stiffly to look about him. 'Then where is this?'

'We are just north of Little Markham.'

'The devil we are.' He flinched again. 'I have no idea how many men attacked me, but my body feels as if it was used as a punch bag. If they took my coat and waistcoat, they clearly intended the cold to finish me off. This wood is too small to attract poachers and they would not expect anyone else to be abroad on so cold a night.' It was as if he was talking to himself and had forgotten her presence, until he glanced up and added, 'They certainly would not expect an eccentric female to be taking a night-time stroll.'

Nancy curbed her temper with an effort.

'This is doing no good at all,' she told him. 'Let us argue the point by all means, but not here. We are less than half a mile from the Black Bull. Let me take you there.'

He struggled to his feet, using the nearest tree for support.

'My good woman, I would never make it half that distance.' He leaned against the trunk, breathing with difficulty as his eyes ran over her. 'You may be a Long Meg, but I do not think you could carry me all the way.'

'Very well, I will return to the inn and get help.'

'No! That's too dangerous.' He added ominously, 'For both of us.'

'Then what am I do to with you?' she cried, exasperated.

'Why, nothing. I am grateful for your help, but the best thing now is for you to go away.' He clung to the tree trunk, his face twisting with pain. 'If you will allow me to keep your cloak, I think I shall survive the cold and hopefully in a while I shall be sufficiently recovered to make my way back to Darlton.'

Of all the pig-headed, stubborn— Nancy sought for words to express her frustration and echoed his earlier exclamation.

'The devil you will!' He did not even blink at her unladylike response, but his brows lifted, as if he was surprised anyone should contradict him. She said, through gritted teeth, 'You had already admitted you could not reach the Black Bull. You would collapse before you covered half the distance to Darlton. I shall take you.'

'No. I have told you, it is too dangerous.'

She continued as if he had not spoken.

'My carriage is at the inn, ready to travel. You will wait here for me and I shall take you up and carry you to your house.' He frowned at her, as if he wanted to refuse. A sudden icy breeze stirred the empty branches and she said bluntly, 'You will not last for long out of doors in this weather so you had best accept my help. There really is no other way.'

He scowled at her. 'As long as you tell no one.'

'If that is what you wish,' she replied, with a touch of impatience. 'You are clearly raving and it behoves me to humour you. Once we have deposited you at your abode we will be on our way. My servants are my own and they are engaged to carry me all the way to York-shire, so no one here need be any the wiser.'

'By God, you are a stubborn woman.'

'But a practical one,' she retorted. 'Now, let me go and fetch my carriage before I, too, become chilled to the bone!'

She turned to walk away, but he called to her to wait. She glanced back, brows raised.

'To whom am I indebted for this signal service?'

'I do not think it necessary for you to know that, since our acquaintance will not be of long duration.'

'But I should like to know.' His teeth gleamed in the light. 'My name is Gabriel Shaw, if that helps.'

The smile and coaxing note in his voice caught her unawares.

'I am Nancy.' Heavens, she was behaving like a giddy girl, responding to a charming flirt! She pulled herself together and added coldly, 'Mrs Hopwood, that is.'

Nancy flew back to the inn, spurred on as much by a sudden excitement as the icy cold. Within minutes of her arrival she had ordered her chaise to be brought to the door and she bundled Hester into it, refusing to answer any questions until they were on their way.

'Now what mischief are you up to?' Hester demanded as she settled herself more comfortably into one corner. 'And for heaven's sake put up the glass!'

Nancy ignored her. It was snowing again, big, fat flakes that settled on everything. One or two drifted in through the open window, but she refused to close it, peering out into the gloom. As they approached the little wood she leaned out and shouted to William to stop. Even as the carriage slowed to a halt she opened the door and jumped down, ignoring her companion's horrified grasp.

'Mercy me, whatever are you about? Miss Nancy. *Madam!*'

'Peace, Hester, I will explain everything in a moment.'

With a word to the servants on the box, Nancy stared into the copse. At first it was nothing but black trunks and shadows and for one frightening moment she doubted herself. Perhaps she had dreamt the whole thing. Worse, perhaps the man had wandered off and collapsed somewhere. Then she saw a movement among the trees, a cloaked figure coming slowly out of the wood.

'There you are!' She ran up to him. 'You are limping. I had not thought—are you badly hurt? Here, let me help you.'

She pulled his arm around her shoulders. Only then did she realise how tall he must be, because she did not have to stoop to support him.

He leaned heavily against her.

'Bruised,' he muttered, 'nothing broken.'

'Tell me where we are to take you.' She walked with him slowly towards the chaise while the snowflakes, big as goose down, settled on them.

'Dell House.' He winced again, and she realised that every step was painful for him. 'A few miles this side of Darlton.'

'On the Lincoln Road. I know it.'

They had reached the carriage and she called to Hester to help her get him inside, then she gave hurried directions to her coachman. The men on the box were clearly bursting with curiosity, but Nancy's tone told them she would brook no objection and they both accepted her instructions with no more than a nod.

It was more difficult to pacify Hester, who had moved to the corner furthest away from the stranger and was staring at him, horrified.

'Nancy, Nancy, what are you about? You have taken up a drunken stranger. He may be a dangerous villain for all we know.' She gave a little cry as the carriage lurched forward. 'Heaven preserve us, have you run quite mad?'

'Not in the least,' replied Nancy, sitting beside Gabriel and holding him steady. Snowflakes still clung to her jacket and to the cloak wrapped about him. She brushed them off with her free hand before they could melt into the wool. 'I am merely being a Good Samaritan. We are going to deliver this poor man to his home.' He was shivering and she added urgently, 'Pray, put your hot brick beneath his feet, Hester, and give me your shawl. I shall wrap the other brick for him to hold against his body.'

Hester did as Nancy bade her, muttering all the time. 'I don't say I understand any of this. Do you *know* this man?'

'Not in the least, but he assures me he is not intoxicated. He told me he had been waylaid.' A laugh escaped her. 'Heavens, what an adventure!'

Hester's snort spoke volumes, but Nancy was more concerned with Gabriel, who had lapsed into unconsciousness. She eased him down until he was lying along the seat, his long legs trailing to the floor. The wound on his skull was no longer bleeding and when she placed her fingers on his neck she thought his pulse was stronger, but perhaps she only wanted that to be so.

'I have done as much as I can for him,' she muttered, sinking to her knees on the carriage floor and resting one hand lightly on his coat, reassured by the rise and fall of his chest.

As they rumbled on she remained at his side, holding him securely on the seat. A rueful smile pulled at her mouth. An adventure indeed, to take up a strange man and drive him to safety. Dell House was only a few miles from her old home. The place she had avoided for more than a decade.

The heady excitement within her faded. Nancy glanced out of the window. The snow was falling steadily and thankfully there was little wind to cause drifting, but she knew that could change in a twinkling. She had been foolish in the extreme to leave the main road, to put herself out for a stranger. She remembered their brief conversation, the sudden, glinting smile that had melted her anger. She had not realised it at the time, but that smile had set her pulse racing. Charm, she thought now. The man had an abundance of charm.

She glanced at his unconscious figure. He was bruised, battered and now dangerously chilled. He would need diligent nursing and nourishing food to return him to health. She could do that. It was her strength, it was what she enjoyed, looking after damaged creatures.

Nancy pulled herself up with a jolt. What was she thinking? This man was not her concern. She must not allow her sympathies to run away with her. Heavens, had she learned nothing in the last twelve years? She shivered and moved on to the seat beside Hester, who patted her knee.

'You've got too kind a heart, Miss Nancy, that's your trouble. We should have told the landlord to fetch the fellow back to the inn. They could have cared for him there.'

'Perhaps, but he was so adamant I should not tell a soul.' Nancy sighed. 'I confess, I shall be glad to leave him with his own people and we can be on our way.'

* * *

However, when at last they reached Dell House, no servants ran out from the house or the outbuildings to greet them. The sky had cleared and Nancy had a good view of the house in its snowy setting. It was a modest gentleman's residence, sitting four-square in its own grounds, and it was in darkness, save for a glimmer of light from the fanlight above the door. Without waiting for her footman, Robert, to climb down from the box, Nancy alighted and went to the door, where she rapped smartly upon the knocker.

Silence.

Robert joined her, his hat and shoulders white with snow. 'Don't seem to be anyone at home, ma'am.'

'There has to be.' She beat another tattoo upon the door. 'Are we sure this is the right house?'

'Aye, ma'am, Dell House. 'Tis carved on the gateposts, clear as day.'

At that moment there was the sound of bolts being drawn back and Nancy gave a sigh of relief.

'At last.' She schooled her face into a look of cheerfulness, but a sudden loud sneeze from behind the door made her step back in surprise.

A man opened the door, a lamp held aloft in one hand. He cut a very sorry figure, standing before them in his stockinged feet and with a blanket hung loosely about his hunched shoulders. His eyes looked heavy, there was the dark shadow of stubble on his face and his hair was tousled, as if he had just risen from his bed.

'Good evening, I—'

She was interrupted by another loud sneeze. The man buried his face in a large handkerchief.

'I beg your pardon.' His voice was muffled by the cloth over his nose but he was clearly mortified. 'A cold!' he managed to gasp, before being overcome by another explosive sneeze.

'Yes, well, we have an injured man in the carriage,' said Nancy. 'A Mr Gabriel Shaw.'

'By baster!'

'Yes, your master.' Nancy was relieved to have that point confirmed. 'We need to get him into a warm bed as soon as possible. Can you—?' She stopped as the man was seized by a paroxysm of coughing. 'Is there anyone else in the house who can help?'

'Do one,' he managed. 'Only be and I'm weak as a cat.'

Nancy pursed her lips. 'Well, we cannot stand here discussing the matter. If you cannot help, then *we* must see to your master. All you need do is lead the way.' She looked past him into the darkened hall. 'Robert, go with him and light some candles in there, for heaven's sake.'

She turned and marched back to the carriage, where Hester was at the open door.

'What is it, ma'am? Are we at the right place?'

'Oh, yes, but the only servant is suffering from a heavy cold. No use to us at all. We shall have to get Mr Shaw into the house ourselves.'

Hester nodded. 'Between us I am sure we can manage. The sooner he is in his own bed the better.'

They wrapped the cloak more securely around the

man and William and Robert carried him up to what was clearly the main bedchamber. Everything was tidy and Nancy noted that the bed was made, but the fire had gone out and the room was distinctly chilly.

'This will never do,' she declared as the men laid their burden on the bed. 'William, you and Robert must go and find kindling and fuel to light the fire. And if there is a fire in the kitchen, then reheat the bricks and bring them back here. This man needs all the warmth we can give him.' She waved at the servant who had let them into the house. 'Take him with you, he will show you where to find everything and he is of no use at all here.' When the men had withdrawn, she turned to her companion. 'Hester, you must help me get him out of his wet things. Come along now.'

'This is no job for you, madam! You must leave it to me—' Hester protested, scandalised, but Nancy cut her short.

'You will never manage him alone, he is a dead weight.'

She set to work on unbuttoning the filthy shirt. Together they removed his clothing and Nancy used the towel hanging near the washstand to buff some warmth into his cold limbs. He was no weakling, she thought, as she rubbed vigorously at his arms. A smattering of dark hair shadowed his deep chest, tapering downwards until it was hidden by the sheet that Hester had insisted upon pulling up decorously over his lower body.

She tried not to press too hard on the bruises that were beginning to show. No wonder he had struggled to walk. She helped Hester to put him into his nightshirt and covered him with quantities of blankets before she started to clean his face.

She refused Hester's offer to help. The man was her patient, she felt a certain responsibility for him.

'Perhaps you could fetch the lavender water from my dressing case,' she suggested. 'We can sprinkle a little on his pillow. And if you go to the kitchen perhaps you could bring up the hot bricks, too.'

'Very well, I will go now. And if the bricks aren't ready, I might be able to put some hot water into a few wine bottles,' said Hester, moving towards the door.

'Yes, yes. Anything to help warm him.'

Left alone with the man, Nancy set to work with a damp cloth, cleaning the wound on his head. Tenderly she smoothed the dark hair from his brow and wiped away the blood, then set to work removing the dirt from the rest of his face.

He stirred, as if awakened by her touch, and opened his eyes. They were a deep blue, she noted. He began to shift restlessly in the bed.

'Hush now,' she murmured, perching on the side of the bed and placing one hand on his chest. 'You are safe.'

He began to mutter, incomprehensible but clearly agitated. She quickly dried his face, crooning as she might to a fractious child. At last he grew calmer; his gaze steadied and became fixed upon Nancy, but he was looking straight through her. Something knotted inside her, constricting her breath. She dearly wanted him to know she was there.

He had freed one hand from the bedcovers and she caught it in her own.

'Safe,' she repeated, smiling down at him.

He grew still, the eyes remained glazed, but his long fingers wrapped themselves about hers, their grasp surprisingly strong. He lapsed into unconsciousness, but Nancy did not move. Even when Hester returned and placed the hot bricks wrapped in flannel under the covers, she remained curled up beside her patient.

'Come away, Miss Nancy, 'tis not seemly for you to be sitting on a man's bed.'

'Why? He does not know I am here.' She saw Hester was looking anxious and smiled. 'Very well, you may bring over a chair for me. But I must stay close. I think he finds some comfort in holding my hand and it makes me feel as if I am doing something.'

'You have done too much for the fellow already,' muttered Hester.

She said no more, for the men had returned and they set to work on the fire, which was soon blazing merrily in the hearth.

'There,' said Hester, 'I think we can safely leave Mr Shaw with his man now, Miss Nancy, and be on our way. Come along.'

But Nancy did not leave her seat. She dragged her gaze from the unconscious man in the bed to the woebegone figure of the servant, leaning against the wall, coughing and wheezing into his handkerchief.

'Oh, I think not.' She looked up at Hester, a rueful smile in her eyes. 'I really do not see how we can leave these two poor men to fend for themselves, do you?'

* * *

Gabriel was surfacing from some deep, black pit. His eyelids fluttered but he did not open them fully, for the light was painful and the slightest movement of his head made it throb. In fact, as consciousness returned, he was aware that his whole body ached like the devil.

He lay still, not struggling to recall what had happened, but allowing memory to return. Still, icy night, the cold bone-deep. The empty lane to Darlton, black shadows and the sudden rush of his attackers. He had thought it was footpads, but those two assailants proved to be no more than a diversion for whoever came from behind and knocked him unconscious. Then he was on the ground, among the trees and being harangued by a female to get up.

Gingerly he opened his eyes. He was in Dell House, in his own bedchamber. Presumably she had brought him here, as she had promised. Another memory stirred. Someone wiping his forehead with a damp cloth, the soothing smell of lavender. The woman's voice, softer this time, bidding him to be still. Now he did make an effort to remember. He closed his eyes again, concentrating. Yes, he had seen her. She had come towards the bed, into the lamplight. A full, womanly figure, dark-eyed, red-lipped, with an abundance of glossy dark hair. She had leaned over him, her face full of concern. The same woman who had found him in the copse. Or had he dreamt the whole?

He heard the click of the door, soft footsteps and Thoresby appeared beside the bed, carrying a tray. The man was so much more than a servant, Gabriel counted him a loyal friend and he was relieved to see him.

'John.'

'Good morning, sir. I am glad to see you awake at last.'

Gabriel frowned. 'You were laid up in bed. I feared influenza.'

'Thankfully it was nothing worse than a bad cold, sir, and I am much better now.' John Thoresby set down the tray on a table that had been pulled close to the bed. With the smallest movement of his head Gabriel could see it held a bowl of something looking suspiciously like porridge. However, that was not his most pressing concern.

'But you were too ill to get out of your bed.'

'That was five days ago, sir.'

'So long!' He tried to sit up and winced as pain shot through his bruised body.

Thoresby came to help him, gently supporting his shoulders and rearranging the pillows. Gabriel muttered his thanks and leaned back, closing his eyes until the pains in his body settled into no more than a dull ache.

'There is laudanum, sir, if you wish it.'

'No. Just a little water, if you please.'

He insisted on holding the glass himself and managed to take a few sips, even though his hands shook. He was glad to relinquish it when he had finished and he leaned back against the pillows, his eyes closed.

'John, there was a woman.'

'Ah, yes. Mrs Hopwood.'

The name struck a chord.

'She brought me here?'

'Yes, she did. And very relieved I was to see you, even though I could scarce drag myself to the door when she knocked. I knew I shouldn't have let you go out alone.'

'Damn it, John, you were too ill to be of use. Feverish, too. That is why I left you sleeping. But never mind that now. The woman. Did she stay here?'

'Oh, yes, sir, she stayed,' said Thoresby. 'She is still here.'

'What!'

John spread his hands. 'It was impossible to stop her, sir. She marched in and took over. I was coughing and sneezing, trying to collect my wits, and the next minute she and her servants were putting you to bed. And no sooner had she made *you* comfortable than she set about preparing rooms for herself and her maid, while her footman and coachman made themselves at home.' Thoresby paused. 'I have to admit, sir, that I could not have tended you without her and that's a fact. She packed me off to my bed and said she would see to everything. Said a good rest was probably all I needed and after a couple of days I'd be up and about again. And before you say I should've protested, I did. I tried, sir, I promise you. And all she said was I should stay away from you, in case I was infectious. It went against the grain, I can tell you, but truth to tell, I was too weak to be much use for the first couple of days.'

Gabriel recognised the truth of this and held his

peace, but he was far from mollified. He glanced again at the tray.

'I suppose *that* is what she considers a fit breakfast for an invalid.'

For the first time Thoresby would not meet his eyes.

'Yes, sir. Porridge. It's what we've been managing to get down you for the past couple of days. That and a little chicken broth she cooked up.'

Gabriel said drily, 'Mrs Hopwood appears to be a very resourceful woman.'

Thoresby allowed himself a wry grin. 'She's helped us out of a rare scrape, sir, and that's for sure. If she hadn't come across you in that wood, you'd have perished by morning. And she and that companion of hers nursed you for the first three days while I was fit for nothing but sleep!'

'And there've been no unwanted visitors, no one skulking about in the night?'

'No sign that you was followed back here, sir. With the snow it's been easy to see that the only tracks around the place are those made by myself or Mrs Hopwood's servants. We've had that much snow the past few days that the roads are blocked now, so nothing's moving by road.'

'Then we must hope our whereabouts are unknown to my attackers. They may come looking for me, though, if they realise I am alive.' He lay still for a moment, considering, then said, with sudden decision, 'It is too dangerous for anyone else save ourselves to be here. You may tell Mrs Hopwood that her help is no longer required.'

'I can try, sir, but I doubt she'll go until she sees for yourself that you are recovered. Perhaps if you were to eat a few spoonfuls of the porridge…'

Gabriel cursed him roundly. 'Take that stuff away and bring me my usual breakfast. Well, what is the matter now?'

'The ladies have quite taken over the kitchen, sir. They have prepared every meal between them since they arrived. I'm not sure…' Gabriel's furious gaze made him say quickly, 'I will go and see to it immediately, I am sure there will be no difficulty.'

'There had better not be.' Gabriel scowled at him. 'After that you may help me to get up. If you won't tell the damn woman to leave, then I will!

Chapter Three

Nancy was trimming a piece of beef when Thoresby came in with the tray. She glanced at the untouched breakfast dish.

'Is your master still sleeping?'

'No, ma'am, he is very much awake, and insists upon his usual morning meal of eggs and ham.'

He announced this with no little trepidation and such an appearance of one prepared to be executed for being the bearer of bad tidings that Nancy had to bite her lip to stop herself from laughing. She had some sympathy with Mr Thoresby, for she knew she had been something of a tyrant in the past few days, but kitchens and cooking had been her domain for over a decade and she felt at home here. She had taken control, organising the meals and producing food suitable for the injured man, once he had been able to eat a little. Her friends laughingly called her a mother hen, wanting to look after everyone. A sudden warmth spread through her body. Not that she wished Gabriel Shaw to think her *motherly*!

She said now, 'I am glad to hear he is feeling so much better. Would you like to prepare something for him? I am happy to leave this and attend to it, but you will know exactly how he likes his breakfast.'

The man quickly assured her that he was more than happy to prepare his master's breakfast and set about finding eggs and fetching the large ham that was in the larder.

Later, when he had taken a fresh tray to his master and then helped him to dress, he returned and issued an invitation to Nancy.

'My master begs that you will join him for dinner tonight, ma'am. In his room. He deeply regrets that he is not yet well enough to manage the stairs.' Having performed his duty, John Thoresby unbent a little and added, 'To tell you the truth, he is weak as a cat and it's as much as he can do to sit upright in his chair beside the fire. But he hopes you will not object to the informality of dining in his chamber.'

Nancy was not fooled. However politely Mr Thoresby wrapped it up, it was clearly a summons. Not that she was averse to having dinner with Mr Gabriel Shaw. She had a great many questions she wanted to put to him.

Just before dinner, Nancy went upstairs to wash away the heat and grease of the kitchen, leaving Hester and Thoresby to put the final touches to the meal. There was no time to wash her hair, so she brushed it well and bundled it up on her head before turning her attention to what to wear. Her trunks held an array of colourful, expensive dresses, the jewel box was full of ostentatious pieces, all designed to attract attention, but she had no wish to display her charms tonight. Quite the opposite, she thought, remembering Mr Shaw's smile and its effect upon her pulse.

She chose the most sober of the evening gowns, a sheath of deep sapphire-blue silk with a high waist and long sleeves that she thought would be a necessity, because the continuing icy weather seemed to permeate the very fabric of the building. She arranged a muslin fichu in the neck of the gown, partly for warmth and partly for decorum. It would also remove the need for jewels. She pushed her feet into the matching kid slippers and took a moment to study herself in the looking glass. She gave a little nod of satisfaction, confident she would pass as a respectable widow, fallen on hard times, which was just how she wanted Gabriel Shaw to see her. Throwing a fine woollen shawl about her shoulders to keep her warm, she set off through the unheated passages.

'Mrs Hopwood, good evening.'

Gabriel Shaw greeted her politely as she entered his room. She had half expected him to receive her in a garish dressing gown, but he was fully dressed in biscuit-coloured pantaloons and a dark evening coat that fitted without a crease across his broad shoulders. Even in the candlelight she could see it was of impeccable cut. He wore it over a gold silk waistcoat and immaculate white linen, and above the intricately tied cravat his face was unmarked, save for the ugly bruise on one cheek. It had been darkening when she had cleaned his face on the night they had arrived. The night she had perched on the bed, holding his hand. The memory evoked a sudden fluttering in her chest, but she ignored it. She had nursed him as she would have done any injured man.

She glanced at him again. There were dark shadows beneath his eyes, but she thought he looked remarkably well. Even the cut on his head was healing and hidden now by the sleek dark hair that was brushed back from his wide brow. No fobs or seals adorned his clothes and his fingers were bare of rings, but she was sure he was no country gentleman. He was as fashionably dressed as any of the men she had seen during her recent sojourn in London. Even more reason to question him.

He was sitting at the little dining table that had been set up before the fireplace and he struggled to get up when she came in. She quickly waved him back to his seat.

'I pray you will not exert yourself, Mr Shaw. You are not yet fully recovered.'

She remembered the purple-black bruises she had seen on his body. A strong, muscular body, she recalled, and hastily buried the thought, hoping the sudden heat in her cheeks was not noticeable.

'I am well aware of that,' he said ruefully, dropping back into his seat. 'I shall have to leave it to John to escort you to the table.'

He lifted a hand and beckoned to his manservant, who was hovering in the shadows. Nancy smiled her thanks at Mr Thoresby and while he filled her wine glass, she removed her shawl and arranged it over the back of her chair. She was surprised how nervous she felt to be dining alone with a man and needed time to compose herself.

Thoresby stepped back and gave a little bow. 'If you are ready, ma'am, Mrs Yelland and I will serve dinner immediately.'

When the man had left them, Gabriel picked up his glass and saluted her. 'I am greatly in your debt, Mrs Hopwood.'

'It is no more than any Christian would do. I could not leave you to perish in the cold.'

'Come, madam, you have done so much more than that. Not only did you save my life, but for the past several days you have helped to nurse me and yet, Thoresby tells me, you have never once pressed him for an explanation.' He looked at her, a gleam of laughter in his blue eyes. 'Not many women would have been so forbearing.'

She felt a smile tugging at her mouth.

'The poor man has lived in fear of my interrogation, but I thought it best to wait until *you* could tell me everything.'

A sudden draught announced the opening of the door. Hester and Thoresby came in. Nancy watched them, a feeling of pride warming her as she saw the food she had planned and laboured over placed on the table. Gabriel, too, was regarding the array of dishes with blatant appreciation.

'I fear I have greatly inconvenienced you, madam,' he remarked. 'You have had to break your journey. Will that not make people anxious, friends, family?'

'Robert, my footman, has gone ahead with a message. He is a resourceful fellow and, with a full purse, I have no doubt he found a way to reach his goal. My friends will know I shall be perfectly safe with William Coachman. And there is Hester, too. My companion.'

She smiled up at the older woman, who was setting out the remainder of the dishes on a small side table.

Hester bent an unsmiling gaze upon Nancy and said pointedly, 'Would you like me to stay, madam?'

'No, no, we shall serve ourselves, thank you, Hester. Go now and enjoy your own dinner.' Noting her friend's hesitation, she added, 'You may be sure I shall call you if I need you.'

When they were alone Gabriel cocked an eyebrow. 'Does she fear for your reputation?'

'Very likely.' Nancy laughed. 'I really do not think I have anything to fear from you in your present state. After all, you can barely stand up.'

Again, that glinting smile in his eyes.

'I might beguile you with my charm and ready wit.'

'You might try,' she agreed cordially, accepting another glass of wine from him, 'but you will not distract me from my reason for agreeing to dine with you.'

'And that is?'

'I want an explanation, of course. Why you were attacked, why you are living here with only Mr Thoresby to look after you. He says he is your valet, but he is able to turn his hand to almost anything.'

'Yes, he is indispensable to me. But before we discuss anything more we should eat,' he suggested, surveying the table. 'It looks and smells very inviting. I believe you cooked everything yourself?'

'With Hester to help me.'

'Then, pray tell me what we have here.'

'There is beef brisket, cooked in wine, and stewed mushrooms—I found a jar in the larder, very neatly labelled and dated, for which I am grateful to whomever left it there!—an apple tart and a hash of wild duck from a fine bird that my coachman acquired when he went to buy the vegetables.' She noted his sudden wariness and added, 'Pray calm yourself, Mr Shaw. William was very discreet. I sent him to the market in East Markham, rather than Darlton.'

'What makes you think there is a need for discretion?'

His innocent look did not deceive her. 'Everything about you!'

He laughed. 'Very well, we shall discuss that later. For now, let us eat!'

It was surprisingly enjoyable, dining alone with Gabriel Shaw. She had expected to feel ill at ease, she had certainly intended to keep the man at a distance, but it took only a short time in his company for her to relax and she found herself talking to him as she would to an old friend. Not that she trusted him, of course. She knew nothing about him. But he was good company, he spoke like an intelligent man, and made no attempt to patronise or flirt with her.

He tried most of the dishes, which was gratifying, but he did not eat heartily. Unsurprising, she thought, considering he had only that morning risen from his bed. When he had finished his meal, he pushed away his empty plate.

'My compliments, madam. The food is excellent. Where did you learn to cook like this?'

'From a Frenchman. I spent many hours in his kitchen as a child and he thought it better that I should be working than to have me getting in the way.'

He raised his glass to her. 'Then you proved an apt pupil.'

His praise warmed her, but it also set alarm bells ringing. She must not allow herself to fall for his undoubted charm. Time to make him aware of her menial status.

'He was an excellent teacher. Cooking is now how I earn my living.'

He sat back, his brows raised in surprise. 'Yet you have your own carriage and servants.'

'My employers insisted upon it.'

'They must think very highly of you to allow you to travel in such style.'

'Good cooks are difficult to find and even more difficult to keep.'

'But you were not born a servant, Mrs Hopwood.'

She hesitated. 'No.' She gathered up the empty plates and carried them to the side table. 'I am a widow and must needs make my living where I can.'

He reached out and caught her hand as she passed his chair.

'This is an expensive wedding ring. Surely your husband made some provision for you?'

Nancy glanced down at the heavy gold band on her finger, a necessary accoutrement for her masquerade as the relict of a wealthy man. Harder to explain on the hand of a poor cook.

'His death was…unexpected. This is all I have left of him. I could not bear to part with it.'

She felt the weight of guilt growing heavier with every embellishment of her story. It made her uncomfortable to lie to him, she did not want to do it. Her only consolation was that as soon as the road was clear she would leave Dell House and the enigmatic Gabriel Shaw. Mrs Hopwood would disappear for ever and she could once again be plain Miss Nancy.

She was startled to feel such little comfort in the thought. She loved her life at Prospect House, didn't she? She had her friends there and more than enough work to fill her days. Standing here with this man, this stranger holding her fingers, she suddenly realised why she threw herself into her work each day. It was to tire her, to help her sleep through the lonely nights. She withdrew her hand and returned to her seat.

'But I did not come here to talk about me.'

'Ah.' He refilled the wine glasses. 'Now we get to it.'

'Yes. I want to know about *you*, Mr Gabriel Shaw.'

'How flattering.' He sat back and smiled at her. 'Very well. I am not married, and have no intention of taking a wife. Why limit myself to one woman when I can have a dozen mistresses?' He added wickedly, 'So I am quite unattached at the present time, Mrs Hopwood, if that is what you were wondering.'

'That is not what I meant at all!' Nancy bit her lip, blushing.

He was teasing her, trying to distract her. She could not allow that. Yet now that the moment had come she did not want to ask him about his business here. She was suddenly afraid that she might not like the answers. But it must be done. Nancy squared her shoulders and looked him in the face.

'Who *are* you, Mr Shaw? How do you come to be living here?'

'I came here from London, to, er, rusticate.'

'You are running away from some scandal, perhaps?' It would be a woman, she thought, remembering the jolt of awareness she had experienced when he had caught her hand in his own, strong grasp. With his handsome face and undoubted charm, he was almost irresistible.

Another thought to be firmly quashed.

'Something like that.' He fixed his eyes on his wine glass, twisting it round by the stem. 'I brought only one servant. As you have noticed, John Thoresby is much more to me than a mere valet. We have been together for years. He is a man of many talents and I need no one else to look after me while I am here.' He looked across the table at her. 'So, there you have it, Mrs Hopwood, I am an ordinary single gentleman, on a repairing lease.'

He was smiling at her, his blue eyes warm, and she had to fight against the sudden tug of attraction. He was trying to bamboozle her and she was having none of it.

She said, 'I do not believe you are what you say, Mr Shaw. Ordinary gentlemen might be set upon, robbed and left for dead, but footpads do not normally take the trouble to strip their victim of his coat and then carry him several miles to a secluded spot to die. When William returned from East Markham he told me the snow had been much worse there. Several inches had fallen and the continuing icy weather means there is no sign of it thawing. If I had not found you, your body might have been lying in that copse for weeks.'

'Since my attackers did not speak to me, I cannot tell you why they chose to do that, but it is no matter. I am alive, thanks to your timely ministrations, but I have imposed enough on your goodwill, madam. There is no longer any need for you to delay your journey, I am well on the way to a full recovery.'

'On the way, yes, but you are barely able to walk without help.'

'My strength will return very quickly now I am up and about. John Thoresby can do all I need.'

But the puzzle of the attack upon Gabriel Shaw was preying upon Nancy's mind. She shook her head.

'Mr Thoresby may be well enough to wait upon you, but he is not yet fully recovered from his cold. A trifling illness in itself, perhaps, but he would need all his strength and his wits, too, should it be necessary to defend you.'

'Defend me!' He laughed. 'What nonsense is this?'

She was not tempted to smile. 'You told me yourself, when I came upon you in the wood. Someone wants you dead, Mr Shaw.'

* * *

Gabriel looked at the woman sitting opposite and felt his exasperation growing. He did not want her mixed up in his affairs, yet she was proving damnably difficult to shift. Perhaps he had been too polite.

'And if they do, what concern is it of yours, madam?'

Her brows went up. She said lightly, 'After the effort I have put into saving you, I do not intend to let anyone kill you now.'

'Very well, let us admit there is some danger. Staying here might jeopardise your own safety. I cannot take you into my confidence—'

'Well, you should.'

'Damnation, woman, I do not *want* you here!'

She sat back in her chair and folded her arms, giving him back look for look.

'Since you are not yet well enough to physically throw me out of this house, Mr Shaw, I think you should give in gracefully, do not you?'

His sense of the ridiculous got the better of him and his lips twitched. She did not miss it and her own generous mouth widened into a broad smile.

'That is much better, sir. Now, I will call Hester and we will take these dishes to the kitchen—'

'No. I pray you will allow John and your companion to take care of that. I should like you to stay and talk to me.'

'That I cannot do.' She walked to the fireplace and tugged at the bell pull. 'You need your rest, sir. Hester and I will clear everything away and your man can help you back to bed.'

Confound it, she refused to quit the house, even though he had said she was in danger. But now she wouldn't give him the pleasure of her company! Damned contrary woman.

She turned to look at him, saying innocently, 'I beg your pardon, did you speak?'

He gave a growl of frustration. 'You are the most managing female I have ever encountered.'

Her eyes gleamed with mischief and she was not a whit offended.

'Hen-witted, too. You called me that in the wood. And eccentric,' she added thoughtfully.

'I did? I don't remember it. Most likely I was trying to get rid of you.'

'You were clearly suffering from the blow to your head, so I forgave you for your incivility. But I could not leave you then and I will not leave you now.'

With that she took a tray of dishes and sailed out of the room.

Chapter Four

Gabriel lay in his bed, exhausted by the effort of spending just a few hours out of it. The widow was right, damn her, he needed his rest. But strangely, now John had left him and he was lying alone in the darkness, he did not want to sleep. He was fortunate, he had numerous bruises, but nothing broken, and surprisingly, no broken ribs. Apart from the blow on the head which had rendered him unconscious, his injuries were most likely caused by being bounced around in a cart for the five-mile journey to the wood on the Great North Road. He should never have gone to the tavern in Darlton without John to watch his back, but what else could he do, when the fellow was so ill?

His mind wandered to the more pleasant subject of Mrs Hopwood. Nancy. He had some vague memory of her telling him that was her name. She had joined him for dinner, demurely dressed with no jewellery save her wedding ring, but not even the plainest gown could disguise the voluptuous figure beneath that blue silk. It had clung to her full, high breasts and shim-

mered over her hips when she walked. She had pinned
up her hair, leaving just a few glossy ringlets resting
against the back of her neck. In his mind he imagined
what could have happened if she had not left him so
quickly after the meal. He might have helped her rise
from the table and slipped one hand around the ivory
column of her neck, feeling the silken curls tickling
his fingers as he pulled her towards him until he could
kiss her full, red lips.

The thought made him stir restlessly, reminding him
that his bruised and battered body was in no state to
make love to a woman. He should sleep. He needed his
rest, but when he closed his eyes Nancy's image taunted
him. She was not conventionally beautiful, her face was
too strong for that—the high cheekbones and straight
nose suggested a forceful character and, by heaven, he
knew that to be true! Her generous mouth was made
for laughter and he suspected she laughed often, for
she had a keen sense of the ridiculous. Those choc-
olate-brown eyes had twinkled at him several times
during the evening.

He frowned. But who was she, *what* was she? He
tried to recall what she had said, when she had brought
him to Dell House. When he had told her where he
lived, she had said she knew it. So, she was no stranger
to this area. Indeed, she must be well acquainted with
it to know such an out-of-the-way place. And she was
a gentlewoman by birth, he would swear to it, even
though she said she earned her living.

A cook! He would not have believed it if he had not
seen and tasted the proof of it for himself. And why

should she not be? After all, many women of good birth fell on hard times and were obliged to make a living where they could. But something jarred with him. The way she moved, the way she talked. Her energy and sheer vivacity—he could more readily think her a courtesan than a cook, for she was a dashed attractive woman.

He shifted uneasily in his bed and then winced as his aching limbs protested. She might be Aphrodite herself, but this was no time for dalliance, even if he had been fit for it. He had a job to do and the recent attack had only served to convince him he was getting close. Time to try a different approach. Tomorrow he must arrange for something to be inserted in the papers to announce that a body had been found on the Great North Road near Tuxford. If the snow was as bad there as Nancy had said, it was unlikely anyone would be able to challenge the truth of the notice and whoever was behind the attack on him might believe they had succeeded in removing him.

But he could not proceed with his plans while he had the telltale bruise on his face, or until he was well enough to defend himself. It would mean lying low for at least another week, maybe more, but that could not be helped. His thoughts strayed once more to Nancy. John had told him there were no signs of anyone prowling about Dell House, so perhaps he should not be in such a hurry to be rid of her. If he had to live quietly for a while, why should he not enjoy the company of an attractive widow? She appeared intent upon looking after him, too, so he would only be allowing her to do what she wanted.

He closed his eyes, a sudden smile tugging at his lips. Who said one could not have one's cake and eat it?

When John Thoresby came up with Gabriel's morning coffee, he announced in a voice of doom that it had been snowing all night.

'Drifting, too. That man of Mrs Hopwood's says the road is already blocked. No one will be going very far today, save on foot, across the fields.'

'Capital,' Gabriel replied, sanguine. 'Let us hope it is the same on the Great North Road.'

John helped him to sit up and handed him his cup.

'You've changed your tune. I thought you wanted our visitors gone?'

'I do, eventually, but the snow will prevent my assailants from becoming anxious that my remains have not yet been discovered. Which reminds me, John, we need a notice in the *Markham Courier* to that effect. And possibly in the *Intelligencer*, too. That is widely read in Darlton, I believe. You say it is possible to get out across the fields? Good. I want you to go to East Markham and send a message, express, to…er…our friends in London. They will arrange the whole.'

'Very well, sir. And what do you plan to do next?'

Gabriel eased himself back against the pillows and sipped his coffee. 'I really have no idea,' he said cheerfully. 'But this weather will give us a little extra time to make a new plan. Do not worry, John. I will think of something!'

* * *

Gabriel had taken his breakfast in his room and then allowed his manservant to help him dress. His muscles were still stiff and sore, but he felt much more himself. Well enough, in fact, to leave his room. Knowing John would want him to rest for at least another day, he had waited until he had set off on his errand to East Markham before sallying forth and it was thus a little before noon that he made his way downstairs.

He found Nancy in the kitchen. She was absorbed in stirring the contents of a copper pan on the stove and did not notice him come in, which gave him time to study her. She wore a linen pinafore wrapped around her over her gown, a cheerful yellow muslin with a frilled hem that was more suited to a London salon than a country kitchen, but its bright colour reminded Gabriel of spring flowers. It suited her, too, the yellow contrasting well with the deep rich brown of her hair. She had swept it up hurriedly out of the way and small dark curls framed her face. Several glossy tendrils had escaped at the back, drawing his attention to the elegant neck rising from the low-cut bodice.

For a moment he considered stealing silently up to her, slipping his arms about the dainty waist and dropping a kiss upon the soft skin of her shoulder, but common sense prevailed. She was stirring a boiling pot and he was not at all sure that she wouldn't throw the contents over him if he took such a liberty. He decided it would be safer to cough to attract her attention.

'Oh. Good morning, Mr Shaw.'

She turned from her task, not a whit embarrassed to be discovered at her work. Her eyes appraised him and he was not sure if she approved of what she saw. He felt a flicker of apprehension and laughed at himself. By heaven, he could not be such a coxcomb that he needed a woman's approval!

'You look better,' she said at last. 'I trust you are feeling better?'

'Very much so, madam, thanks in part to an excellent meal last night.' He walked further into the room. The air was warm and deliciously scented with spices and vanilla. 'John has gone out and I came in search of coffee. To make it,' he added quickly. 'I do not expect you or Mrs Yelland to wait upon me.'

He was rewarded by a wide smile.

'How wise of you. As you see, I am busy and Hester is in an outhouse, plucking one of the older hens for the pot. There is some hot water in the kettle, it will not take long to boil, and you will find coffee and the pot over there on the shelves.'

She moved aside to allow him to reach the kettle, but concentrated on her saucepan while he busied himself making coffee. They did not speak, but Gabriel thought it felt pleasantly companionable.

'May I offer you a coffee, too, Mrs Hopwood?'

'Why, thank you, yes. I am just finishing the custard pudding for tonight's dinner; it should thicken in a few moments, then I can put it on the marble slab in the larder to cool.' She paused, lifted the spoon to check the consistency, then continued with her stirring. 'The morning room fire had not been lit when I went in there earlier, so I suggest that we drink it here. This is by far the warmest room in the house at present.' She looked up suddenly, frowning. 'Apart from your bedchamber. I gave instructions that the fire should be kept in all night.'

'And it has been,' he assured her, 'but now I am recovered, I dare not invite you to join me there to drink coffee.'

'Or for anything else.'

'No, of course. Not on such a short acquaintance.'

He knew he was being provocative and he wondered if she would take offence. Instead she laughed at him. It was a happy sound, loud and full-throated. *Infectious*, he thought, smiling inwardly. *Joyous*.

'Indeed not.' She gave her custard a final stir and lifted it from the stove. 'Pray, take the coffee to the table, sir, and we can enjoy it here. I believe there are some biscuits somewhere that Hester baked yesterday.'

She took the saucepan to the larder and returned a few moments later carrying a small jar. When she opened it, the smell of lemons wafted into the air.

'I commend your previous housekeeper, Mr Shaw. She left the larder very well stocked. Even preserved fruits. I find it very unusual,' she continued, as he took a biscuit, 'to have a house with no servants. Did you turn them all off?'

'Not at all. The family that lived here did not wish to renew their lease and moved out at Michaelmas. I knew I might need a retreat and had the house furnished with all the necessities. Including a well-stocked larder. That was vital, with winter approaching.'

'It is your house, then?'

'Most assuredly it is my house. I purchased it only this summer.'

'And you prefer to live here with no staff.'

'I do.'

'But you are a gentleman. You must be accustomed to having servants. A cook, housekeeper.'

Her dark eyes were fixed upon his face, intense, questioning. He gave a little shrug and said lightly, 'The needs of a bachelor are far simpler than those of a married man, madam.' She gave a tiny hiss of exasperation and he laughed. 'The truth is that Thoresby and I spent some time in the army. We are perfectly capable of looking after ourselves, Mrs Hopwood.' She looked so frankly disbelieving that he laughed. 'Very well, on this occasion your help was very much appreciated.'

'Grudgingly appreciated would be more accurate.'

'Was I unpardonably rude to you?'

'Outrageously so.'

'I shall blame it upon the blow on the head that I received.'

'Fustian! You do not like having your will crossed.' She rested her arms on the table and leaned towards him, her plump, rounded breasts rising from her low décolletage. Desire stirred and he tried to ignore it.

'I wish you will tell me why it is dangerous for me to stay here.' She read his thoughts and blushed. 'Apart from the obvious, of course.'

'Is that not reason enough?'

'I have Hester with me and, in your current state of health, I do not fear you.'

'I would not have you fear me at all, madam, especially as we are snowbound here for a few more days at least. If you believe nothing else of me, believe I am a gentleman.' He raised his brows. 'Why do you look at me like that, do you doubt me?'

'My experience of *gentlemen* is that they take what they want of their servants—of any woman—and damn the consequences.'

He frowned. Not at the unladylike language but at the bitterness in her voice. He had not heard that note before and it disturbed him.

'Not all gentlemen behave like that, Mrs Hopwood,' he told her. 'And you are *not* my servant.'

'No, indeed.' She gave a faint smile, her eyes softening, then she seemed to recollect herself and withdrew from him. 'Since the snow makes it impossible for you to be rid of me for a few days, I had best get on with preparing dinner for this evening.'

She made to rise and he put out a hand to stop her.

'Not yet. Take a moment to drink your coffee.' She sank down again and he said, 'You are an unusual woman, Nancy Hopwood. Tell me about yourself.'

She shrugged. 'My story is no different from many other respectable women. I have no man to support me—and no wish for one!—and I was fortunate enough to find a position as a cook.'

'And your employer, he is good man?'

She smiled at that. 'My employer is not a man at all, it is a charity. I work at a house in the north of England that takes in women who have no other home. There is a small farm attached where we grow what we need and sell any surplus and we all do what we can to support ourselves. Those who are good with their hands make things we can sell, such as knitted purses, or stockings. My passion is cooking, so it was natural I should take over the kitchen.'

'Then what were you doing in Tuxford?'

'I have been to London. On business. I was on my way back when I came across you in the wood.' Her shoulders lifted a fraction. 'I am not one to ignore any creature in trouble.'

'Which was fortunate for me.' He refilled their cups. 'But how long can this charity spare you?'

'As long as I am needed here.' She met his eyes, a challenge in her own. 'We may differ on how long that will be, but you will admit that while the snow continues I cannot leave.'

And it was safe enough for her to remain. For the moment.

He said: 'I freely admit that you cannot quit this house today, ma'am, and most likely you will be here tomorrow, too, but you should go as soon as may be. I am going on well enough now. John and I are quite capable of looking after ourselves.'

'And you will not tell me why you are so eager for me to leave?'

'Will you believe me if I say I might forget I am a gentleman if you stay here much longer?'

She smiled at that, but shook her head. 'Of course I will, but that is not the only reason. There is some mystery about you and I wish you would share it with me.'

'It is best that you do not know, ma'am.'

'Then I am obliged to conclude you are here upon some unlawful business.' She sighed and her mouth drooped. 'I do not wish to think of you as a villain.'

It was his turn to smile.

'You need not think it, but neither will your gusty sighs persuade me to tell you.'

'I thought I might as well try.'

She peeped up at him from under her lashes, a roguish look that made him catch his breath as the simmering desire turned to a bolt of pure lust. It required a supreme effort to remain still and keep his countenance impassive.

She finished her coffee. 'Thank you, sir, for the refreshment and the company. But now I really must get on.'

As she pushed the cup away he reached out and caught her wrist.

'Will you dine with me again? I think I am well enough to sit in the morning room this evening. We could of course use the dining room but it is large and draughty. Dashed difficult to heat.'

Nancy was shocked at the way her skin reacted to his touch. Darts of electricity shot through her arm, setting her pulse racing. It was as much as she could do not to cry out or pull away.

She said, as calmly as she could, 'I believe you dined here in the kitchen with Mr Thoresby, prior to our arrival.'

'Well, yes, but—'

He released her and the disappointment she felt was

a further surprise. Alarming, too. He might be a gentleman, he might not mean her any harm, but he was surely dangerous. It was in her own interests to keep him at a distance.

'Then I suggest we all eat in here together,' she told him. 'There is a strong argument in favour of the arrangement, the food will be hotter when it reaches the table.'

'I have no objection, if that is what you wish.'

She was relieved he had accepted the suggestion so readily. Much as she had enjoyed his company last night, she knew it would be safer to dine with the others. She found Gabriel far too attractive and was in no doubt that it would be all too easy to succumb to his charm. Heaven forbid he should realise the effect he had on her. Now she threw him a pitying look.

'I am the cook, Mr Shaw. I am quite accustomed to eating at the kitchen table.'

'Who is eating at the kitchen table?' Hester came in, carrying the plucked chicken and bringing with her a blast of cold air.

'Everyone,' Nancy replied. 'It will be more convenient for us all to eat together.'

'Oh, no, madam, we cannot do that.' Hester stopped in her tracks. 'You are a lady, Miss Nancy, even if you have fallen on hard times. You will dine in the morning room with Mr Shaw.'

Nancy gave a little tut of frustration. 'It is not seemly for us to dine alone.'

'It is seemlier than you both sitting in the kitchen,' Hester retorted. She stomped into the larder to deposit the chicken, saying when she returned, 'And from what I've seen of this gentleman, I don't believe you'll come to any harm.'

Gabriel beamed at her. 'Thank you, Mrs Yelland.'

'You may be right about this…*gentleman*.' Nancy threw him a scorching look. 'However, it will be a lot less work for everyone if we all eat together. And you won't need to carry the food through those draughty passages!'

But Hester was not to be moved. She folded her arms.

'If you won't think of yourself, madam, think of Mr Thoresby and William. It'll quite put them off their dinner, to have to eat it in your presence.'

'But we dined together when we arrived here,' Nancy protested.

'That was from necessity. What with Mr Shaw at death's door and the rest of the house unheated and unprepared, there was only the kitchen fit to use. But now everything's different. We will all be much happier if the two of you are dining elsewhere and we can get on with our own meal in peace.'

Gabriel gave a little cough. 'You would not wish to make the others uncomfortable, Mrs Hopwood.'

'No, of course not, but since I shall be preparing the meal—'

Hester interrupted her. 'We managed yesterday and we shall do the same this evening. I am sure Mr Shaw will agree that you work hard enough as it is. The least we can do is to see to it that you enjoy your dinner.'

Nancy stared at her in silence, frustration bringing an angry colour to her cheeks.

Gabriel rose from the table, chuckling. 'And you said *I* did not like having my will crossed. I shall leave you now, but I look forward to joining you for dinner later, Mrs Hopwood. In the morning room!'

Nancy watched him walk out and it was as much as she could do not to pick up something from the table and hurl it at the door.

'Of all the arrogant, high-handed—'

'Very much like yourself,' Hester commented. 'Come along now, Miss Nancy, there's no time for a tantrum. We must get a move on or we will be eating dinner at midnight.'

Nancy returned to her cooking, muttering to herself, but gradually the discipline of preparing the meal soothed away her anger and by the time she went up to her room to change for dinner she was resigned to her fate. She put on the blue silk again, knowing it was the only evening gown that was decorous enough for a poor and modest widow.

Gabriel was just coming out of his room opposite her own as she stepped out on to the landing. With a bow he offered her his arm. She hesitated, still angry with him for not supporting her decision to eat in the kitchen.

'It is not gallantry,' he informed her. 'I am still unsteady and I need your assistance to descend these stairs.'

A laugh bubbled up, dispelling her anger.

'You are a complete rogue,' she scolded, placing her fingers on his sleeve.

'Unfair, ma'am, when you yourself say I am not yet fully recovered.'

'I was wrong. You are much improved, although I am relieved to see you are using the handrail.'

They reached the hall and she withdrew her hand and preceded him into the morning room, where the shutters had been closed and the fire was burning merrily. The small dining table was already set for dinner and Gabriel stepped forward to hold her chair.

'If you are afraid for your virtue, we could always leave the door open,' he suggested.

'And lose the benefit of the fire? No, I thank you.' She glanced up at him. 'I will risk being alone with you.'

It was no hardship, she thought, as they settled down to their meal. Gabriel was good company. He was intelligent, his conversation was both witty and entertaining and she soon relaxed and began to enjoy herself. She had forgotten to put the muslin fichu about her neck, but there was nothing in Gabriel's manner to cause her alarm. His eyes did not linger on her breasts, nor did he try to flirt with her. They talked companionably about various subjects with the ease of old friends, and the evening sped by. When the long-case clock in the hall chimed the hour, she exclaimed in surprise.

'Is that the time already? I had no idea it was so late.'

'Eleven o'clock cannot be considered late, ma'am.'

'It is for an invalid such as yourself. You need to rest.' She rose, but waved to him to remain in his seat.

'Pray do not get up.' She walked to the side table to collect a decanter and a glass and bring it to him. 'There, I will leave you with your brandy and bid you goodnight, Mr Shaw.'

When he reached for her hand she gave it to him without thinking. He pressed a kiss upon her fingers and let her go. A friendly gesture, she told herself. Nothing more.

'Goodnight, Mrs Hopwood.'

'Mr Shaw.'

Oh, how she wanted to stay! Her whole being protested as she turned away from him and her spine tingled with the knowledge that he was watching her. He would not object, she was sure, if she remained to drink another glass of wine with him, but then what? There was only one way the evening would end if she showed such a preference for his company. And though her body might cry out for relief from the longing that disturbed her nights, Gabriel Shaw was too charming, too attractive, and she feared she might grow too attached to him. She would not risk her heart for a moment's pleasure. She walked out, closing the door quietly behind her, and kept walking until she had reached the safety of her bedchamber, where she resolutely turned the key in the lock.

Gabriel watched Nancy leave the room. She was a tall woman and built on queenly lines, but she moved with an almost liquid grace that made him long to see her in a ballroom. He poured himself a measure of brandy and sipped it, his mind filled with the agreeable image of Nancy gliding across the dance floor, the skirts of her gown shimmering in the candlelight as they swayed about her hips.

A line of poetry came into his head and he murmured it aloud.

'"*How sweetly flows that liquefaction of her clothes!*" Who wrote that? Herrick, of course.' He bethought him of another line from Herrick, this time writing of Julia's breasts.

Between whose glories there my lips I'll lay.

With something that was almost a growl he shook off his reverie.

'Confound it, such thoughts will do me no good at all!'

Finishing his brandy, he pushed himself to his feet and made for the door.

Nancy lay in her bed, her head, her whole body buzzing. She was not in the least sleepy and wished she had been able to stay talking with Gabriel into the early hours. It had been years since she had enjoyed a man's company so much and the thought set alarm bells ringing. He roused in her a longing for more than just conversation. She wanted to touch him, to feel his arms about her. To assuage the terrible loneliness that she had barely acknowledged until now. Over the years she had learned to protect herself where men were concerned. A single woman could not afford the luxury of letting down her guard. Only once had she lost her heart and she knew the pain of loving a man who could never be hers. She would not risk that again.

She tensed, clenching her hands at her sides. She had her work and her friends at Prospect House, was that not enough? The traitorous voice inside told her no. She wanted a man's touch, a man's kiss. But it was not just the physical need that alarmed her. She felt, nay, she was certain, that if circumstances had been different, Gabriel Shaw could have been a friend. Someone to laugh with, to share jokes. To share worries.

Impatiently she rolled on to her side. Heavens, what was happening to her? She was far too old for such a foolish infatuation. But when she was with Gabriel she felt giddy and reckless, ready to throw her cap over the windmill. With a sigh she sat up and turned her pillow. Oh, this would never do. Her friends at Prospect House relied upon her for her good sense and here she was behaving like a schoolgirl, losing her head over an attractive man about whom she knew nothing. Less than nothing.

She remembered her father's housekeeper, Mrs Crauford, saying 'Handsome is as handsome does' and she must keep that in mind, because Gabriel was most definitely handsome. She felt a sigh building and fought it back, determined to be sensible. If Gabriel had indeed been left to perish by his enemies it might make him a victim, but it did not mean he was a good or an honest man. That remained to be seen.

She settled down again, snuggling her hand against her cheek. Relaxed and warm within the comfort of her bed and with the door securely locked, she allowed her thoughts to wander freely. There was no denying Gabriel was very attractive, with his dark hair and charming smile, and those eyes… She took a moment to consider his eyes. They were as blue as the borage flowers she used to decorate her salads and when he looked at her, *just so*, it felt as if his glance was piercing her very soul. Yes, even with the fading remains of that bruise upon his cheek he was handsome enough to turn a girl's head. Lucky then, she thought sleepily, that she was no longer a girl…

Chapter Five

'Wind got up last night, Miss Nancy. William Coachman says nothing will be moving by road for a while yet.'

From the cosy comfort of her bed, Nancy heard Hester's news with a sinking heart. She had spent a restless night, dreaming of Gabriel, holding him, kissing him. Waking with her body burning and aching for his touch. She had crawled out of bed to unlock her door, and by the time Hester came in with her morning tea and hot water, she had decided that the less time she spent in Gabriel's company the better for her peace of mind. Before climbing into bed, she had peeped out of the window. The snow had stopped and she had thought it felt a little warmer, giving rise to the hope that a thaw might set in. The news that she must remain longer at Dell House was a blow. She sat up, rubbing her eyes. Outside the first glimmer of dawn was painting the sky a dull rose.

'Can we not push through any drifts and at least make our way back to Tuxford?' Suddenly almost anywhere seemed better than remaining in the same house as Gabriel Shaw.

'Aye, we might do that on the lane, but William has just come in after walking Darlton way and said the roads in every direction are blocked.' Hester picked up the poker and began to rake over the ashes. 'Looks like we shall be obliged to remain here for a few more days yet, ma'am.'

'Well, what cannot be cured must be endured.' Nancy threw back the covers and slipped out of bed. The floor struck chill even through the thick rug under her feet. 'Don't bother with the fire, Hester, I will wash quickly and join you in the kitchen as soon as I am dressed.'

'Work,' she said to herself as she splashed the warm water on her face. 'There is plenty of work to be done in the kitchen and that will keep me out of Gabriel's way.'

But she had reckoned without the attraction of a warm room and the delicious smell of baking that drew everyone into the kitchen at noon. William had already come in from the stables and was enjoying a plate of bread, cheese and onion which he declared would keep him going until dinner time, while John Thoresby had persuaded Hester to cut him a slice of the game pie left over from yesterday. The room was redolent with the scent of lemon and spices by the time Gabriel appeared, looking so impossibly handsome that Nancy's heart gave a little skip. He came in wearing breeches and top boots with the full sleeves of his white shirt rolled up to expose muscled forearms.

Nancy was standing over the mixing bowl, the ingredients for a cake spread out on the table before her. Frowning, she bent her head and gave her attention to beating together the flour, eggs and sugar. It was easy to ignore the banter going on between Hester and John Thoresby, and William was happily ensconced in a chair by the range, lost in his own thoughts. Gabriel, however, after helping himself to a slice of pie, eased himself on to the bench across the table from Nancy, determined to talk.

'You slept well, I hope, madam?'

'Perfectly, sir.' A lie, but what was one supposed to say? 'You are well enough to work out of doors, I see.'

He grimaced. 'A few logs and I was done. I must content myself with chopping kindling. Which reminds me, John tells me the coal scuttle in your room did not require filling this morning. I hope you are not skimping on your own comforts. I assure you we have plenty of fuel.'

'I prefer a cool bedchamber.'

'That may be, but in this extreme weather a room can become icy in no time. I would not have you catch a chill when you retire tonight.'

The words were perfectly innocent, but his deep voice conjured images at once shocking and enticing. Nancy pictured herself lying with Gabriel before the roaring fire, their naked bodies pressed together as they shared long, lingering kisses. She bent her head and beat the cake mixture even harder, trying to ignore the thrumming of hot blood through her veins.

'I am not such a poor creature,' she muttered.

'I have never believed you were. I think you are quite remarkable.'

His voice was low and warm, like a caress. Flattery. It was nothing but flattery and she must not take him seriously.

She managed a laugh and said lightly, 'Your words have more butter in them than this cake! If you are wheedling for more food, I suggest you turn your charm upon Hester. I am not one to succumb to such blandishments.'

'Thank you, no, this pie is sufficient for me.' He climbed to his feet. 'John, I pray you will join me in the study when you are finished.' He reached out and stole a few of the currants she was about to beat into her cake. 'Until dinner, Mrs Hopwood.'

Nancy's pulse was jumping erratically. She told herself she was glad he had left the kitchen but there was no denying she enjoyed his teasing. She was torn between exhilaration and panic at what might occur if she spent too long in his company. She was tempted to suggest once more they should all eat together in the kitchen, but abandoned the idea. The others would not agree and it would signal to Gabriel that she was not immune to his charms. Better to bluff it out, she thought.

She looked up, giving him a bright smile. 'Until dinner, then.'

Nancy spent the rest of the afternoon in feverish activity. She cooked, cleaned and tidied, ignoring Hester's protests that there was no need for her to mop the

floor or sweep the stairs. The inclement weather made
it impossible to go out and Nancy needed an occupation to try to keep her thoughts away from Gabriel.
She was dismayed at how much she wanted to throw
caution to the winds and give in to the mutual attraction that sizzled between them whenever they were
together. And she was not helped by the insidious voice
of temptation that whispered in her ear.

*After all, what have you got to lose? You are too old
to worry about your virtue. Enjoy a brief liaison with
an attractive man. Before it is too late.*

Madness, she told herself. To allow Gabriel into her
bed and enjoy his lovemaking would only make the
inevitable parting even harder to bear. She had good
friends in Compton Parva and the living she earned at
Prospect House provided her with a measure of independence that she would be foolish to jeopardise. So
she threw herself into her work, only stopping when
Hester reminded her that she must change for dinner.

'You will need to bathe, first, Miss Nancy,' declared the older lady. 'You cannot sit down at the table
with Master Gabriel in all your dirt. And there's no
need to fret,' she continued, with the glimmer of a
smile, 'I have been heating up the copper all afternoon for you.'

Hot water was hurriedly carried upstairs, but once
she had bathed, Nancy was forbidden to help empty
the hip bath, Hester explaining that she and John
Thoresby would clear the room while she was having dinner.

'You've worked hard enough today, Miss Nancy.

Now, you rest and dry your hair in front of the fire while I get on with dinner. Then you can enjoy your meal.'

Enjoy! Nancy felt again a guilty flush of pleasure. Her stomach swooped at the thought of dining alone with Gabriel. They had been getting on so well, so companionably. They laughed together and teased one another as if they had known each other all their lives. As if they were lifelong friends. And yet they were strangers. The truth sobered her. Gabriel had told her nothing of himself and had no intention of doing so. Every time she attempted to discover his history, he turned the conversation. It was neatly done, he gave no offence and in all other respects proved himself an entertaining companion who appeared to enjoy her company.

As she sat before her fire, letting the thick curtain of hair fall in front of the flames to dry, she sank into a pleasant reverie of the moments they had spent together.

If one put aside Gabriel's propensity to flirt, there had been many pleasurable and quite innocent moments these past few days, such as Gabriel's making coffee for her to share, helping her in the kitchen by stirring a pot so that she might get on with something else, hunting for eggs with her in the henhouse and carrying the precious finds back to the kitchen. Menial tasks but necessary, and all the more enjoyable for doing them together.

The striking of her bracket clock, sitting on the mantelshelf, reminded Nancy of the time and she jumped up with a little cry of alarm. There was less than half an hour until dinner! She piled her still-damp hair on top of her head and set about finding something suitable to wear. Time was short, but she did not want to put on the blue gown again and hastily rummaged through the trunks of clothes. Thankfully most of her gowns were cleverly designed so that she might dress herself, for she dared not drag Hester away from the kitchen to help her.

Brightly coloured evenings gowns with their ornate frills and flounces were held up, but hastily discarded, one after the other. In the end she decided on a half-dress of Pomona-green sarsenet. It had a double flounce around the hem, but it was relatively plain, being intended to be worn about the house when there were no visitors. The demure neckline needed no lace or muslin to cover her breasts and, like the blue silk, it had the advantage of long sleeves, which would help to keep out the winter chill.

There was no time to pack everything away. Nancy scrambled into her gown, picked up her shawl and hurried downstairs, thankful that Hester had refused all her offers to help her serve up the meal. She went directly to the morning room, where Gabriel was waiting. He was drawing the curtains when she came in and when they were securely closed he crossed the room towards her, scooping up two glasses of wine from a side table as he passed and handing one to Nancy.

She said, by way of greeting, 'I hope you are feeling even better today?'

'Much better, thank you. Allow me to escort you to the table.'

She was all too aware of his hand on her back, the merest touch, but her skin tingled beneath the layers of fabric. He held her chair for her and she half expected his fingers to brush the back of her neck. When they did not and he took his own seat, her disappointment was almost physical.

Stop it, Nancy. Just enjoy the evening. Ask nothing, explain nothing.

Was that possible? Their discourse on the previous occasions had been varied and wide ranging, but the subjects had been innocuous. Interesting, enjoyable, but giving away very little of themselves. Surely there could be nothing left to talk about. However, within minutes of their being alone they were once more engaged in lively conversation. Nancy began to relax as they discussed books and music and the theatre. Gabriel asked her no probing questions and she curbed her own curiosity, enjoying his company far too much to risk his withdrawing behind a wall of politeness.

John and Hester came in to carry away the last of the dishes and Nancy only made a half-hearted protest when they insisted she should not return with them to the kitchen to help clear up. Instead she watched them working, folding her hands together in her lap. They felt softer than they had for years. A lady's hands. During her sojourn in town she had not been obliged to do anything more taxing than write letters and, since they had arrived at Dell House, Hester had tried to ensure they remained that way by taking on most of the heavy work.

'You are smiling,' Gabriel observed, as Hester and John left the room. 'What are you thinking?'

'That I am being thoroughly spoiled.'

'No, why should that be when you have been working all day? I saw you, you know, polishing the handrail on the stairs with all your might.'

She blushed and shook her head. 'Everyone has been busy today, even you.'

'Not as much as I would like.' He refilled their glasses.

'But you have not yet recovered your full strength.'

'And nor shall I, if I am not allowed to do anything more strenuous than chop kindling and light a few fires.'

She laughed. 'You must learn patience, sir. You will recover all the quicker if you do not overstrain yourself. You need to rest. And having said that, the clock struck eleven some time since. It is late.'

He sat back, grinning.

'Oh, no. I allowed you to persuade me of that yesterday. Today I am much better. I intend to take my wine and sit by the fire. Will you join me?'

Common sense and self-preservation told Nancy she should bid him goodnight and go to bed, but for the life of her she could not resist the temptation to stay. They sat, one on each side of the fireplace, and Gabriel filled their wine glasses before placing the bottle on the hearth. She sipped her wine, then cradled the glass between her hands and watched him. He was sitting back in his chair, his long legs stretched before him and crossed at the ankle.

A frisson of excitement ran through her. She had nursed him, washed him and tended his bruises. She knew that beneath the thin layers of fine cloth he had the body of an athlete, the muscles finely sculpted over his broad shoulders and deep chest, his long legs shapely and powerful. He was staring into the fire, the shadows enhancing the clean lines of his cheeks and jaw. It was a strong face, she thought. Intelligent, determined, perhaps even a little ruthless. Certainly dangerous.

He looked up suddenly and caught her gaze. She said, 'Tell me who you are. Why you are here.'

'Madam, it is a subject too dull for conversation.'

'I doubt it.'

'It is to me. I want only to enjoy the company of a beautiful woman.'

She blushed. 'I will not be diverted by your compliments.'

'I am merely telling you the truth.' He paused. 'I should very much like to kiss you.'

The words were soft, a caress in themselves, and her throat dried.

'I do not think that would be wise.' But her heart told her it was what she would like, too.

'No, not wise at all.'

A candle was guttering on a side table. He pushed himself out of his chair and walked across to pinch it out. She noted that he was moving easier, little sign of the stiffness of yesterday. He did not need a nurse. She had no excuse to stay here any longer, she could return to Prospect House as soon as the weather allowed. She wondered why the thought did not please her more.

'John tells me there are signs of a thaw,' he said, keeping his back to her.

'Yes.'

'You will be able to continue your journey.'

'Yes.'

And I shall never see you again.

She put down her glass. She should have drunk less wine. It was going to her head, weakening her resolve just when she most needed to be sensible. 'I should retire.'

He turned. 'Then I will escort you.'

The words were polite enough, but the tension in the room was tangible, thick and dangerous as flour dust. Nancy was well aware that a single spark would ignite it. Silently she threw her shawl about her shoulders and accompanied Gabriel from the room. The hall and stairs were dimly illuminated by the occasional candle in its wall sconce, but their eyes soon grew accustomed to the gloom. Nancy's bedchamber was the first room off the landing and as they ascended the stairs the bead of light beneath the door reminded her that she had rushed out in a hurry and had forgotten to turn down the lamps.

She had resolved what she must do. At the door she would pause to say goodnight and at the same time she would reach for the handle so she could slip quickly away, but when they reached her bedchamber, her thoughts and her wayward body froze. Gabriel stopped and turned towards her, his frame blocking what little light there was. She was enveloped in his shadow. Wrapped in the powerful, charismatic presence of the man. Perhaps it was his height—there were very few people taller than Nancy—and having to look up into

Gabriel's shadowed face made her heart beat a little faster. As if controlled by some will other than her own, Nancy put her hands on his shoulders and stretched up to kiss his mouth. For a moment he did not move, then the whole world exploded.

His arms came around her and he was kissing her, a fierce, savage kiss that made her senses reel. He pushed her against the wall, his powerful chest crushing her breasts. She could feel the iron strength of his thighs against her legs. She slid her arms about his neck, clinging to him while she responded to his mouth's demands, her lips parting to allow his tongue to explore her mouth. He was hard and aroused against her, his hands roving over her body, cupping her breasts. She felt the heat of his palms through the thin silk of her gown and her body stiffened. She sighed against his mouth. Her very bones were melting.

He raised his head and stared down at her, naked desire in his eyes.

'May I come in?'

'Yes. Oh, yes.'

In one swift movement he swept her up into his arms. For an instant he fumbled with the door handle and then they were through, into the golden lamplight. Gabriel strode into the room and set her on her feet. She clung to him to get her balance. After the darkness of the passages the lamps were dazzling, illuminating the jewel-like colours of the discarded gowns that were spread in rich and vivid confusion across the bed and draped over the furniture. Nancy gave a little tut of impatience.

'I left in a hurry, I will move them—'

'No. Wait.' He kept his arms about her, but he was looking around the room, frowning. 'What is all this?'

He released her and went to the bed, lifting and fingering the rich, colourful silks. Still dazed and shaken by his kisses, Nancy could only stand and watch as he walked across to the open trunk and picked up a scarlet ballgown. He tossed it aside and reached into the trunk, pulling out her jewel box. When he opened the lid, the gems winked and glittered in the lamplight.

He lifted out a diamond necklace and held it up to the light.

'This is real.' He dipped his hand in and lifted several more pieces. 'As are these.' He let the jewels slip back through his fingers. 'There is a king's ransom here.'

The hot, urgent passion of that kiss had gone. There was no burning desire in Gabriel's eyes now when he looked at her, only cold suspicion. Nancy felt her own exhilaration drain away, leaving her nervous and on edge. She ran her tongue across her dry lips.

'I know how this must look—'

'What is this?' He stared at her. 'What *are* you?'

'I—I wore these in London—'

'You are a rich man's whore.'

She winced. 'No.'

'You stole them, then.'

'No! Nothing like that.' She put up her chin, trying not to be cowed by the accusation in his eyes. 'I was hired to wear them. By Lord Quinn.'

His brows went up. 'Well, he is rich enough, I'll

grant you that. You must be an excellent lover, if Rufus Quinn rewarded you with all this.'

'How dare you!' Anger scorched her cheeks. She glared at him. 'It was not like that at all.'

'No?' His lip curled. 'Then you had best explain it to me.'

He walked to a chair, picked up the gowns thrown over it and dumped them on the floor before sitting down. For a moment she was tempted to say it was none of his business, but her temper was cooling. She owed him an explanation. She had told him she was a poor widow, earning her living as a cook, and now he had discovered that she was in possession of gowns and jewels worth hundreds if not thousands of pounds.

'It is a delicate matter,' she said. 'Can I rely upon your discretion?'

'Oh, no, madam, I will make you no promises until I have heard your story.'

Despite his suave tone, his eyes glittered dangerously. He was furious and with good reason. No man liked to think he had been duped. With a sigh she rubbed one hand across her eyes.

'Quinn's wife is related to a friend of mine, Mrs Charles Russington, who set up Prospect House, where I live and work as a cook. Serena—Lady Quinn—was being threatened with ruin by Sir Timothy Forsbrook and she needed…extricating. It was impossible for Quinn to call him out without causing the very scandal they were trying to avoid. When I heard about it, I suggested I could distract him. Lure him away.'

How sordid that sounded now, yet at the time, when

Molly had told her of the dilemma, it had seemed straightforward. She had been eager to take on the role. Perhaps even then she had been finding her life a little dull, only she would not admit it. She glanced at Gabriel. His arms were folded across his chest, his face was stony, impassive, like some terrible god sitting in judgement.

'Go on.'

The tone was not encouraging. Nancy pulled her shawl about her and began to pace slowly about the room.

'Do you know Sir Timothy?' She did not wait for an answer. 'He is a fortune hunter, but he is also a spiteful man. When his attempt to abduct Serena was foiled he was determined to ruin her, out of revenge. I masqueraded as a wealthy tradesman's widow, to draw him off. He took the bait and courted me, spending a great deal of money to convince me he was a rich man. He ran up huge debts, believing my fortune would soon be his, but I disappeared and he was left, facing ruin.' She raised her head, returning his gaze steadily. 'Perhaps it was wrong to deceive Sir Timothy, but he had no qualms about marrying me for my money. He pretended he had fallen head over heels in love with me, but there was no true affection in him.' Her lip curled. 'I was the means to an end. I learned afterwards that he had planned to put me away in some isolated house once he had control of my supposed fortune. Quinn settled with him, gave him enough money to pay his debts on condition that he left the country.

'My fee for this charade was that I would keep all

the gowns and the jewels. Not for myself. They will all be sold and the proceeds will go to the charity that runs Prospect House.' She waved her hand towards the trunks. 'The gowns and the jewels reflect the character I played: dashy, loud, and totally without breeding, but Forsbrook was not deterred. He thought my fortune sufficient compensation for taking such a wife.' She stopped and turned to him. 'So, there you have it. It is a sordid little tale, but it was done to protect Lady Quinn's good name.'

'And what of your own reputation?'

She shrugged. 'I did not have one to lose. I forfeited my good name the day I ran away from home.' She added, with a touch of defiance, 'I have supported myself by my cooking ever since and I am proud that I have been able to do so. I do not consider myself a fallen woman.'

In the silence that followed her confession she dragged together what shreds of pride she could muster and went about the room, packing up the gowns and carefully putting them back in the trunks.

Gabriel said slowly, 'I have spent little time in town these past few months so I have no idea if your story is true, but I am acquainted with Sir Timothy Forsbrook. I know him for a grasping, treacherous scoundrel.'

She shuddered. 'He is a horrid little man. I cannot regret tricking him.'

'And do you regret deceiving *me*?'

She turned to look at him. 'I did not deliberately deceive you, save to call myself Mrs Hopwood, the name I used in town. Everything else I have told you about myself is true.'

'And your real name?'

She shook her head. 'I shall be leaving here very soon, there is little point in you knowing that.'

'I see.' He rose. 'Thank you for explaining the matter to me.'

He left her, closing the door quietly behind him. Nancy continued to pack her clothes in the trunk, telling herself it was just as well he had gone. What good would it have been to succumb to temptation and spend a night of passion with him? It could never be anything more.

But when at last she climbed between the sheets and blew out her candle, she thought her bed had never felt so cold and lonely.

Chapter Six

When Nancy awoke the next morning, the sky was as grey and overcast as her spirits. She dressed and went directly to the kitchen, where she found John Thoresby busy at the stove. Hester, who was trussing the chicken, peered closely at Nancy. 'You are looking a bit pale, ma'am, if you don't mind my saying so.'

'I did not sleep well.' It was not a lie. She had spent a restless night, regretting that she had ever let Gabriel into her room.

'Then why don't you go back to bed, my dear? There is very little to be done here. Mr Thoresby and I can manage and, to be frank, another body would be very much in the way.'

For once Nancy did not have the energy to argue. She decided to take her coffee into the morning room, where the remains of last night's fire would still be emitting some warmth. There might even be enough life in the embers for her to revive the fire and, if not, she was perfectly capable of kindling a new one.

But when she walked in she discovered that Gabriel

was there before her. He had added fresh logs to the fire and was dusting off his hands when she entered. Nancy wanted to withdraw immediately, but he had already seen her.

'Please, do not run away.' He gestured to one of the chairs beside the fire. 'Will you not come in and sit down? I wanted to talk to you.'

'I do not think there is anything more to be said.' But despite her words she carried her cup across the room and perched on the edge of the chair. 'I am only sorry I cannot leave Dell House today.'

He sat down. They were in the seats they had occupied last night, only now they were both sitting upright and Nancy at least was ill at ease.

He said, 'I should not have ripped up at you as I did last night. I beg your pardon. I was at fault, I admit it. My nature is cynical, from having lived so long in the fashionable world. I am far too ready to think the worst of people. After all you have done for me I had no right to say what I did.'

'No, you did not.' She looked down at the coffee cup, clutched between both hands. 'But it prevented our making an even greater error.'

'Do you think so?'

'I do. Most assuredly.' She lifted her head and met his eyes. She had expected to see his eyes gleaming with laughter, ready to flirt, to tease. Instead he looked unusually sober. She went on. 'I do not hold you wholly responsible for what happened between us. I cannot deny that I...wanted you.'

Her glance slid to the fireplace, where the flames

crackled greedily around the logs. Want. Such a poor, thin word to describe the strength of desire that had overwhelmed her last night. How long had it been since a man had roused her to such a fever of longing? She had thought herself too sensible, too old for such things.

'Shall we agree to blame it on the wine?'

'Yes,' she said bleakly. 'I think we must.' She finished her coffee. 'I am obliged to remain here for another day or two yet. I would not have the others know what has occurred between us. We should continue to dine together, if we are to avoid questions and speculation. I hope we may at least be civil to one another.'

'I think we might manage that.'

His voice was smooth again, with just that hint of laughter she found so attractive. She would not give in to it again, Nancy told herself. She had learned her lesson.

'Good. Until dinner, then.' She left her seat and went to the door. As she opened it he called her name and she looked back.

He was standing before the fire, a faint, rueful smile curving his lips.

'It will not do, I'm afraid. I want to kiss you as much this morning as I did last night.'

His words caused a sudden flutter in her breast. He still desired her! Her spirit leapt at the thought. However, pride would not allow her to let him see it. She shrugged.

'Alas, sir, we cannot always have what we want.'

And with that she left him, but the day suddenly seemed a little brighter.

* * *

Gabriel waited until the door had closed before sinking back on to his chair. He had seen the shadows fly from Nancy's eyes, replaced by a glimmer of mischief when she made that last remark, and he was surprised at how much that pleased him. His actions last night had ruined the easy friendship that had been growing between them. It was bad enough that he had tried to make love to her, but then to accuse her of heaven knew what!

He closed his eyes, reliving the moment he had seen the gowns. For an instant it all made sense: her sensuous beauty, the passion that had flared so instantly when they kissed. He had recalled his original assessment of her, that she was more courtesan than cook, and he had allowed his anger and disappointment to cloud his judgement. Of course, he only had her word for it that she was not playing some deep game of her own, but his gut instinct was to trust her. Yet could he do so? *Should* he do so?

Gabriel rubbed his hand over his eyes. The sooner this commission was over the better. It was making him suspicious of everyone. And it was unjust to accuse Nancy of having secrets, when he had so many of his own.

'Mrs Hopwood, the snow has stopped and the sun has come out. I wonder if I might invite you to take a turn around the grounds with me?'

Nancy almost dropped the baking dish she was carefully placing in the oven when she heard Gabriel's voice.

She had come down to the kitchen to help Hester with dinner, determined to put last night's encounter out of her mind. It was over, he had apologised. They understood one another. And yet…

And yet part of her could not help regretting their quarrel, that he had not taken her to bed and assuaged the longing that now slumbered, but was still there, deep inside. Which was why it was so infuriating to have him address her so cheerfully when she was still struggling with what might have been. She closed the oven door and schooled her face to a look of polite unconcern as she turned to look at him. The refusal was already on her lips when Hester spoke up.

'Now that's a grand idea, Master Gabriel. It has brightened up and Miss Nancy could do with a breath of fresh air. I said this morning she was looking peaky.'

Nancy glared at her. 'Thank you, Hester, but I have not yet finished here.'

'Tush, ma'am, there is nothing to do now but clear away and I am far better at that than you. Off you go now and fetch your cloak.'

Still Nancy hesitated.

Gabriel said, with a diffidence that was at odds with the teasing gleam in his eyes, 'I am very much recovered, but John refuses to let me go out alone, lest I should suffer a sudden relapse. He is exceeding busy, however…'

Hester tutted. 'Good heavens, Master Gabriel, if John Thoresby is to escort you out of doors, then who will do all the fetching and carrying that is required in the house? I think it much better that Miss Nancy should go with you to make sure you come to no harm.'

'My thoughts exactly, Mrs Yelland.' Gabriel was smiling, his eyes full of laughter, but Nancy read understanding in their blue depths, too. He said, 'If you are concerned for your skirts, ma'am, there are very few drifts in the grounds, nothing a stout pair of shoes cannot cope with. I feel sure the fresh air would do us both good.'

Ten minutes later she was outside with Gabriel, their feet scrunching through the fresh snow on the path.

'You realise I only agreed to walk out with you because everyone else is busy,' she told him crossly.

'Yes, I gathered it was not what you wished to do at all. That was very evident when you flounced out to fetch your cloak.'

'I did not flounce!'

'No, of course not.'

His soothing tone made her gasp in indignation before her ready sense of humour took over. She laughed, her anger evaporating like their cloudy breath in the bright, cold sunshine.

'Odious creature! You deliberately set out to tease me!'

'I admit it, but only to dispel any restraint between us. I have not yet apologised for kissing you.'

Her cheeks flamed and she averted her face. 'We agreed not to discuss that. It was the circumstances. Being so much in each other's company.'

'And dining alone.'

'And the wine,' she added.

'Yes,' he said quietly. 'One becomes prey to temptation.'

She swallowed, trying not to think of just how tempted she had been. 'Quite.'

'Madness for two elderly people such as ourselves to be carried away on a tide of passion,' he remarked thoughtfully.

Nancy glanced at him sharply. *She* might consider herself over the hill, but Gabriel was in his prime. Why, he could not be more than five-and-thirty. His handsome face bore little more than laughter lines around the eyes and his dark hair had only the faintest touch of silver at the temples. And she knew from nursing him that his body was lean and athletic.

Nancy felt again the knot of desire uncurling inside and her instinctive retort, that she was not yet in her dotage, withered on her lips. He might take her protests as encouragement, or at the very least think she wanted to flirt with him. A man like Gabriel would have the pick of society's young beauties. How could she compete? It was better not even to think of it.

She managed a very convincing laugh.

'Quite ridiculous, I agree. I pray you will forget it. I have.' She tucked her hand into his arm, as if to prove she did not fear contact with him, and they began to walk on. 'You no longer need nursing, so as soon as my coach can get out to the main road, Hester and I shall continue our journey north.' She could not resist adding, 'We will leave you to whatever nefarious activities you are engaged upon.'

He chuckled. 'My activities as you call them are not nefarious, madam, I assure you. Covert, but not detrimental to King or country.'

'But they *are* dangerous?'

'Naturally.'

They had walked full circle around the lawns and were now back at the door to the house. As Gabriel stood aside to allow her to enter she stopped and turned to him.

'Then I pray you will take care, Gabriel. Not that it matters to me,' she added quickly, 'but I should hate to think that all my hard work in saving your life has been wasted.'

'I shall do my best to obey you.' He caught her gloved hand and raised it to his lips. 'Until dinner time, Nancy.'

She flushed, only then realising she had called him by his first name and thus given him an excuse to use hers. With as much dignity as she could muster, she withdrew her hand from his grasp, picked up her skirts and fled.

Gabriel felt the now-familiar desire flooding through him as Nancy hurried away. It was useless to deny it and he did not want to, but it made it damned difficult to concentrate upon anything else when she was near him. He made his way to his room to remove his greatcoat, thanking providence he had not been wearing it the night he was attacked, else he would have lost that along with the very expensive coat he had purchased from Stultz that very Season.

The memory of the attack sobered him. A coat might be easily replaced, even at ten guineas, but if his attackers should learn of Nancy's part in his rescue—it was better that she should be well away from Dell House before he ventured into Darlton again, so despite the attraction he felt for her he must hurry her departure. He would not risk any harm befalling her.

The time dragged until dinner, even though Gabriel kept busy. With so many extra people in the house there were more rooms to keep warm. John Thoresby and William Coachman shared the heavier duties between them, such as fetching and carrying coal or logs up to the rooms, and Nancy and Mrs Yelland had commandeered the kitchen, so Gabriel was left with little to do except tidy his and John's bedchambers and light the fires in the principal rooms. His man thought such tasks were beneath his master's dignity, but Gabriel had never been one to allow his servants to do everything for him and in their current situation it was necessary for them to work together.

He did not see Nancy as he made his way about the house, but suspected she was in the kitchen, helping to prepare the meal. He had enjoyed their dinners together and hoped this evening they would be able to meet with at least some semblance of ease.

At the dinner hour he made his way to the morning room in good time. The table was already set, candles lit and a good fire crackled in the hearth. He was at the side table when he heard the faint whisper of the door opening and looked around to see Nancy coming into the room. She greeted him coolly and accepted his offer of a glass of wine.

'I am constantly amazed at how civilized Dell House has become since you and Mrs Yelland arrived, ma'am. Do you never rest?'

She accepted the wine and his question with a faint smile.

'Hester and Thoresby are determined to observe the niceties. Theirs is the industry, not mine.'

He did not choose to argue the point. The fact that she was here, talking to him, dining with him, was more than he had expected and he had no wish to jeopardise the mood. He escorted her to her chair and had barely taken his own seat opposite when the door opened and Hester Yelland came in with the first of the hot dishes.

He exerted all his charm during dinner, introducing unexceptional topics of conversation, offering his companion the very choicest meats and keeping the wine glasses filled. He was careful not to issue fulsome compliments or to make any remark that might be misconstrued. His efforts paid off and by the time the meal was ended, they were once more talking easily together.

However, he knew it was a fragile truce so he did not suggest they sit by the fire. Nancy seemed content to remain at the table, sipping her wine and occasionally selecting a dainty morsel from the china dish of nuts and dried fruits that Hester had brought in when she and John came in to remove the covers.

'Another excellent meal,' he remarked, raising his glass to her. 'My compliments, ma'am.'

'Thank you.' She reached out to pick a dried apricot from the dish. 'You are wise to appreciate good cooking while you can. This snow cannot last for ever and when Hester and I leave, you and Mr Thoresby will have to fend for yourselves again.'

'Which we can do. No doubt you will be relieved to continue your journey.'

'Yes. My friends will be growing anxious if they do not have word of me soon. And you.' She glanced up. 'Do you have family, friends who worry about you?'

He was not expecting the question.

'I have one or two good friends. As for family…' his mouth twisted '…I am a younger son. They are never of much value.'

She looked up, surprised, and he suddenly realised how bitter that must sound. She did not question it, however, merely ventured a light, teasing remark.

'Younger sons can also be expensive, I believe.'

'Yes, but my parents are fortunate that I have my own income.'

'Indeed?' She leaned on the table, propping her chin on one hand. 'Do they want to see you setting up your own establishment?'

'I am sure they do, although they are far too wise to say so. I don't doubt they would like me to take a wife and settle down.'

'And will you do so, some day?'

'I very much doubt it. I have been a bachelor for too many years to wish to change my situation now.' He sipped at his wine. 'You do not look convinced. Do you think perhaps I might one day lose my heart? If that was going to happen, I think it would have oc- curred long before now.'

'I agree.' She laughed and raised her glass to him. 'One of the advantages of growing older is that one is no longer a prey to these starry-eyed notions of ro- mance!'

They drank silently, Gabriel relieved that they were remaining on good terms and surprised at how relaxing it was to dine with a woman who was not constantly looking for compliments. Or trying to persuade him into marriage. He heard the distant chime of a clock, reminding him that the evening was far advanced, but he did not want it to end just yet.

He said, 'Tell me about the house where you work. It is a charity, you say?'

'Yes. Prospect House provides a safe and respect- able home for women who have nowhere else to go. Fallen women, you might call them, although most are guilty of little more than being far too innocent and trusting of men. Once a woman loses her good character she must survive as best she can. Without references a servant cannot find work and for ladies the situation can be worse, they do not know *how* to work. Their education is often poor or non-existent and they are trained only in the accomplishments they require to become wives or companions.' She looked at him. 'You said that younger sons were of little account. Daughters have even less value, unless they find a rich husband.'

'And how did you come to Prospect House—did you need a refuge?'

'I ran away rather than marry the man my father had chosen for me. A rich man, notorious for his excesses.' Her lip curled. 'It was not only the fact that he was old enough to be my grandfather, but I knew he was a lecher with a cruel temper. The idea of shackling myself to such a man was not to be considered.'

'So you ran away and used your talent for cooking to support yourself.'

'Yes.'

She fell silent and he observed the sudden shadow in her eyes, as if the memories were painful. He wanted to reach out to her, to offer some comfort, but even as he lifted a hand she straightened and gave her head a little shake. 'Then, three years ago, I learned about Prospect House and was fortunate enough to be taken in.'

'So recently?' He frowned at her. 'How old were you when you ran away from home?'

'Eighteen.'

'And you are now…?'

'I shall not see thirty again.'

'Then how did you live for the intervening years?'

'I did what was necessary to survive.' The closed look on her face told him quite clearly she would not talk of it. 'When I arrived at Prospect House, everyone was sharing the chores, but it was clear that having one person to run the kitchens would be an advantage. My experience proved useful and I took charge.' She chuckled. 'As you have already said, I am a very managing female, but in this instance, I put the trait to good use.'

'And you are happy there?'

'Why, yes. I enjoy helping the women who come to us. Some are no more than girls, frightened, often desperate. We look after them, nurse them if they are ill, help them to learn new skills and try to find them a way to earn a respectable living. Some have become dressmakers, housekeepers, even a lady's maid. Everyone who moves on leaves a bed free for someone else. And believe me, sir, there is always another poor unfortunate needing a sanctuary.' She looked up, blushing a little. 'I beg your pardon. I have been rattling on.'

'Not at all. You have a kind heart, Nancy, but then I knew that already.'

'Because I rescued you from the snow?' Her shoulders lifted slightly. 'Anyone would do as much. And you have been wishing me at the devil since!'

'I do not deny I did so at first. I shall miss—' he saw the warning look in her eye and continued smoothly, '—your culinary skills.'

Her lips twitched. 'I am sure you will.'

Nancy closed the door of her room and leaned against it, letting her breath out in a long sigh.

There, that was not so bad. She had survived dinner with Gabriel—nay, she had *enjoyed* it—and returned to her room unscathed. But of course that did not mean she did not want to move on. Away from Dell House. Away from Gabriel.

Chapter Seven

The weather continued to play havoc with her plans to leave. Nancy busied herself in the kitchens all morning and as she did not see Gabriel, she suspected he, too, was anxious to avoid a meeting. However, it did nothing to lessen the attraction that sparked between them when they met for dinner. It was intoxicating, thought Nancy, like the thrill of an electric shock.

She tried to ignore it as Gabriel held her chair for her, but when his fingers grazed the back of her neck it was as much as she could do not to jump out of her seat. They sat in silence as Hester brought in the first dishes, but even when they were alone they spoke little. Gabriel seemed distracted and Nancy thought that he, too, must be aware of the charged atmosphere. She forced herself to make light conversation and was grateful when he followed her lead.

Nancy tasted next to nothing of the meal and it was almost a relief when the covers were removed. Neither of them had taken much wine and the decanter was still half-full. Gabriel held it up, his mouth twisting.

'John will think I am ailing if I leave this much.'

She feasted her eyes on the long fingers holding the decanter as he topped up his glass, imagining them on her skin, slipping around her neck and pulling her close. The very thought of it made her stomach swoop and set her heart pounding. He glanced across at her, lifting an eyebrow in enquiry, and she shook her head.

'Thank you, but I must not drink more. I need to keep a clear head for the morning.' She pushed herself out of her seat and went to the fireplace. 'William thinks the road will be clear enough to drive the coach to Markham tomorrow.' She salved her conscience with the thought that he had said it *might* be clear. 'From there we can pick up the Great North Road. I want to be packed and ready.'

'You are impatient to be away from here.'

'Why, yes.' She began to straighten the ornaments on the mantelshelf, refusing to turn and look at him. He was too adept at reading her thoughts. 'I have been here for more than a se'ennight—'

'Nine days.'

His voice was very close and Nancy's spine tingled. She had not heard him leave the table, but he must be standing just behind her. She gripped the mantelshelf, not daring to turn around. She stared down into the fire, every nerve end screaming.

'You feel it, too, don't you?'

His voice was a low caress that set her nerves tingling. She shook her head.

'It is just…being shut in like this. We agreed.'

'Being so much in each other's company,' he murmured, his breath warm on the back of her neck.

'D-dining alone...'

Her throat dried as she felt his lips on her skin. It was no more than a butterfly's touch, but it sent a thrill skittering down her spine. For the life of her she could not stop her eyes closing and her head going back as he trailed light kisses down to her shoulder.

'And the wine.' His voice was ragged as he turned her to face him. He cupped her face with his hands. 'One becomes prey to temptation.'

His blue eyes were hot, burning with desire, and her lips parted, inviting his kiss. He did not hesitate. She made no pretence of resistance when he captured her lips. Instead she answered him hungrily, twining her arms about his neck and clinging to him while he plundered her mouth, drawing up the desire from deep in her core. Her legs felt weak, she thought she might swoon with the delightful havoc he was wreaking within her body and she gave a little mewl of protest when he raised his head.

His sigh was deep and heartfelt. He held her close, resting his cheek against the top of her head.

'Ah, no. Much as I want to, I must not compromise you further. Tomorrow you may be leaving. We can be strong for one more night.'

Every nerve in her body cried out against that. The blood was pounding through her—she was stunned by the hot, aching need that suffused her body. Suddenly everything was clear.

'No,' she said, her voice calm, steady. 'I want you,

Gabriel. Even for one night, if that is all we have. I want that memory to carry away with me.'

'Nancy—'

She put her hands against his chest and looked up into his face. 'Please, Gabriel. I am thirty years old and no innocent, I know what it is that I am doing. I want no promises, no ties. Just take me to bed.'

His eyes blazed and she stared back boldly. Without a word he caught her hand and led her out of the room. Silently they crossed the empty hall and made their way up the stairs.

'My room,' he muttered, leading her past the door of her bedchamber. 'We shall not be disturbed there.'

No candles burned, but the firelight was sufficient for their needs. Nancy was already untying the ribbons of her bodice by the time Gabriel had locked the door. He pushed the satin gown from her shoulders and it slid with a whisper to puddle around her feet. She forced herself to keep still as he ran a finger along her collarbone and down into the valley of her breasts, but when he hooked it into the top of her stays and pulled her close she gave a shuddering sigh and with a growl he dragged her into his arms, capturing her mouth for a fierce, hungry kiss. She responded eagerly, clinging to him as he swept her into his arms and carried her across to the bed.

For a few moments there was a frantic scramble in between the hot kisses. Shoes were kicked off, Gabriel's coat, waistcoat and breeches were discarded before Nancy clutched at his billowing shirtsleeves and dragged him down on top of her, too impatient to wait any longer. Her body moved instinctively against his, hips lifting towards him, inviting him to enter her. It was a wild, joyous coupling born of need and only afterwards did they remove the remainder of their clothes and slip, naked, beneath the covers.

Gabriel gathered her in his arms and kissed her hair, murmuring, 'Why did you not tell me?'

'What?'

'That you were a virgin. I beg your pardon, I thought, assumed…from your manner, the things you have told me—'

She said bitterly, 'In my experience, men find unprotected virgins irresistible.'

'Not I.'

'Oh.' She bit her lip, her sudden anger fading as quickly as it had come. 'How did you know? Was I not…satisfactory?'

His arms tightened. 'More than satisfactory, but let us just say I am…experienced in these matters.'

'You have had many women?'

'Enough, but I had made it a rule never to seduce a virgin. Unfortunately, by the time I realised, it was too late.'

He sounded rueful and she wanted to reassure him.

'You did not seduce me,' she said, raising herself on one elbow. 'I asked you to take me to bed and I do not regret it.'

'I hope I never give you cause to regret it. But if I had known—'

She put her fingers on his lips to silence him.

'If you had known you would not have done it?'

'Oh, yes, I would! But I might have been a little more gentle. And a lot more circumspect.'

She shook her head at him. 'I did not want you to be gentle! And I am fully aware of the possible consequences of what we have just done. I am old enough to deal with it. I will not ask anything more from you than a night's pleasure. At thirty, I have no expectation of marriage, and I am quite content to return to my friends in the north and continue my life there, I promise you.'

'Nancy—'

'Hush now and let us enjoy this moment.' She snuggled down against him. 'I wanted this as much as you, Gabriel. Perhaps more, since it was a new experience for me.'

He chuckled sleepily. 'Then I hope I did not disappoint you.'

'Oh, no.' She closed her eyes, smiling in the darkness. 'You did not disappoint me at all.'

Nancy awoke some time later to near darkness, the fire no more than a sullen glow. She turned towards Gabriel, who responded immediately. She felt the delicious swoop deep inside when he pressed against her, hard and aroused. This time they made love slowly. He gave his attention to every part of her and she moved restlessly beneath the gentle but unrelenting pleasuring he inflicted with his hands and tongue. Her whole body was singing and she ran her own hands over him, exploring and caressing, revelling in the firm contours of his muscled body.

When the ripples of excitement began to overwhelm her, she gave a little groan and gripped his shoulders while he covered her and they moved together, soaring, flying, hurtling towards that final joyous climax. Their cries rang out in the darkness. Nancy clung to him as her body bucked and writhed and Gabriel held her, safe within his arms, until at last they sank back on to the bed, sated, exhausted.

Nancy stretched luxuriously as she awoke from a deep, dreamless sleep. Slowly she became aware of the smooth cotton of her nightgown against her skin and the fact that she was in her own bed. At some point in the night she and Gabriel had agreed that she should return to her own room. The glowing embers of the fire had provided sufficient light for her to dress, putting on just enough clothes to be decent and carrying the rest back to her own room, so that when Hester came in with her morning coffee, there would be no sign that anything untoward had occurred. A smile of deep satisfaction bloomed inside and curved her lips. No outward sign, at least.

It must have been her companion's brisk step that had awoken her, for almost immediately the door opened and Hester came in, wishing her a cheery good morning. Nancy sat up slowly, blinking as Hester dragged open the curtains to let in the grey morning light. She drank her coffee while the older woman built up the fire.

'Thank you, Hester, but I will see to that,' she said, when her companion turned her attention towards the tangle of satin and linen thrown over a chair. 'You have more than enough to do without waiting upon me.'

'Well, if you are sure, ma'am, I *would* like to get on with preparing breakfast.'

Having assured Hester that she could manage perfectly well and sent her away, Nancy put down her coffee cup and snuggled back beneath the covers. She did not want to get up just yet. She wanted to go over every moment of her night with Gabriel. To relive the wonder of it and remember how safe she had felt in his arms and how much she had enjoyed his caresses. He had been so gentle, so tender, there had been no pain, no fear.

With my body I thee worship.

Restlessly Nancy threw back the covers and slipped out of bed. Why she should think of those words from the marriage service now she really had no idea. She had told Gabriel she wanted nothing from him save one night to remember and it was true. The fact that the night had been so...so *delicious* would make the coming parting all the more difficult, but she did not regret a moment of it.

She scrambled into her day gown, but when she had put up her hair she stood for a long moment, staring into the looking glass, wondering if anyone would notice the added sparkle in her eyes, the faint, hectic flush upon her cheek. And even if they missed those telltale signs, surely she would give herself away when she and Gabriel met again.

Gabriel. Just the thought of him knotted her insides, but there was a cautionary voice in her head that told her not to expect too much. Her experience might come mostly from the stories she had heard from her friends at Prospect House, but she knew that for most men the excitement of the chase was everything. Now that Gabriel had bedded her, he would probably show her no more than common politeness.

'Which is all to the good,' she told her reflection. 'We both have our own lives to lead and the sooner we get on with them the better!'

And on this salutary note, she made her way downstairs.

Her courage faltered for a moment when she entered the kitchen to find Gabriel sitting at the kitchen table. He was talking to Hester, who was busy cooking his breakfast. They looked up as she came in and she managed a general word of greeting before moving swiftly across to the larder, pointlessly moving bottles and jars as if checking on the ingredients required for dinner. When at last she felt sufficiently collected to return to the kitchen, she was greeted with news that should have been welcome.

'William and Mr Thoresby have gone off to Markham,' Hester told her. 'William heard tell that the road was clear for a carriage now. He had it from a farmer's boy who went by at first light, so they've ridden out to see for themselves. William thinks it would be as well if we set off later today and we can follow the night mail northwards.'

'I see.' She poured herself a cup of coffee and took a seat on the opposite side of the table to Gabriel, as far away from him as she could manage without fall-ing off the end of the bench.

'So, as soon as we have finished breakfast I shall go and pack your trunks, Miss Nancy, ready to be on our way this afternoon,' declared Hester.

She put a plate of bacon and eggs before Gabriel, who said now, 'There is no definite news yet about the Great North Road?'

'No, sir, but if we can get to Markham that will be a start.'

'Perhaps it might be best to wait another day,' Gabriel spoke casually, giving his attention to cutting up his bacon. 'I do not like to think of you ladies setting out until we know the main road is clear.'

'Perhaps we *should* wait until we are sure,' remarked Nancy, avoiding Hester's eye. 'We have tarried this long; another night is neither here nor there.'

'Quite,' said Gabriel. 'Although I have to confess I have a vested interest in your remaining.' He sent a glinting smile down the table. 'I shall be loath to re-turn to John's cooking.'

'Oh, Miss Nancy, you've spilled your coffee!'

'Yes, how clumsy of me.'

As Hester hurried over with a cloth to mop the table, Nancy threw a swift, indignant glance at Gabriel and was rewarded with a bland look that made her long to hit him.

'Well, I suppose, by the time the men get back, there won't be much daylight left,' said Hester. 'And since we have everything prepared for tonight's dinner, perhaps we should have that, for heaven knows when we might get another good meal on the road.'

Nancy agreed, trying to ignore her soaring spirits. There was no doubt that Gabriel wanted her to remain another day. Another night.

Nancy and Hester were alone in the kitchen when the two men returned from Markham. They came in laden with shopping and a waft of icy air.

'The road to Markham has been cleared of drifts,' said William, putting two sacks down on the table. 'But there's been no word of the York mail.'

Thoresby added his bags to the table, then excused himself and went off to find his master. Hester and Nancy fell upon the shopping while William looked on, his hands wrapped about a tankard of mulled ale.

'There wasn't much at market today, madam, the weather having been so bad, but Mr Thoresby thought we should get what we could, whether you decide to stay or no. I managed to get turnips and potatoes, and some winter cabbage, too. And Mr Thoresby bought four dozen wax candles so you don't have to use those rank-smelling tallow ones in the main rooms. We was fair loaded up by the time we rode away, I can tell you.'

Nancy was quick to thank him for their efforts and, after helping to put away the fresh supplies, she left Hester and William peeling vegetables for the pot while she carried off a box of candles.

The long hours of darkness had taken its toll on their stock of good candles and Nancy wanted to make sure

there were beeswax candles in all the rooms in readiness for the evening. She started with the bedchambers,
knowing everyone was downstairs, before proceed-
ing to the lower floor, including the small room at the
back of the house that Gabriel used as his study. The
thought of finding him there, alone, brought on the
now-familiar lightness inside and she scolded herself
for behaving like a lovesick schoolgirl. She was merely
performing the task she had set out to do and his writing room more than any other required good light.

As she approached she heard the rumble of voices.
Which was good, for that meant she would not be alone
with Gabriel.

*Oh, don't lie to yourself, madam. You know full well
you would like to have him to yourself!*

She heard his deep voice as she opened the door,
speaking most decidedly.

'The key to this is Masserton Court. We need to—'

Nancy stopped by the door and Gabriel broke off
when he realised she had come in. Her thoughts had
become jumbled as soon as she heard him mention
Masserton. What was so important about the Court?

'I beg your pardon.' She swallowed, hard. 'I did
knock.' She held out her basket. 'I, um, have brought
you fresh candles.'

'Excellent.' Gabriel came over to her, no sign in his
manner that there was anything amiss. 'Give me the
ones for the wall sconces.'

It was the work of a few minutes to change the candles and Nancy went out, leaving the men to talk. She
closed the door behind her and waited for a moment,

listening, but they were speaking more quietly now, and she could not make out a word. For a moment she stood, chewing her lip. Part of her wanted to go back into the room and demand to know what was afoot, but after a few moments she decided to carry on with her task. It wasn't but an hour or so until dinner, she would talk to Gabriel then.

The morning room was warm and bathed in a cosy glow of candle and firelight when Gabriel joined Nancy there for dinner. He had spent most of the day thinking about her, about their night together. The way she responded to him, warm and yielding, making him feel like a giant among men. By heaven, it was years since lovemaking had been so satisfying. If ever.

The smile grew inside him as soon as he saw her. She was sitting beside the fire dressed in a ruby-red gown, one of those he had seen strewn over her bed, discarded as too dashy for a poor widow. Clearly, she no longer considered it necessary to hide the fact she had such gowns in her possession.

She rose as he came in, her dark hair glowing like polished mahogany, and she had coaxed a single curl to rest upon her bare shoulder, where it enhanced the creamy whiteness of her skin. He took her hand and bowed over it.

'You look delightful, madam. That colour suits you. Quite ravishing.'

She laughed, blushing adorably as she gently withdrew her fingers and preceded him to the table.

'It is far too showy for a quiet country dinner. But

I thought I might as well wear it as not. You have seen all the plainer ones.'

'I have, indeed, and they are charming in their way.' He held her chair and when she was seated he stooped to kiss her neck. 'This one, however, makes me hope you plan to seduce me. Shall we forgo dinner and slip away upstairs?'

She laughed at that. Gabriel sighed and took his seat opposite her.

'Have you never learned, madam, that it is most *un*seductive to giggle when a man propositions you?'

Her eyes gleamed, but she answered seriously, 'I wish to talk to you.'

'That sounds ominous.'

He was not reassured by the slight frown creasing her brow, but John and Hester came in at that moment with trays of dishes and he could not ask her about it. When they were alone again, Nancy politely invited him to partake of the pork ragout and buttered turnips. She showed no wish to discuss anything other than the food and he followed her lead. Something was on her mind, but he would not rush her. After all, they had all night. Well, not all of it, he thought, glancing at the sofa he had moved closer to the fire. He very much hoped he and Nancy might find more pleasurable ways to finish the evening.

Hester and John had just left another selection of dishes on the table when Nancy said suddenly, 'This afternoon, when I came into your study, you and Mr Thoresby were talking of Masserton Court. Does whatever you are doing here concern the Earl?'

He was spooning rice on to his plate, but paused to throw a warning glance at her.

'I'd rather you did not ask about that, Nancy.'

She toyed with the food on her own plate. 'I know the family.'

'But not well enough to break your journey with them?'

She was avoiding his gaze, which intrigued him, but she answered lightly enough.

'A humble cook cannot invite herself to stay wherever she pleases. But I am curious about your interest in the Court.'

'To use your own words, madam, there is little point in you knowing that, since you will be leaving here soon. In fact,' he added, when she opened her mouth to object, 'it is safer if you remain in ignorance.'

She gave a little hiss of exasperation. 'How do I know you mean them no harm? Perhaps you are planning to rob them.'

He laughed at that. 'I promise you I am no housebreaker. Now, I know how hard you and Hester have worked to produce these excellent dishes, the least you can do is allow me to enjoy them.'

She returned her attention to her food and after a few moments she introduced another totally innocent topic for conversation and later urged him to try the potato pudding or the dumplings Hester had made from the bottled damsons. He smiled to himself. She was too wily to tease him further. Yet. She probably hoped that when he had finished his meal and drunk a few glasses of wine, he might be more susceptible to her cajoling.

It would not work, of course. He had withstood much more experienced interrogators than Nancy. More experienced seductresses, too.

However, he was more than willing to enjoy her attempts to charm him. He wanted to be diverted. He and John had spent hours trying to think of a way out of their current impasse, to no avail. He had hoped a solution might present itself during dinner but so far nothing had occurred to him. However, Nancy's company made up for that. She had a quick wit and conversing with her gave his mind a rest from the problems that whirled round and round in his head. And there was always the possibility that she might allow him to take her to bed again. He wanted to do so, very much indeed, but not out of gratitude for sharing his secrets with her.

When the dishes were cleared away and the covers removed, they remained at the table. Gabriel pulled the dish of hazelnuts towards him and began cracking them between his fingers. Nancy seemed in no hurry to leave. She sipped her wine and watched him.

'I wish you will tell me why you are here,' she said at last. 'I would like to know what your real purpose might be and why someone should wish to kill you.'

He offered her a shelled nut and when she refused he popped it in his own mouth.

'My dear, it is best that you do not know.'

She folded her arms on the table and fixed her eyes upon him. 'Have I not proved myself trustworthy?'

'Eminently, but I would not risk your safety.'

'Surely just being here with you is risk enough.'

She was leaning forward, giving Gabriel a fine view of her full, rounded breasts curving above the low-cut bodice of her gown. He dragged his eyes to her face and grinned.

'Aye, it *is* a risk, in more ways than one.'

He saw the heat steal into her cheeks, but she smiled back at him.

'Pray be serious, Gabriel. I saved your life. I think you owe me an explanation.' She reached across and touched his hand where it rested on the table. 'Won't you tell me?'

Even that gentle contact sent lustful thoughts slamming through him. He understood the impulse to get up and drag her into his arms. What surprised him, however, was his desire to tell her everything. That was unprecedented. He had known many beautiful, intelligent women, but he had never yet taken one into his confidence.

Nancy was watching him, her dark eyes luminous in the candlelight and he suddenly thought, why not? She had told him she knew the family and she might be able to bring a new perspective to the problem that had been plaguing him all day.

'You are right, I owe you some sort of explanation,' he said at last. 'And you might even be able to suggest how we go forward.'

'Of course.' Her sudden smile lit up the room and set his pulse jumping like a firecracker. 'I will help you if I can.'

He took his time refilling their glasses, giving his

body a chance to calm. He needed to think rationally and not be influenced by his carnal desires. It would be safer for both of them if he told her only what was necessary.

'I was sent here by certain…senior figures in the government to try to discover how secret documents are being smuggled out of the country and ending up in the Netherlands.'

'The Netherlands?' Her brows rose. 'Not France? Napoleon was defeated this summer, but he still has some support in the country, does he not?'

'Yes, he does, but they are not the problem this time. Or not directly.' He pushed her glass across the table. 'As you may know, the Congress of Vienna created a United Kingdom of the Netherlands under William I. It was thought that would provide some stability, a buffer against any future French incursion. There were always going to be those who opposed this new state and a new kingdom, in its infancy, is very vulnerable.

'A few months ago, highly confidential documents disappeared from a cabinet office. They later turned up in the Netherlands, in the hands of those who want to see the new kingdom dismantled. And since then, more have gone missing.'

'And that is why you are here, to find them?'

'Yes, and to discover how they are leaving the country. There is now strong evidence that the papers are being smuggled out through a Lincolnshire port, via a halfway house in this area. I was due to meet an informer when I was attacked. John brought me word this week that the source of the leaks has been found—a junior cabinet minister with scandals he would rather not have made public. He was removed, but not before another vital document went missing, this one from the Home Office regarding our Navy working with the Netherlands in Africa. If King William's opponents get hold of those plans not only could it endanger our fleet, it could cause a rift between the British government and the other countries in Europe that are looking to England to keep the peace. All we know is that the documents are no longer in London.'

'But the plans could already be out of the country,' argued Nancy. 'How can you be so sure they are not?'

'I am not working alone. The militia is over-wintering near Markham and I have a small party of men at my disposal. John is in regular touch with their captain. The snow has been even more severe in the east, nothing has been moving there. We know the plans can't have reached the coast yet.'

'You think the documents are at Masserton Court,' she challenged him. 'What proof have you?'

'Not much, admittedly, but I have spoken to a servant at the house. He hinted that his conscience would not allow him to shut his eyes any longer to what was happening.'

'No.' Nancy shook her head. 'I cannot believe it. That might have been a tale made up to lure you into an ambush.'

'Possibly, but the old fellow appeared genuine. He was not one of my attackers, of that I am sure.' He shrugged. 'Perhaps he was warned off. I only wish to heaven he had confided everything to me at our first meeting, but there were other servants around and he was afraid to be seen too long with me. Whatever the case, my being set upon suggests I was getting too close to the truth.'

An icy hand was squeezing Nancy's heart. She stared at her wine glass, turning the stem around between her fingers.

'And you think the Earl is a traitor.'

'It is hard *not* to think it, if our suspicions are correct and the papers are being smuggled out via his principal seat.'

'But what proof have you?' she demanded again. 'You cannot charge anyone, let alone a peer of the realm, if you have nothing more than suspicions.'

'I know that, but it is common knowledge the Earl has squandered his fortune. He might be susceptible to bribes.'

She gave a snort of derision. 'If every penniless peer turned traitor to refill his coffers, the country would indeed be ruined.'

'I agree, but although we have nothing positive, the evidence is compelling.'

'But the minister involved,' she said, 'can he tell you nothing?'

Gabriel frowned and ran a hand through his hair. 'Unfortunately, he died before he could be questioned.'

Nancy's eyes widened in horror and she put a hand to her cheek. 'I heard nothing about that when I was in London.'

'It was all hushed up.' His mouth twisted. 'Passed off as a tragic accident. Which is what my attackers planned would be the verdict when my body was found.'

'And they transported you five miles to keep suspicion away from Darlton.'

'Yes, but they may have caught themselves out. John arranged to have a report of my death put in the local newspapers. Having dumped my body so far from Darlton, and with the snow cutting off the town, they have had no way of verifying those reports. When I do not reappear, I hope they will believe they have eradicated the threat.'

'That is all very well, but you have *not* disappeared. What happens when they see you again?'

'Ah, *then* they will not recognise me, I promise you. They attacked a hesitant, bespectacled country fellow with a thick northern accent. I shall reappear as something very different.' He looked at her, the corners of his mouth quirking upwards. 'What is the matter, Nancy, are you concerned for my safety?'

'I do not like to think of you putting yourself in danger,' she admitted, incurably honest.

He was smiling at her and for a moment she felt like bursting into tears. She wished she had never stopped at the Black Bull and found Gabriel lying in the snow. She wished she had never asked him why he was here. The moment passed and she steadied herself. Crying would do no good. It was impossible to forget what she had learned. She needed to think clearly.

She said, 'You believe the key to all this is Masserton Court.'

'Yes.' He grew serious. 'That is what John and I

have been puzzling over all day. We believe the missing plans are in the Court and we need to get in and find them. The difficulty is how to do that without arousing suspicion. And time is running out. With the weather clearing they will be moving those papers any day now.' He frowned. 'John thought he might be able to find work there, but they are not recruiting anyone from this area. Rather they are turning local people off.' He looked up suddenly, grinning. 'Perhaps we should kidnap the Earl's cook and you might replace him. One cannot do without a cook, after all!' When she did not smile, he said quickly, 'That was a poor jest, Nancy, I beg your pardon. Do not pay any heed to me. Perhaps by morning we will have hit upon something.'

Nancy drew a breath and said slowly, 'That will not be necessary. I can search Masserton Court for you.'

'Really?' He looked up, his brows raised. 'You know it well?'

'Very well indeed.' She paused for a heartbeat. 'I am the Earl of Masserton's daughter.'

Chapter Eight

'You are *what*?'

Gabriel was staring at her and Nancy flushed at the steely coldness of his eyes. Once again, he was all suspicion. However, she had started now. There was no going back.

'I am Lady Ann Chartell, the Earl's younger daughter.'

'Really?' He sat back and folded his arms. 'When we first met you said you were a widow in straitened circumstances. Next you told me you were a cook. What is this latest fantasy?'

'It is true, although the connection is one I would rather forget. I have not seen my father for more than ten years and I have no wish to do so. It is the reason I insisted we press on with our journey rather than putting up at Tuxford, the night I came upon you in the wood. You may ask Hester and William, if you do not believe me. They would have much preferred to sleep in comfort at the Crown.'

'Forgive me, madam, but Mrs Yelland and the

coachman are in your employ. They will corroborate any story you wish to tell.'

Nancy threw up her head. 'You do not believe me!'

'What do you expect, when you have changed your story so often? Let us say I am not convinced. You rescued me from the wood and brought me back to Dell House, and now you tell me you are the daughter of the very man I am investigating. I do not believe in coincidence, so it seems more likely that you are here at the Earl's behest. To keep a watch on me.'

'How dare you! You think I would put myself to the trouble of nursing you, that I would stay in this house—even share your bed—merely to spy on you?' She almost choked on her fury. 'If you are that much of a threat to anyone, they would want you dead, not restored to health!' She jumped up from her seat and glared at him. 'I have offered you my assistance, you stupid creature. I cannot believe my father would turn traitor to his country, but if that is the case then he must be stopped and since you seem to be at Point Non Plus I thought I might help, but believe me, there is nothing I want less than to return to my father's house.' She dashed a hand across her eyes. 'Now look what you have done, you hateful creature. I detest tears! Excuse me—'

She made for the door, but Gabriel was too quick for her.

'No, Nancy. Wait.' He caught her just as she turned the handle. She felt the weight of his forehead on her shoulder. 'Forgive me for doubting you. I have lived for too long in a world of lies and deception. Suspicion comes naturally to me.'

She said icily, 'Release me, if you please. I wish to leave.'

'I wish you would stay.'

'Why, when you do not believe me!'

'Then convince me,' he urged her, his grip tightening. 'I want to believe you, my dear. My heart tells me you are telling the truth, but my head—' He sighed. 'Please, Nancy, stay and explain it to me.'

She stood still, her anger waning. His distrust had cut her to the quick, but in all honesty could she blame him? Gently, Gabriel eased her fingers from the handle and closed the door. Nancy allowed him to lead her to the sofa where he sat with her, holding her hands.

'Now, tell me why you are estranged from the Earl.'

She gazed into the fire. Her instinct was to leave, to run away, but that was what she had been doing for years, was it not? Perhaps now was the time to face the truth, to live with her past rather than trying to bury it. Slowly she began to speak.

'I have already told you. My father planned to marry me off to one of his cronies, Viscount Packington, a hard, vicious man thirty years my senior. When my father told me his intentions I refused to countenance it, but it soon became clear that my wishes were of no consequence. If I resisted I would be forced, by one means or another, to accept the match.'

'So, you ran away.'

'Yes. I put together a small bundle of possessions and left Masserton Court.' She raised her head. 'I took nothing that did not belong to me: the jewels I had been given for birthdays, a little pin money I had managed to save. It was enough to pay for the coach fare and to get me away from Masserton.'

'And since then you have supported yourself by using the skills learned in your father's kitchens.'

Nancy's lip curled. 'You are sceptical, but why should you be? My governess did nothing to inspire me, although I admit I was a wilful child and difficult to teach. She managed to give me a rudimentary education—how to reckon and write, a little music—I doubt she was capable of anything more. And she had her own problems. When she was in her room, drowning her sorrows in a bottle, I escaped to the servants' quarters, where I received more kindness than I ever found above stairs. The tyrant who held sway over the kitchens found it easier to put me to work than to turn me away. He insisted his minions find things for me to do and when he discovered I had a talent for cooking he took me under his wing.' For the first time since making her revelation, she smiled. 'Whatever else my education lacked, I learned to speak French like a native!'

She hurried on, afraid he might offer some sympathy for the neglected child she had been. She did not want that, especially from him.

'Since leaving my father's house I have looked after myself. Finding work without references was not easy but I managed. And then I met Molly Morgan, who is now Mrs Charles Russington. She invited me to move to Prospect House, which is now my home.'

'And your family, did they make no attempt to find you?'

'Very little. I have kept in touch with my sister, Lady

Aspern, but her correspondence is delivered to a post office. Even after I learned Lord Packington had died of the pox, I would not risk anyone finding me.' She wrapped her arms about her, conscious of a sudden chill in the room. 'It was Mary who informed me of my mother's death, a few years ago.'

'That must have pained you.'

She shrugged. 'My mother and I were never close. Giving birth to me almost killed her and she was unable to bear more children. I was the reason she could not provide my father with the heir he needed. I was never allowed to forget that.'

'I am very sorry. '

She waved one hand. 'But all this is by the bye. I cannot prove I am who I say, save by appealing to those who knew me before I left Masserton. I do not think they could fail to recognise me. That is why I was loath to stop at Tuxford. Our family is well known at the Crown.' She added carelessly, 'If you want my help, you will have to trust me. If not, I shall leave here in the morning. Whatever you decide, it makes no odds to me.'

But Nancy was lying. She desperately wanted him to believe her. She waited for his answer, schooling her expression into one of indifference.

'Tell me one more thing,' he said, his gaze so sharp and steady she felt pinned beneath it. 'When you left your father's house why did you not go to Lady Aspern? Surely your sister would have given you refuge.'

'I did.' She ran her tongue over her dry lips. 'I did go to Mary. I begged for her help and she took me in, but her husband—'

She stopped, colour suffusing her cheeks as she re-lived the terror of travelling alone, the relief of reaching Mary's house safely, pouring out the story to her sister and brother-in-law, only to find he considered *her* to be at fault. His words still taunted her: 'If you insist on quitting the protection of your father's house, then you must take the consequences.'

And then, that night, he had come to her room and climbed into her bed, pawing at her, tearing her night-gown. She shuddered at the memory.

Gabriel was watching her closely and he nodded. 'Lord Aspern is one of those who cannot resist an... er...*unprotected virgin.*'

'Yes.' Nancy put up her head. After all, she had nothing to be ashamed of. 'When I resisted his...his *attentions*, he said it was what I must expect, now I was alone in the world. He wanted to set me up as his mistress. He offered to put me in a discreet little house somewhere convenient, so that I might still see my sister, although she was not to be told what was going on.' She looked down at her hands, twisting together in her lap. 'Mary is very much in love with her husband, you see. When I told her why I was leaving she did not quite believe me, but neither could she bring herself to believe Aspern, when he said I was to blame, that I had thrown myself at him. Mary and I have not seen each other since, although we correspond occa-sionally, in secret. So, there you have it. The story of my life, such as it is.' She forced herself to meet his eyes. 'That is the truth, Gabriel. More than I have ever told anyone before.'

'Then I am honoured by your confidences. You have been singularly unfortunate in your experiences with men.'

'I do not believe that is the case. The girls and women who come to Prospect House have suffered far worse. Aspern is a product of his upbringing, taught to believe women are of little consequence. We have already said that daughters are worthless, except as a marriageable commodity. A great match requires either beauty or a good dowry, preferably both. I had neither. My father considered himself fortunate when Lord Packington offered to take me off his hands and to pay handsomely for the privilege. I was an ill-favoured child, too thin and awkward to be considered worthy of attention.'

'Then you have changed out of all recognition,' he remarked, smiling a little.

She blushed and waved one hand. 'I am in no mood for compliments.'

'I intended none, it is merely the truth. And from our conversations I see nothing lacking in your education.'

'Thank you. I have always been a voracious reader and my father's library was well stocked, if a trifle out of date. Reading is a habit I have tried to keep up. But we digress. I do not know what else to say to convince you of who I am.'

'You have done more than enough. I am sorry I doubted you.' He lifted her fingers to his mouth. 'Can you forgive me?'

He was smiling at her, setting her pulses jumping. She resisted the temptation to melt into his arms and tell him she would forgive him anything, but it was a struggle.

'You need someone inside the Court,' she said, withdrawing her hand and trying to sound businesslike. 'Someone who can search the house. I can do that, although I will tell you now, I do not believe there is anything to be found. My father is many things—weak, blustering, something of a bully—but I cannot believe he is a traitor to his country.'

'And you are willing to return to your family home to prove it?'

'Yes.' She met his eyes. 'I will do my best to discover the truth, whatever it may be.'

Now the decision was made, she realised how much she disliked the thought of returning to her father's house. Not that she feared for her safety, it was the unhappy memories that disturbed her. The answer was not to think of them.

Nancy turned her mind instead to practical matters. She must write to Prospect House again and tell them she had been further delayed. Then she would need to prepare for her arrival at Masserton Court. Gabriel was deep in thought, his brow creased, and she guessed he was about to refuse. Having made up her mind to do this, she was affronted by even this slight hint of opposition.

'You think a mere female too weak for the task? I assure you I am not.' She looked at him, saying, 'You said yourself you had no other idea how to proceed.'

'True.'

'Very well then. I think it would be best if William

Coachman took me back to Tuxford and I transferred there to a hired chaise.'

'And your reason for going back?' he asked her, re-filling her wine glass.

'A wish to be reunited with my family. I shall prostrate myself at my father's feet and beg him to take me in.' She paused. 'I doubt he will welcome me with open arms, but if I am suitably remorseful I do not think he will turn me away. I shall then be well placed to discover if there is anything untoward going on.'

Gabriel pushed himself to his feet and paced the floor, his hands behind his back and his brow furrowed in thought.

'No, I think not,' he said at last. 'The risk for you is too great. From what you have told me, to put yourself back into your father's power—'

She laughed at that, a genuine moment of humour. 'I am thirty years old, I do not think he will attempt to find me a husband.'

'But even so, you thwarted him. He will resent that.'

'He will be even more angry if he discovers the true reason I am there!'

'There is that, too.' He stopped before the fireplace and looked at her. 'No. It is too dangerous. The Earl is still your father, Nancy. I cannot let you involve yourself in this.'

She sat back in her chair and folded her arms. 'I do not think you have any choice.'

Gabriel thumped his fist on the mantel.

'I cannot let you—' He broke off as the door opened and John Thoresby came in.

'I beg your pardon, sir, madam. It is getting late and I wondered if you might require any more wine this evening?'

Nancy looked at Gabriel. 'Perhaps you should ask Mr Thoresby for his views on the matter.'

She sat quietly while Gabriel explained. When he had finished John Thoresby rubbed his chin.

'It sounds like a good plan, sir. If Mrs Hopwood is willing.'

'Mrs Hopwood is very willing,' put in Nancy. 'And perfectly capable, too.'

'You would be taking Mrs Yelland with you?' John Thoresby asked her.

'Of course, if she will come, once I have told her why I am going to Masserton. I think she will.'

'So, too, do I.' He looked towards Gabriel. 'I have formed a good opinion of that lady, my lord. I believe we can take her into our confidence.' He saw his master was not convinced and added, 'In truth, my lord, it is the only plan we have, is it not?'

Gabriel frowned, not pleased to be reminded of that fact.

He turned to Nancy. 'But your friends in the north will be expecting you.'

'William can take a letter to them. Well?' Nancy rose and walked around the table to stand before Gabriel. 'Mr Thoresby and I are agreed. What do *you* say?'

Gabriel still looked troubled. He glanced at his servant.

'No more wine tonight, John. You may go.'

When Thoresby had withdrawn she reached out and took Gabriel's hands.

'You need me to do this,' she said. '*I* need to do it, if only to prove my father is no traitor.'

He looked at her, his eyes unusually sombre. 'And if you prove otherwise?'

Then I shall have sent my father to his death and it will always be between us.

Not that it mattered, she thought bleakly. This was only a brief interlude, a snowbound idyll. She put up her chin.

'I am prepared to face that. I shall not fail you, Gabriel.'

'I know that.' He drew her into his arms. 'Will you cry friends with me again?'

His smile was like balm to her battered spirit, as if the world had righted itself. She put her head against his shoulder and gazed up at him.

'More than that.'

Her voice was husky. The steely light in his eyes deepened to a hot blue flame as his mouth came down upon hers.

'If you want to change your mind, about going to Masserton Court tomorrow, I shall understand.'

Gabriel had walked into Nancy's bedchamber to find her at her dressing table, brushing her hair. She had not turned, but watched his approach in the mirror. When he put his hands on her shoulders, he was all too aware of the fragile bones beneath the flimsy linen of her nightdress and was overwhelmed by the desire to protect her.

Her reflection was calm, resolute.

'No. I am determined to do this.'

'It might be dangerous for you.'

'Then I shall expect you to rescue me.'

'Be serious, Nancy. This is no game.'

She rose and put her arms about him.

'I know it and I am taking it seriously, I promise you. But I cannot walk away without at least trying to discover the truth.'

'Perhaps it would be better not to know the truth.'

She shook her head. 'I should always wonder if my father was a traitor. I have to do this, Gabriel.' She slipped her arms about his neck. 'But we can have one more night together.'

He felt the now-familiar desire rising as she pressed herself against him.

'There will be many more nights, I promise you.'

She did not reply, but pulled his head down and kissed him hungrily. He pushed all the doubts and worries from his mind, giving himself up to the pleasure of making love to her. She responded eagerly to his caresses, rousing him to a white-hot passion. He reined it in, holding himself back until he had brought her with him to the edge of wild abandon. Only then did he grant them release and they toppled together from the heights. Half-laughing, half-crying, they fell back against the pillows, where he pulled her into his arms and held her close until sleep claimed them.

Gabriel stirred. He reached for Nancy but found only cool sheets. He opened his eyes. She was sitting up, her hair loose about her shoulders and her naked back gleaming white in the moonlight.

He turned on his side to look at her. 'Is something wrong?'

She did not turn to look at him, merely shook her head, sending a glint of silver rippling over her tumbled curls.

'Not really. I could not sleep. I want to tell you something. Before I leave for Masserton Court.'

'Go on.'

'There was a man in my life, once. An officer. A major who employed me as cook in his household. He was a good man, but his wife was very ill and he needed…comfort. He…he pleasured me and taught me how to satisfy him, but we never…' She stopped, her shoulders lifting in a faint shrug. 'He would not risk giving me a child when he was not free to marry me.'

Gabriel resisted the desire to run a finger down her spine. This was not the time to tease her, when she was confiding in him about someone who had clearly meant a lot to her.

He said softly, 'What happened?'

'I left him.' The words were matter of fact, but the bleak note in her voice tore at something in his chest. 'He was too good, too honest. The guilt of our affair was tearing him apart, but he could not bring himself to send me away. And I was falling in love.' A sigh, barely audible. 'I slipped away one day while he was out of the house. I left him a note, begging him not to try to find me.'

Gabriel frowned. 'But if he was as good a man as

you say, surely he would have provided you with a character, a reference, if you had asked him.'

'I am sure he would, but having made up my mind to go I had to do it quickly. If I had seen him again, if he had begged me to stay, I would not have had the strength to deny him.' He saw her hand go up and guessed she was dashing away a tear. 'I never saw him again.'

'He did not deserve you!' Gabriel ground out the words, unfamiliar emotions knotting painfully in his chest. Sympathy, envy? He said quietly, 'And you loved him.'

'Oh, yes.'

The words were soft, little more than a breath, but they sliced into him as painfully as any knife. But why that should be, he did not know. He was fond of Nancy, he enjoyed her company, and if he had helped her to forget her lover then he was glad of it, but neither of them wanted or expected more than this short interlude together.

Did they? Did *he*?

No, no, no! There was no denying Nancy was beautiful and their lovemaking was exquisite, but he had no intention of becoming a tenant for life with any woman. He had seen too many of his friends go down that route, moonstruck at first and swearing undying love, but eventually both parties went looking for pleasures outside the marriage bed. Even his own parents now lived their own lives and had done ever since they had concluded the business of producing enough sons to ensure the family line. They still lived together, and he thought they were fond of one another, in their own fashion, but while his father's latest mistress enjoyed the luxury of a house in town, his mother's cicisbeos were constant guests at whichever of their houses they happened to be occupying. He had long ago decided he was not such a hypocrite as to tie himself to any one woman, to promise to love, honour and obey until death parted them and then forget the vows when he tired of her.

He glanced at Nancy. Her head was bowed, her shoulders drooping. Fury blazed within him against the man who had caused her to feel so dejected. It was quickly followed by frustration that he could do so little to put it right and a sudden irrational anger with Nancy herself for allowing it to happen.

'I have had a great deal of experience of this sort of thing,' he said lightly, ignoring the instinct that warned him to keep quiet. 'The trick is not to lose one's heart.'

'That is easier said than done.'

He heard her sigh again and he said, 'I am very sorry if he hurt you.'

He watched her straighten, then she twisted back towards him, smiling.

'That is all in the past. I am much happier as I am, looking after myself. I value my independence, Gabriel, I wanted you to know that. To know that you do not need to worry about me, when all this is over.'

Still smiling, she rolled on top of him and kissed him. Her body was like cold silk against his skin, but she used her mouth and tongue to such effect that he was instantly aroused. Their lovemaking was heady and passionate, and afterwards she nestled close to Gabriel, who pulled the covers about them and held her in his arms.

Why had she told him that story now? He remembered how fiercely she had made love to him. As if it was the last time they would lie together. She was saying goodbye. Well, that was not unexpected. They had to part at some point. He should be pleased to know she wanted nothing more from him. No commitment, no obligation.

But he discovered that the idea did not please him. It did not please him at all.

Chapter Nine

Tuxford was bustling when Nancy and Hester arrived to meet the coach that John Thoresby had hired to carry them through the snowy landscape to Masserton Court.

They had spent days with Gabriel and John Thoresby, planning how Nancy should make her entrance. In the end they had agreed she should continue to masquerade as Mrs Hopwood. After all, she already had her story prepared for that role and the Earl would find widowhood a far more acceptable fate for his daughter than being a serving woman, however respectable. She had filled a single trunk with some of the gowns and the jewels she had worn in London and brought them with her. To her mind they were garish and ostentatious, but they were well made and clearly expensive, and that would give her a certain standing when she returned to the family fold.

By the time the carriage bowled along the drive to Masserton Court, Nancy was feeling slightly sick with nerves. She twisted the heavy gold wedding ring round and round beneath the thin kid glove, until Hester reached across and put a hand over both of hers.

'Whist now, Miss Nancy, you stop that. You will fret yourself into a fever.'

Nancy drew in a long, steadying breath. 'I know, Hester, but it was one thing to masquerade in London among strangers, quite another to do so in my father's house.' She added, with the ghost of a smile, 'Thank you for agreeing to come with me.'

'As if I would leave you to face this alone.' The older woman gave her fingers a final squeeze and sat back in her corner. 'Take comfort now, ma'am. We have played these parts before, so we know what we are about.'

'I pray you are right,' murmured Nancy, turning to the window in time to catch the first sight of her old home.

Masserton Court was a large, sprawling house built at the beginning of the last century in the Baroque style favoured by Vanbrugh and Hawksmoor. Two symmetrical wings curved around to form a courtyard on the north front, where the main entrance was flanked by Corinthian pilasters. A sweeping drive meandered through landscaped parklands and all too soon the carriage was pulling up by the shallow steps that led to the double doors. Nancy waited for the hired lackey to open the door and she stepped out, head high, with all the confidence she could muster. When Hester had alighted Nancy led the way up the steps to where the elderly butler was waiting by the now-open door. There was a puzzled frown upon his face, but it changed to dawning recognition as Nancy came up to him. She greeted him cheerfully.

'Good day to you, Mickling. Yes, it is I. Pray have my dresser shown to our rooms.' She pulled off her gloves and regarded him, her brows raised in feigned surprise. 'You look surprised. Surely you had my letter?'

'Lady Ann! No, my lady, that is, I—'

'My father is here, is he not?' John Thoresby's enquiries had already ascertained the fact, but she had a role to play and she was determined to do it well.

'He is, my lady. His lordship is presently in the yellow saloon.'

'Very well.' Nancy turned to her companion. 'I pray you wait here with the luggage, Hester. Mickling had best go ahead and announce me to my father. If my letter has gone astray, this might come as something of a shock.'

The pregnant glance Hester laid upon her almost made Nancy burst out laughing, despite her nerves. She turned away and followed the butler to the yellow saloon.

The marble hall was even colder than Nancy remembered. As she went further into the house the memories reared up. Not happy images of childhood—those were confined to the kitchens and servants' quarters—but the dark, lonely times spent in the oppressive splendour of the main house. Once she had left the schoolroom, Nancy had found living above stairs as confining as the tight lacing that her mama had insisted would produce the sort of figure a man required in a wife.

A respectable female had been hired to accompany

her everywhere. She was no longer allowed to slip away to the nether regions of the house and she was forbidden to climb trees or ride astride and bareback through the park. There were to be no more torn gowns or grazed knees, no more red, chapped hands. She was old enough to be wed and her father thought it might be possible to marry her off well. She was at last considered to be of some value to her parents.

After the chill of the great hall and statue-filled passages that led to the family apartments, the warmth of the yellow saloon was very welcome. Nancy's steps faltered as she followed the butler through the door, taking in the all-too-familiar surroundings, the faded grandeur of the wall hangings, the smoke blackened paintings and worn furniture. Her heart seemed to swell and block her breathing when she saw the stout figure of her father in a plum-coloured frock coat, sitting close to the fire. He was dozing in his chair, an open book in his hand.

Twelve years ago he had held her future—her very life—in his hands. She had never been frightened of him, despite the beatings and punishments meted out to the wayward child she had been, but she had always known he was unscrupulous enough to force her to bend to his will if she remained within his orbit. Now, with a greater knowledge of the world and how cruel it could be, uncertainty tremored through her. What had she done, putting herself back in the lion's den?

Mickling announced her in sonorous accents and the Earl gave a start. He got to his feet, pushing himself out of the chair with some difficulty. The years had not been kind to him, Nancy decided. He had always been a big man, but he had put on a great deal of weight since she had last seen him. His iron-grey hair was fashionably short and curled about his face, which was more lined than she remembered, the cheeks and nose reddened by excessive indulgence.

With a jolt she realised he was an old man and she was obliged to quell a sudden spurt of sympathy. He had always been a bully and a petty tyrant and she had no reason to think that had changed. It behoved her to be cautious. She returned his stare with a faint smile.

'Good day to you, Father.'

'Fore Gad!' The book dropped from his hand. 'It *is* you.'

'It is indeed.' She walked forward, aware of a momentary alarm when she heard Mickling withdraw and close the door upon them. 'I wrote to apprise you of my coming, but it appears you have not received my letter,' she said with apparent calm.

His face darkened. 'You have a nerve, coming back here after all this time.'

'Not the most effusive greeting,' she murmured, 'but I suppose I should expect nothing else.'

'You *deserve* nothing else! By Gad, it must be all of ten years.'

'Twelve,' she corrected him.

'And now you come crawling back.'

Her head went up.

'Hardly that.' She spread her hands and glanced down at the stylish bronze-velvet travelling dress with its elaborate frogging. She considered it ostentatious, but there was no question that it positively shrieked affluence. 'I am not throwing myself upon your charity, if that is your fear. I have means enough to support myself.'

That was true enough, she thought wryly. No need to tell him she could only do so by earning her living as a cook.

'Then what do you want?'

It was as much as she could do to stand her ground. There was no affection in her father's look, only suspicion, distrust and something more. Dislike. He had not forgiven her for upsetting his plans to marry her off.

Old feelings of rebellion and bitterness resurfaced and the force of them rocked her. If the hired post-chaise had not driven away, she would have been tempted to turn around and leave immediately. But she had a role to play and, if Gabriel was telling the truth, this was far more important than her masquerade in London. That had been to secure the happiness of one young woman. Now she needed to prove her father was not a traitor, or at least to prevent him further undermining the security of the country. A daunting task.

'What do I want?' she spoke lightly, stretching her lips into a smile. 'To return to the bosom of my family, naturally.'

He looked sceptical, but not totally disbelieving. His lip curled.

'Twelve years is a long time—how low did you have to sink to survive?'

'Not as low as you would have had me go!' she

flashed back. 'I was very fortunate. I met John Hopwood, a rich tradesman. A good man,' she added,
'nothing like the fiend to whom *you* were willing to
sell me.'

'Packington was prepared to make a good settlement. Better than you had any right to expect.'

'He was a depraved libertine with a taste for cruel
practices. It would have been no better than rape!'

His face darkened angrily, but before he could reply
they were interrupted. A soft, female voice spoke from
the doorway.

'Oh, I beg your pardon, my lord. I did not realise
you had a visitor.'

The speaker, a willowy, sylph-like figure in a
sheath of figured cream muslin, entered the room and
glided across to the Earl, the skirts of her gown sway-
ing around her hips. Her only ornament was a gold
chain, from which hung a pendant that drew attention
to the creamy breasts swelling up from the low-cut
bodice. Her beautiful face was delicately boned and
framed by a head of glorious golden curls piled high.
Nancy thought the woman was not much older than
herself, but as she came nearer she could see the net-
work of fine lines that fanned out at the edges of the
cerulean-blue eyes and deepened to creases around
her mouth as the sculpted lips stretched into a faint,
questioning smile that she directed towards the Earl.

He said, 'Ah, Susan, my dear. Come in.' The lady
stepped up and slipped a proprietorial hand on to his
sleeve. 'Let me present to you my daughter Ann.' There
was more than a hint of smug triumph in the gaze he

fixed upon Nancy. 'This is Lady Craster, my future wife.'

Wife! Nancy tried to keep her face impassive, but it was an effort. Lady Craster's smile grew and she uttered a soft laugh.

'You look shocked, Lady Ann, but you can be no more surprised than I. Until this minute I was not aware of your existence.'

'And I would not have mentioned it,' barked the Earl, 'had she not arrived on my doorstep without so much as a by your leave.'

'It appears my letter never arrived,' Nancy said smoothly, 'but I came hard upon it, never thinking I would be turned away.'

'More fool you!'

Nancy ignored the Earl's bad-tempered growl and addressed Lady Craster. 'Pray accept my felicitations, ma'am.'

She sketched a curtsy, silently damning Gabriel to hell and back. He must have known of this and deliberately kept it from her. She knew why, of course. She could almost hear his deep, mellifluous voice explaining that if she had known her father's fiancée was in residence, then her reaction to the news might have lacked conviction.

'Shall we all sit down?' Lady Craster had taken charge and was even now inviting Nancy to make herself comfortable in a chair. She guided the Earl to a sofa and sat down beside him. Then she folded her hands in her lap and fixed her blue eyes upon Nancy.

'Now, I am all astonishment at the news that my dear Hugh has another daughter.'

'I don't.' The Earl's denial was brutal. 'This woman forfeited any claim upon me when she left this house.' He scowled. 'I suspect her sister has kept up some sort of correspondence, but I have forbidden her name to be mentioned in my presence.'

'I quite understand that,' murmured Lady Craster in soothing accents. 'But, my dear sir, should we not at least enquire what has brought her back?'

'I am now a widow,' Nancy explained. 'I thought, Father, you might welcome my company and wish me to run your house for you. Mary told me Mama was gone, but I did not know you were planning to remarry.'

'Even if I was not about to take a wife, I would not wish you back again, you damned, ungrateful creature! You can leave this house immediately.'

'And how am I supposed to do that? My hired chaise has departed.'

'You may walk. In fact, you can spend the night in a ditch for aught I care!'

'Now, now, my dear Hugh, let us not be too hasty.' Lady Craster put a calming hand upon his sleeve. 'How would it look if it became known that your errant daughter had come back and you had turned her away? Think of the scandal.'

'Scandal be damned,' he retorted. 'She has done pretty well for herself until now, by the looks of it, so let her continue to do so!'

'Hush now, my lord.' Lady Craster broke in, turning her lovely smile upon the Earl. 'I will not allow you to let your temper run away with you. Lady Ann has come here to heal the rift and it would be very uncharitable to turn her away without a hearing.' She pouted. 'And your neighbours would be sure to say it was my doing. And then there is the ball.' She looked across at Nancy. 'Your father is giving a ball in my honour. It is all arranged for next week, when the moon will be almost full to light the way home for our guests.'

'And what has all this to do with Ann?' barked the Earl.

'My dear Hugh, think how well it would look to have your estranged daughter back with us.'

'I don't care a fig how it would look!' he declared, adding irascibly, 'And we are in uproar because you are in the process of decorating every bedchamber.'

'Oh, my love, you know that is not true! The Chinese room is quite ready and one or two of the others could be made comfortable in a trice.' She raised melting blue eyes to his face. 'Surely allowing her to remain here for a few days, or even a few weeks, would not be so bad?'

It took a little more cajoling upon Lady Craster's part before the Earl agreed and allowed his daughter's trunk to be taken upstairs to the Chinese bedroom.

Nancy herself went up shortly after and found Hester arranging her gowns in the linen press. She waited only until she was sure they were alone before throwing herself into a chair and giving a long sigh of relief.

'Well, thank heavens that is over!'

'Bad, was it?' Hester gave her a grim smile. 'I take it your father did not welcome you with open arms.'

'He was more inclined to throw me out on my ear! Thankfully his inamorata took my part and persuaded him to let me stay, at least for a few days.'

'That would be the thin-as-a-broom female who crossed the hall as I came up the stairs,' stated Hester, her nose wrinkling in distaste. 'Swanning around as if she owned the place.'

'Yes.' Nancy chuckled at this masterly description. 'Susan, Lady Craster. She is my father's fiancée and not at all pleased to have me here, I think, but she is even more anxious to avoid unfavourable gossip.' She folded her arms. 'She seems to have my father wrapped about her little finger and it may be that she fears I shall come between them.'

'Is she jealous of you, do you think?'

Nancy laughed at that. 'She has no need, as my father showed by his reception of me!' She sobered and a frown creased her brow as she continued. 'It is not inconceivable that he hopes she will provide him with an heir, but it is more than that, Hester. I think he truly loves her. Or at least he is infatuated. He fawns over her like a moonstruck schoolboy, but for all her soft looks and caressing words I do not think she loves him. There is something odd here, Hester. She knows he is not rich, so she cannot be a fortune hunter.'

'Perhaps she is eager to be a countess. Some women would sacrifice a great deal for a title.'

'That is possible, I suppose,' Nancy conceded. She fell silent for a moment, then said slowly, 'Despite her honeyed words, there is something cold and calculating about Lady Craster that puts me on my guard. For all my father's angry bluster, I think the lady is the more dangerous of the two.'

An awkward dinner was followed by an uncomfortable hour in the drawing room and it was with relief that Nancy pleaded fatigue and retired early to her room. She was relieved to be installed in the newly decorated guestroom, where there were no childhood memories to oppress her. Lady Craster had suggested Nancy might prefer her old rooms in the east wing, but on this point even his affection for his fiancée would not move the Earl. He had obstinately refused to acknowledge that Nancy was anything more than a guest in his house. And an unwanted guest at that.

She had dealt easily with the enquiries about her past, thankful that the preparation for her masquerade in London had been thorough enough to bear scrutiny and she was reasonably satisfied that her father believed her story, that she had fallen on her feet and met an honourable merchant who had made a respectable woman of her. Not that the Earl would ever approve of anyone connected with commerce.

Her father also thought it natural that she should want to take up her position again in his household. However, Nancy feared Lady Craster was not so easily convinced. In response to her questions as to why a widow of independent means should choose to return to the home after so many years, Nancy hinted that she had never felt comfortable in the less-than-genteel world of trade.

'Well, if you are thinking you might be able to catch

yourself another husband, then think again,' her father told her, adding with brutal honesty, 'As a tradesman's widow you are soiled goods, not fit to join the ranks of the *ton*.'

Nancy held on to her temper, but it was an effort. She assured him quietly that she had no wish to marry again.

'I merely want to live quietly, in the sphere in which I grew up.'

Her weary, submissive tone had the desired effect: a look of contempt swept across Lady Craster's delicate features. It was gone in an instant, but Nancy had seen it, and she hoped she had done enough to allay the woman's suspicions.

When Nancy went down to breakfast the following morning, it appeared that her plan had worked. She found the Earl deep in conversation with his fiancée. They broke off when she came in, but she had barely taken her place at the table when the Earl addressed her.

'I was discussing with Susan how best you can make yourself useful.'

He sounded much more cheerful this morning and was clearly reconciled to her remaining at Masserton, at least for the present.

'Of course, Father. If there is anything I can do...'

'Well, as a matter of fact there is.' Lady Craster spread butter on a hot muffin with small, precise strokes of the knife. 'You may help me with the final arrangements for the ball next week. Goodness knows *I* do not want one, but your father insists we invite every-one in the neighbourhood with any claim to gentility.'

'Aye, I do. If I'm taking a wife, then they all need to know of it. You've been here for over three months now and scarce know anyone.'

'But, my dear Hugh, you know I came here to be with you, not to be gadding about visiting all and sun-dry. And I have been very busy, all the decorating, I have not wanted to invite anyone to call…'

'That's as may be,' muttered the Earl. 'But I don't care to be on a bad footing with any of my neigh-bours.'

Susan tried, but not very hard, to hide a sigh. 'Apart from the odd baron, a couple of knights and a few bar-onets, there will be no one of higher rank than your father, which is a great pity, but there you are.'

The Earl waved his fork at her. 'I told you we might invite the militia, if you wanted to fill your rooms, my dear.'

The lady wrinkled her dainty nose. 'I am not des-perate to fill the house with young officers who have been starved of good company. No, this ball is for your neighbours, my dear, and we shall keep it so. Perhaps, Lady Ann, after breakfast you will attend me in the morning room and we will discuss what still needs to be done. Then you may relay my instructions to the staff. I find these country folk do not always seem to know what is expected of them and Mrs Crauford is really too old to be a housekeeper, but there, your fa-ther is adamant she must stay.'

'Aye,' growled the Earl. 'Crauford has been here for

as long as I can remember. Why, she was a maid here in my father's time and I ain't having her pensioned off. No question of it.'

'Quite, my dear.' Susan's smile was thin. She turned back to Nancy. 'So you see how useful you will be, Lady Ann. I shall leave it to you to make sure my orders are understood and carried out.'

'Of course, ma'am. I shall be delighted to help.'

Nancy smiled. It could not be better. Running errands would give her the perfect excuse to go to all corners of the house. She could search for the documents that Gabriel was convinced were secreted somewhere in the Court and make discreet enquiries of the staff. If there was anything untoward going on at Masserton, then they would know of it.

The Earl refilled his tankard from the jug of ale that stood beside his plate.

'Perhaps Ann could help you choose the wallpaper for the Blue Bedroom,' he suggested. 'Damned business has been going on for ever.'

Lady Craster leaned across and patted his hand. 'Bless you, my lord, but choosing the correct paper is not the work of a moment and I want it to be perfect.'

He grunted. 'You have been trying to decide on the right pattern for months, samples flying back and forth to Lincoln! Perhaps you need to find another paper-hanging warehouse, if Hewitt has nothing suitable. My late wife used Masefields on the Strand.'

'Mayhap I shall, if I do not find what I want in the latest samples he has sent me. But you will remember I told you, my lord, that his prices are so much more reasonable than the London warehouses. Why, I expect to save a hundred pounds or more by the time I have done all the bedrooms. And how much cheaper it is to have the paper hangers travel only from Lincoln rather than London!'

Nancy said, 'I would be happy to look at the patterns with you, Lady Craster.'

'Do, pray, call me Susan, my dear. And I thank you for your offer, but this little task is very special to me. Besides, there will be plenty for you to do, with the ball only days away.' She patted her lips with her napkin and rose. 'If you are ready, perhaps we might make a start on that now?'

With the exception of the butler and housekeeper, Nancy knew very few of the staff at Masserton Court. She had been away for so long that it was not surprising many of the older servants had gone. She learned with some regret that Monsieur Paul, the chef who had taught her to cook, had quit the Earl's service once Bonaparte had been banished to St Helena and had returned to France.

Those that did remember Nancy were touchingly pleased to see her and she spent a pleasant and informative hour drinking tea with the old housekeeper, as she reported to Hester when she went up to change for dinner later that day. She kept her voice low, in case anyone was listening at the door.

'Mrs Crauford has been housekeeper at Masserton since before I was born. If anyone would see any difference in my father, it would be she, but it appears he goes on very much as before. There is no sign that he has come into any extra funds recently and that is the only reason I can believe he might turn traitor. There is no talk of anything suspicious going on at Masserton and she told me that, apart from neighbouring families, there have been no visitors here.'

'Excepting Lady Craster.'

'Yes, there is the lady,' Nancy agreed. 'Crauford says that as far as anyone knows, my father met her at Brighton this summer and brought her back here as his fiancée. She has been his constant companion since then.'

Hester sniffed. 'From what I have gleaned, my lady rules the roost here now. They say the Earl is quite besotted.'

'I believe he is,' Nancy agreed. 'Crauford would never be disloyal, but from the little she said, I do not think she approves. Lady Craster has turned off a number of staff in the interests of economy and her own coachman and Lucas, her groom, are in charge of the stables. But my father's people may well have been growing too old, so there is nothing wrong in bringing in younger staff. I cannot believe the Earl has anything to do with the missing documents, whatever Gabriel Shaw may say. He and his lady have been living here since early September, smelling of April and May, according to the housekeeper, and apparently quite content with one another's company.' She chuckled. 'If the lady's plans to decorate the place are anything to go by, she intends to remain in residence for some time yet.'

'I can't help thinking we are here on a fool's errand, Miss Nancy. Master Gabriel should be looking elsewhere for his traitors, not wasting his time here.'

'Well, he is not wasting *his* time, is he?' Nancy replied tartly. She sighed. 'I confess I do not like being here, it is too oppressive. But I promised Gabriel I would search the house and I must do that. I cannot leave until I am sure there is nothing to be found here.'

Chapter Ten

By the evening of the ball, Nancy had rummaged through every cupboard, desk and drawer she knew of in the house, but to no avail. She even found an excuse to go into the attics that very morning, but the layers of dust on every surface convinced her that nothing had been secreted here recently. She felt an immense sense of relief. She had heard and seen nothing to suggest Masserton Court was hiding any secrets. She had discharged her promise to Gabriel and now she wanted nothing more than to quit the house with all haste. The Earl remained hostile and he lost no opportunity to belittle her. Lady Craster's dislike was more subtle, little pinpricks of criticism or disapproval that chipped away at Nancy's comfort and temper.

But it was not merely the behaviour of her father and his fiancée that disturbed her peace. She was missing Gabriel. So much it was like a constant ache inside her. He haunted her dreams. When she tried to read, his glinting smile intruded and, worst of all, her nights had never felt lonelier. Allowing him to make love to her had been a mistake, she acknowledged now. She should never have given in to the temptation.

Or I should have found myself someone who was not such a good lover, she thought with wry humour as she made her way downstairs from the dusty attics.

The major—the only man she had ever loved—had taught her how to please a man and how to take pleasure from his touch, but he had never roused her to such heights of ecstasy as she had shared with Gabriel. She had never felt so beautiful, so alive as she did when she was in his arms. But Gabriel was an expert. He made no secret of the fact that he had had any number of mistresses and that he intended to have many more. He was not the faithful type. He had told her so.

'Beggin' your pardon, my lady.'

Nancy jumped as the footman addressed her. She had reached the main landing and the man was coming up the stairs from the hall, so she hoped he would think she had just left her room. She summoned a slight, careless smile.

'Yes, James, what is it?'

'Lady Craster is looking for you, my lady. She begs that you will join her in the Blue Bedroom.'

'Of course. I will go now.'

Nancy remembered the guest room as a gloomy, cluttered place full of heavy furniture from an earlier age and dark, damp-stained walls. Now, when she walked in, she found it had been stripped of its old damask wallcovering and frames of stretched canvas were on the walls, covered with lining paper in readiness for the new paper hangings. The great bed had been dismantled and removed and the remainder of the furniture was gathered in the centre of the room and shrouded in holland covers. A small side table had been moved in front of the window and Lady Craster was standing over it, slowly turning the pages of a large book of wallpaper patterns.

'You wished to see me, ma'am?'

'Ah, yes. Lady Ann. And do, pray, call me Susan. I am, after all, soon to be your stepmother.' Lady Craster spoke with the false sugar-sweetness that set Nancy's teeth on edge while sorting through an untidy pile of papers beside the pattern book. She picked up a single sheet. 'There are a few little matters outstanding regarding tonight's ball and I would like you to deal with them. I have written you a list.' She held out the paper. 'I would see to it myself, of course, but you can see how very busy I am here. I am determined to make a decision about the paper for this room today. I am thinking of this one, the blue flock. It is almost the same hue as the original wallcoverings, but I think the Earl will prefer that, do not you? He is not one for change...' She paused, watching as Nancy scanned the list in her hand. 'Is there anything you do not understand, my dear?'

'No, indeed, Susan.'

Nancy gave a smile as false as the lady's own. Having searched the house from top to bottom, she felt her mission here was finished and had little desire to continue running errands. However, it would look odd if she were to object now, so she went off to do as she was bid.

* * *

By the time the short winter day was fading she had braved the wrath of the cook and passed on Lady Craster's latest changes to the menu, made sure there were sufficient chairs and tables in the supper room and discovered which of the footmen were to be employed at the main door. Finally, she double-checked all the final arrangements for the evening.

Having completed all her tasks Nancy went in search of Lady Craster, knowing she would want to be assured that everything was in order. She saw Stobbs, Susan's very superior maid, coming down out of a bedchamber and asked if her mistress was within.

The maid sniffed and looked down her nose at Nancy.

'My lady is writing letters in the morning room and is not to be disturbed.' Her tone was so haughty that Nancy instinctively stiffened. Something in her eyes must have told the maid she had gone too far, for she dropped a reluctant curtsy and added, 'My lady.'

The maid hurried away, but Nancy tarried on the landing. Opportunities to enter Lady Craster's room were rare. Her first search had been necessarily swift and it might be worth taking another look. She slipped quietly through the door.

The bedroom was much as she remembered it from the few times she had been allowed there to visit her mama. Pale silk, patterned with leaves, still covered the walls and the *chaise longue* remained at the foot of the painted four-poster bed. The same large gilt mirror adorned the space between the two windows. Nancy expected to feel something, a sense of loss or remorse, perhaps, but there was nothing. Perhaps it was because the room smelled differently now. Lady Craster favoured a light and undoubtedly expensive fragrance that was nothing like the heavy, cloying scent of roses Nancy remembered was her mother's favourite.

A memory surfaced as Nancy looked at the dressing table, littered with an assortment of bottles and silver vials, glinting in the weak sunlight. She and Mary had been brought in to say goodbye to Mama, who was about to set off to join their father in town. Mary had perched quietly on the *chaise longue*, but Nancy, always curious, had wandered to the dressing table, attracted by the profusion of jewels scattered there, waiting to be packed into her mother's jewel case.

'Do not touch those with your grubby hands!' Her mother's angry voice still rang in her head, the memory of it more painful than the sharp slap across the head she had received. 'Why can't you be a good girl and sit still, like Mary? Let me tell you, gentlemen do not like inquisitive young ladies and since you are neither beautiful nor graceful you had best cultivate some attractive manners or you will never get a husband! Merciful heavens, what did I do to deserve such a burden?'

No time now for self-pity, thought Nancy, shaking off the memory, she must concentrate on searching the room. Being inquisitive. Her besetting sin, according to her mother. And she did not have long. The fire had been built up and an empty hip bath had been placed before it, so it was most likely the maid was gone downstairs to order the hot water to be brought up.

Her eyes scanned the room. There were no letters tucked behind the ornaments on the mantelshelf, no notes hiding in the lady's dressing case, nothing sinister lurking among the clothes neatly folded away in the clothes press. She went to the bed and checked beneath the pillows. Nothing. Any letters the lady might have would be in her writing box, which she would have taken to the morning room.

Her eyes strayed to the frothy confection of lace and satin spread over the bed, the new gown Susan had ordered for the ball. The maid had unpacked it and discarded the empty box on the floor, tissue peeping from under the lid and the maker's trade card fixed to one corner. There was also the courier's stamp: Meldrew and Sons, Bridge Street.

A servant's voice in the passage reminded Nancy that it was getting late. There was no time to search any further. She went to the door and listened. A distant door opened and closed, then silence, so she slipped out of the room and hurried back to her own bedchamber to change her gown. When she went in, Hester was busy laying out her evening dress, a flamboyant creation of burgundy shot silk, lavishly embroidered with gold thread that winked and gleamed in the candlelight.

'Come along, Miss Nancy, there's hot water in the jug there, but we need to get a move on if you are to be ready before the first guests arrive for dinner. Hurry yourself, now.'

She helped Nancy out of her clothes and pottered about, tidying the room while Nancy washed away the dirt and tiredness. But she could not wash away her reluctance to attend tonight's revelries. She was not enjoying the role of prodigal daughter.

By the time she stood before the mirror in her freshly laundered chemise and boned stays, Nancy felt more restless and uneasy than at any time since she had arrived at Masserton Court. She exhaled, a loud sigh.

'Oh, Hester, could I not cry off? I really do not want to be sociable this evening. I have spent the afternoon ensuring that all Lady Craster's instructions for this evening's entertainment have been carried out. It would be no wonder if all that work had given me a headache.' She looked hopefully at her companion. 'You could run down and give my apologies.'

'That I could not, Miss Nancy.' Hester threw the gown over her head and twitched it into place. 'The Earl and his lady will expect you to put in an appearance.' She stood back to admire the effect and after a moment gave an approving nod. 'You will draw every eye this evening, madam, you mark my words.'

'I would much rather keep to my room!'

Hester gave a little tsk and said bracingly, 'Come now, you carried off this role in London to great success, you can do the same here, I am sure. And you must keep your eyes and ears open. Who knows, you might learn something important to Mr Shaw's investigation.'

Nancy felt a little knot of loneliness inside her

tighten at the mention of Gabriel. There had been no word from him since she had left Dell House. Not that she had expected any. He had told her that if she had anything to report, a message addressed to a Mr London at the Black Ram in Darlton would find him. If not, she would hear from him in due course, but how or when he did not say.

Now her anxiety and frustration found expression in anger.

'I am sorely tempted to quit this place tomorrow! It goes against the grain to spy on my own father.'

'I am sure it does, my dear, but you know you are doing it in the hope of proving him innocent.' Hester clasped the collar of diamonds about Nancy's neck, then took her shoulders and turned her towards the looking glass. 'There now. I dare say you will outshine your hostess tonight, even though she has a new gown, delivered from a fashionable London modiste this very morning.'

'I have seen it,' Nancy told her. 'White net over blossom-coloured satin. It is quite lovely and far less brazen than this creation!'

'Whist now, that gown suits you perfectly and well you know it,' retorted Hester. 'You are the Earl's daughter, Miss Nancy, whether you like it or not. 'Tis not as if you was aping your betters.' She sniffed. 'And it will be one in the eye for that hoity-toity piece who is Lady Craster's maid to see you dressed so fine. She's been boasting non-stop for days about the fine gown her mistress has ordered, so much so that some of the staff below stairs was hoping the snow might prevent it arriving. If we was only a few miles further north or east, then it would not have got here. Pity.'

Nancy laughed. 'Pray do not be so uncharitable, Hester. We are not in competition. And I have to admit that if I had a choice, I would prefer to be wearing something else.'

She studied her reflection as she spoke. The silk bodice clung to her generous figure, its low neckline and high waist accentuating the creamy swell of her breasts while the skirts fell in soft folds about her hips and shimmered in the candlelight. The gown had been purchased with the intention of attracting attention and she knew there was only one way to wear such a creation, with total confidence. Smothering a sigh, Nancy straightened her shoulders and summoned every ounce of self-assurance for her forthcoming performance.

'Wish me luck, Hester!'

She made her way to the drawing room where the Earl would welcome his guests for dinner. He was in the middle of the room as she entered, but had his back to her, issuing some last-minute instruction to Mickling.

'I am here, Father.'

Dismissing the butler, the Earl turned, his eyes widening at the sight of her. She schooled her face to indifference as his eyes scanned her from head to toe, but his surprise gave her some little satisfaction. He nodded with reluctant approval.

'By heaven, you never showed so much promise when you were at home.'

'Perhaps because I was never shown so much kindness at home as I have received elsewhere.'

He ignored that and looked past her. She turned to see Lady Craster had entered the room. Nancy did not miss the lady's appraising look and the fleeting shadow of displeasure that marred her beautiful features, but it was gone in an instant and Lady Craster was smiling at her.

'My dear Lady Ann, how very well you look.' She glanced down at her own softly flowing robe. 'Personally, I cannot wear such strong colours, but we shall look very good standing together, will we not? A perfect foil for one another.'

The announcement of the first dinner guests precluded any further conversation and Nancy knew it was time to play her part as the errant lamb returned to the fold. She had to admire Lady Craster's aplomb as she smilingly explained her presence.

'And here is Lady Ann, Masserton's youngest. Widowed, sadly, but we rejoice that she has returned to us, do we not, my lord? It is an ill wind, as they say.'

Nor was the lady at a loss when confronted by those neighbours who remembered Nancy and her scandalous flight from the family home.

'We cannot tell you how delighted we are that Lady Ann has decided to return to us. The past is quite forgot…'

Just sixteen persons were sitting down to dinner, all local families. Nancy was acquainted with most of them and could not think that any one of these respectable, stolid neighbours could have any connection with smuggling government secrets. She took her seat among them and played her part in the conversation, but all the time she was listening for any word, any hint that might suggest illicit dealings. However, it was all very innocuous, the subjects ranging from winter crops and spring plantings to hunting and who had the best coverts. The talk turned to the weather and Susan declared how wise they had been to invite only neighbouring families.

'Of course, initially that was because we are having the guest rooms refurbished,' she continued, smiling around the table. 'But with the snow setting in so fiercely I fear anyone from further afield might not have been able to reach us.'

'Aye, well, 'tis clear enough here at present, but I've told my driver to keep an eye on it and send in word if he thinks we need to leave betimes,' said the Squire, who was sitting to her right. 'Not that I think we shall have to do so, but 'tis best to be prepared. They say nothing is moving out o' Lincoln.'

'Oh, dear,' Lady Craster gave a sigh. 'I do hope it will not prevent Hewitt collecting the sample book tomorrow. I do so want to get the paper ordered for the guest rooms.'

'And if my lady hadn't been in such a tearing hurry to decorate them all we might have offered to put you up, Squire,' interjected the Earl, with a laugh. 'But there, you know what these ladies are…'

And so the conversation continued to ebb and flow around Nancy. Her father played his part as the genial host and presided over the dinner with bluff goodwill while Lady Craster smiled in a manner that Nancy thought condescending rather than charming.

When the meal was over Nancy moved across the hall to the ballroom, where Susan had insisted she should stand with her and the Earl and be introduced to all the guests as they came in. For the second time that evening she braced herself for the introductions, turning aside malicious comments with a smile, welcoming the genuine sympathy of some who remembered her, but all the time wishing the musicians would strike up and provide a diversion. At last the line of new arrivals dwindled to a trickle and Nancy turned her head to survey the crowded ballroom. By any standards the event must be considered a success, she thought. Not one family had refused the Earl's invitation and the room was comfortably full. She was wondering if they might safely move away from the door when she heard the sound of voices on the stairs.

More guests, she thought, smoothing her long gloves and composing herself for more smiles, more glib words. She heard her father greeting Lord and Lady Blicker and presenting them to Lady Craster. She recalled they were mild-mannered neighbours who lived at Hollybank, a small gentleman's residence a couple of miles away. They had been very kind to her as a child and she felt herself relaxing. There was nothing to fear from such kindly people. She turned, prepared to greet them with real warmth, but instead her gaze was drawn to the tall gentleman standing beside Lady Blicker. She froze in shock.

Chapter Eleven

Stunned, Nancy could only stare at Gabriel. He was elegance personified in immaculate linen and a silk waistcoat, his dark coat moulded to his form and white silk knee breeches and stockings that did nothing to disguise the power in those long legs. His hair, black and glossy as a raven's wing, was brushed back from that handsome face with its vivid blue eyes and chiselled good looks.

'And this is your unexpected house guest.' Lady Craster was speaking, her voice suddenly low and seductive as she held out her hand. 'Lord Gabriel Ravenshaw.'

'Aye. This is Baxenden's youngest,' declared Lord Blicker in his hearty style. 'The Marquess is one of my oldest friends, so when the young reprobate landed on my doorstep a few days ago I couldn't turn him away!'

Nancy watched as Gabriel took Susan's outstretched hand and bowed over it with practised ease.

'I was on my way north and obliged to break my journey because of the snow.'

'Aye, roads quite impassable,' declared Lord Blicker. 'Lucky to get as far as Hollybank.'

Lady Blicker gazed anxiously at her hostess. 'I do hope you did not take my hurried note amiss, ma'am.'

'Not at all, my dear Lady Blicker,' murmured Lady Craster, her appreciative gaze remaining firmly fixed upon Gabriel. 'You are very welcome, my lord.'

'And you are all kindness, ma'am. I am particularly indebted to you for allowing me to come here at such short notice.'

Nancy observed with mixed feelings how the lady melted beneath the full force of that charming smile. Heavens, she thought, Susan was almost purring at the man!

'I should not have forgiven Lord and Lady Blicker if they had left you behind. We are quite delighted to have you here, my lord. I believe the Marquess, your father, spends the winter at his Alkborough estate. No doubt you were going there to join him?'

'I was indeed,' came the smooth reply. 'With hindsight, it would have been better if I had remained with my friends at Belton rather than attempt the journey to the very north of Lincolnshire in this weather. Then again, if I had done that, I should have been denied this pleasure.'

Another smile, another little bow before his glance shifted to Nancy. He gave the merest start and his brows rose fractionally, as if he had just set eyes on a beautiful stranger. One day, thought Nancy from the recesses of her shocked brain, she would be able to think coolly about this meeting and appreciate

Gabriel's ability to act. He was looking back at his hostess, clearly seeking an introduction.

'Lord Gabriel, let me present you to Lady Ann, my lord's younger daughter, who has recently returned to us.'

The tolerantly affectionate note was now missing from Lady Craster's tone, but Nancy barely noticed. It was as much as she could do to dip into a curtsy without her legs buckling beneath her. Gabriel appeared to have no such problem maintaining his composure. His greeting was practised and graceful, followed by a polite and deferential request that she allow him the honour of standing up with her.

'That is, if you are not already engaged, my lady?'

Nancy had been thrown off balance by Gabriel's unexpected appearance and she found his cool assurance infuriating. She would dearly have liked to refuse to dance with him, but they needed to talk and he was offering her the perfect opportunity. She drew in a deep, angry breath. If he could play this game, then she could, too. She dropped a demure curtsy and kept her eyes modestly lowered as she responded.

'I am but very recently arrived at Masserton, sir, and not engaged for any dance.'

'Then I am fortunate, indeed, and will secure your hand for the first *two* dances, if I may?' At that moment the music began. Almost as if he had planned it, thought Nancy crossly. He held out his arm to her. 'Shall we?'

She accompanied him on to the dance floor, aware of the attention they were attracting.

'It would have been polite to invite your hostess to stand up with you,' she muttered.

'But you are an earl's daughter. Lady Craster is merely the widow of a baronet.'

She was not above enjoying a moment's satisfaction at taking precedence over Lady Craster, but it did nothing to mitigate her anger against Gabriel.

'Allow me to say how magnificent you look this evening, my lady.'

'Do not try to turn me up sweet,' she returned in a furious undervoice. 'Tell me instead what you are doing here.'

He laughed. 'I came to see you, of course.'

'You are living very dangerously, pretending to be the son of a marquess. If you are found out, they will eject you without ceremony!'

'Well, that won't happen. You see, I am indeed Lord Gabriel Ravenshaw.' When she raised her head to stare at him he merely smiled at her. 'No need to look so shocked. It is true.'

His insouciance was maddening. She refused to look at him and maintained what she hoped was a dignified silence as they moved apart. Her partner, however, appeared in no wise discomposed and when the movement of the dance brought them back together, he took the opportunity to provoke her even further.

'I thought you would be pleased to see me.'

She gave him a glittering smile.

'I *am* pleased, you odious creature. I need to talk to you.'

'Good. We shall make it quite obvious that we have

been slain by a mutual attraction and I shall whisk you away to a secluded corner as soon as possible. No one will think it odd if we conduct a little flirtation.'

Her smile slipped a little.

'They will think it most odd,' she contradicted him angrily. 'I am a respectable widow.'

'You do not look like one in that gown.'

This accorded so much with her own opinion that Nancy was obliged to laugh. Her anger melted away. It was just so comfortable to have Gabriel at her side.

'It looked much more dashy in town, I assure you, when I added any number of ribbons and brooches and positively *drowned* myself with jewellery.' She added cheerfully, 'I was outrageously, gloriously gaudy.'

'I wish I had seen it.'

Suddenly Nancy wished he had, too, but only if he had been party to the charade. Then they might have laughed about it together. Impossible, of course. If he had been in town when she had been playing her part as a tradesman's widow on the catch for a title, he would have regarded her with contempt. Instead he knew her now for what she was, a prodigal daughter, a fallen woman. A creature suitable to bed, but never to wed.

They completed the final steps of the first dance and Gabriel remained beside her until the musicians struck up for the second. He was attentive, gazing at her with blatant admiration and barely glancing at anyone else. Nancy kept her own eyes modestly lowered, knowing the telltale flush on her cheek would be evidence to any onlookers that she was not indifferent to Lord Gabriel. When the dance ended he bowed over her hand and made a great show of lifting her fingers to his lips.

It was all an act, Nancy was well aware of it, but still she felt disappointed when he moved away. Not that she was left to play the wallflower. A succession of partners followed for every dance, from gauche, tongue-tied young men to the elderly, avuncular neighbours who had known her as a girl. However, when supper was announced Gabriel appeared at her side, ready to carry her off.

In such a crowd it was a simple matter for them to disappear, but the practised ease with which Gabriel whisked her away made her suspect that he was a master of country-house flirtations. In a matter of minutes he had found a small sitting room, illuminated only by the moon that shone in through the unshuttered window. There was no fire in the room and the chill struck at Nancy's exposed flesh.

'We will not be seen here, if someone should look in.' Gabriel led her to a sofa in one shadowy corner and pulled her down on to his lap, wrapping his arms about her. 'Lean against me, I need to keep you warm.' He said it as if it was the most reasonable thing in the world. 'And besides, if we are discovered, it will leave no one in any doubt that we are flirting.'

'So much for my reputation,' she murmured, succumbing to the temptation to snuggle closer.

It was surprisingly comfortable, cuddled against Gabriel's broad chest. Nancy allowed herself to relax and dropped her head on to his shoulder. She breathed in the familiar smell of his skin, overlaid with a hint of soap and warm spicy scents. Her eyelids drooped languorously, while her body tingled with memories of the nights they had shared.

'That's better,' he murmured, his breath stirring her hair. 'Now, tell me what you have discovered.'

Disappointment crushed the little bud of desire that had been unfurling deep inside. How could she be so foolish as to forget the reason she had come back to this house? Scolding herself, she turned her own thoughts to business.

'Nothing at all. I fear you are looking for a mare's nest. My father and his fiancée are the very model of domestic bliss.'

'Perhaps that is for your benefit.'

'Not on my father's part, I am sure. He is quite besotted.'

'And the lady?'

'I cannot think she loves him, but she seems determined to make Masserton Court her home. She is in the process of decorating the whole house, starting with the guest bedrooms. And at her own expense, I believe, since my father has barely a feather to fly with. Such industry suggests she is planning a long stay here.' She sighed. 'I, on the other hand, cannot wait to leave.'

'Pray bear with it a little longer, if you can.'

'But there is no evidence that anything untoward is going on. Pray believe me, Gabriel, Hester and I have searched the house, asked discreet questions and been on the alert for anything out of the ordinary. My father's post consists of little more than demands for payment and Lady Craster has received only one letter since I arrived, a single sheet from Mrs Wells, the modiste, to advise that her new gown had been despatched. As for visitors, there has been no one.' Her mouth twisted slightly. 'My father and his lady appear to live only for one another. In fact, they appear to have shunned company since coming here from Brighton. That is the reason my father insisted on holding the ball, to introduce his future wife to his neighbours.'

'Hmm.' Nancy had been listening to the soft thud of his heart, but that was lost as his deep voice rumbled against her cheek. 'My sources have confirmed that the last papers to go missing are still in England. It is vital we find them, they contain details of orders already sent to our naval commanders in the Mediterranean. The operations there cannot now be stopped.'

'Then lives might be at risk if the orders fall into the wrong hands.'

'Yes.'

The cold silence of the room settled around them. Nancy sighed.

'I wish I could help, Gabriel, but there is nothing suspicious going on at Masserton, I am sure of it. I have searched high and low, but everything is as it should be. Even Lady Craster, whom I confess I cannot like, appears above suspicion. From what I have managed to glean from the servants, Lord Craster was a respectable man who left his widow with a handsome settlement. She met my father in Brighton this summer and four months ago he brought her here, as his fiancée. They have been here together ever since. There is no evidence that she has been in touch with anyone from London, other than her dressmaker. I have myself had sight of the invoices for her gowns. They are expensive, but nothing more than one would expect, and I am sure Mrs Wells is above suspicion, because I happen to know that she supplies dresses to Princess Charlotte.'

There was silence for a moment. 'When did the last gown arrive?'

'Yesterday.'

'Do you know who delivered it? Was there any mention of the carrier?'

'Not on the bill, but I did see something on the box. The maid had left it in the room and I saw it this afternoon.' She frowned, trying to conjure up a mental picture of the box. 'Meldrew.' She sat up, saying more confidently, 'Meldrew and Sons, Bridge Street, Westminster. Could they be involved, do you think?'

'It is highly likely. Well done, Nancy. I will send word to London in the morning and they will make enquiries. If there is anything suspicious about them, we will soon know it.' He drew her down and kissed her. 'I knew it was a good idea to have you here.'

'Nonsense, you wished me at Jericho! Which reminds me.' She pushed herself away so she could frown at him. 'You knew, did you not? When we made plans for me to come here, you were already aware that my father was to be married again.'

'I confess I *did* know. Thoresby had discovered as much, but I thought it best not to tell you.'

'You are despicably high-handed,' she told him, although her scolding lacked any real anger.

He reached up and cupped her face. 'I know,' he

murmured, drawing her down to kiss her lips. 'Can you forgive me?'

'I suppose you were afraid I might not look sufficiently shocked.' She subsided against him once more. 'I understand that. I admit I was stunned when I learned of it, I do not think they could have been in any doubt of that.'

'It was only part of the reason I did not tell you. I thought you might be loath to meet the woman who is about to take your mother's place.'

Her breath hitched in her throat. She had not expected such consideration from him. It aroused emotions she did not understand, something so fierce it was like a hard knot under her ribs.

'That was kind of you,' she said at last, 'but your consideration is misplaced. I have already told you my mother holds no special place in my affections. Indeed, I barely knew her. Even when she and my father were in residence here at Masserton, my sister and I saw our parents for only a few moments each day. We were reared by a succession of nannies until Mary went off to school.' Now she had started telling him about her past she found she did not wish to stop. 'She was the pretty one, you see. My parents considered it worthwhile providing her with the accomplishments required of a lady and packed her off to a very select seminary in Bath.'

'But not you?'

'No. I was left in the care of a governess.'

'Who, you told me, was far more interested in the

contents of a wine bottle than teaching you. My poor darling.'

Sympathy was more than Nancy could stand. She struggled in his arms and he released her immediately.

'It is of no consequence.' She could not bear the thought that he might remember her as someone to be pitied. She slipped off his lap, saying briskly, 'I can hear the orchestra tuning up again. We should return, before we are missed.'

He followed her to the door, but when she reached for the handle he stopped her.

'Wait.' He drew her into his arms and kissed her, swift and fierce. 'It will not do for me to stand up with you again,' he said at last, 'but tomorrow I shall come a-courting Lady Ann Chartell.'

How could he speak so calmly while she was reduced to trembling like a blancmange by his touch? Pride came to her rescue and she managed to reply with at least the outward appearance of calm.

'An excellent cover, Lord Gabriel.'

He looked down at her, his shadowed face unreadable. 'It is not *just* a cover, my lady.'

His words set her heart thudding so hard against her ribs she could scarce breathe. Then Gabriel kissed the end of her nose and let her go. Without another word they slipped out of the room and back into the ballroom.

When Lord and Lady Blicker carried Gabriel away with them after the ball they were full of speculation about the reappearance of Lady Ann. Gabriel knew his own behaviour towards the lady could not have gone unremarked and he feigned sleep in order that the kindly couple might feel free to say what they wished. Listening to their chatter, he soon realised Nancy had not exaggerated the story of her upbringing.

'Some people shouldn't have children if they don't know how to rear them,' declared Lady Blicker, with uncharacteristic force. 'The Earl was always a fool. Two healthy daughters should have been a blessing, yet he treated it as a curse. And the Countess was no better. You'll remember, my dear, how relieved and delighted I was when Aspern offered for Lady Mary. Thankfully he was rich enough to satisfy the Countess's greedy eye.'

Lord Blicker gave a loud sigh. 'Mary was such a pretty-behaved child—there was never any doubt she would do well. 'Twas a pity Ann was not more like her sister in temperament, for I always thought her the more intelligent of the two.'

'Alas, poor Ann was never expected to amount to very much,' said his wife. 'She had no looks or figure to recommend her, but even so the Earl offered her up to the highest bidder!'

It was as much as Gabriel could do to stop his hands from clenching into fists as he listened. He thought of young Nancy, innocent and vulnerable. Unloved by her parents, who planned to sell her to an elderly rake for his pleasure. He forced himself to keep still as Lady Blicker continued.

'How shocked we were when it was announced she was to wed Packington. I thought it quite outrageous!

I remember saying something to the Countess at the time, but she gave me short shrift. Told me plainly to mind my own business.'

'At least you tried, my love. I don't think anyone was particularly surprised when the child ran away.'

'And it seems she fell on her feet, thank heavens.' Gabriel heard the rustle of silks as the lady settled back in her corner with a contented sigh. 'She was looking quite a picture tonight, did you not think so, my dear sir?'

'Aye, my love, Lady Ann is one of those women who develop their beauty late. Well, good for her, I say.' Lord Blicker gave a rich chuckle. 'She caught the eye of more than one gentleman present tonight. Shouldn't wonder at it if she don't marry again.'

Yes, Gabriel had noticed how the men had looked at Nancy, with her voluptuous figure, creamy skin and those thick, shining curls glowing in the candlelight. She was no shrinking debutante, but a woman to raise the interest of any red-blooded male. There was no reason why she should not find herself a husband.

Not himself, of course, thought Gabriel. He was too set in his habits to change his way of life now. No woman had ever kept his attention for more than a few weeks and he could think of nothing worse than to be leg-shackled for life to a partner one could not care for. He had seen too much of that in his world. Cuckolded husbands, wives abandoned once they had provided their spouse with an heir, bitter couples trapped in an unhappy alliance and providing choice gossip for society.

No, marriage was not for him, but for Nancy—he

did not like to think of her returning to her life as a cook. She had told him she had been in love once and it was not too late for her to find happiness again. Perhaps one of the fellows there this evening would find favour with her. A good, respectable man who would not care about her past. One who would make her happy, make her laugh. A man who could please her in bed as well as out of it—

'No!'

'Oh, heavens, whatever is it, Lord Gabriel? A bad dream, my lord?' Lady Blicker exclaimed in alarm as he gave an involuntary growl and sat up.

'Yes. Yes, I think it was.' He passed a hand over his eyes. 'I beg your pardon. How foolish of me.'

Chapter Twelve

When the last of the guests had departed, Nancy wandered back into the drawing room to say goodnight to her father. She found only Lady Craster there, who told her that the Earl had retired.

'Then I shall see him in the morning,' said Nancy.

With the outside doors open, the empty rooms had cooled rapidly and she made her way to the fire to warm her hands. Behind her she heard Lady Craster's silky voice.

'Well, my dear, you appear to have found yourself a beau. Baxenden's son, no less. He made it quite plain to me he wishes to further his acquaintance with you.'

Nancy shrugged. She said carefully, 'I think he is merely amusing himself.'

'Well, it might not be easy, but you would do well to secure his interest, if you can,' said Susan. She walked to the door and stopped. 'Let me make it plain, my dear, your father neither needs nor wants you at Masserton.'

She went out and Nancy realised she was shaking. It was no more than the truth—she had always known it—but to hear Susan express it, so stark and plain, wounded her deeply and it was some minutes before she could compose herself sufficiently to leave the room.

The Earl's charity towards his prodigal daughter did not extend to allowing the fire in her room to be rekindled in the mornings, which encouraged Nancy to get up while there was still some little heat in the embers. The day after the ball was no exception for her, despite not getting to bed until the early hours, and she was up and dressed before daylight. With Susan's words still ringing in her ears, she decided to avoid the breakfast room and went to the kitchens to beg a piece of bread and butter, before making her way to the stables to see if there was a horse she could ride out later that day.

If there was no suitable mount, she decided she would take a brisk walk. Anything to relieve the distress Lady Craster's remark had caused her. It would suit Nancy very well if the woman proved to be a traitor, but she knew she must be careful not to let her dislike of her father's fiancée cloud her judgement.

An iron-haired groom was sweeping the stable yard by the light of the flickering wall lamps as she walked in through the arched entrance. He glanced up when he saw her, then stopped and leaned on his broom, a slow grin spreading across his weather-beaten face.

'Why, if it ain't Lady Ann! I wondered how long it would be before you found your way to the stables.'

'Davy!' For the first time that morning she felt a

genuine smile tugging at her mouth. She went across to him. 'I should have sought you out long before now, can you forgive me?'

'Nay, m'lady, there's nought to forgive. You can't be expected to remember all the old servants.'

She touched his arm. 'How could I forget the groom who took me out riding as a child? You helped Peter to put me on my first horse.' She looked around. 'I suppose Peter has been retired now, has he?'

Even in the dim lamplight she saw a shadow cross the groom's face.

'Dead, m'lady. Went into Darlton one night and didn't come back. Lucas found him at the roadside next morning.' He shook his head. 'A stroke, they said, poor old fellow. He must have collapsed and died on the spot. Mortal cold it was that night.'

'My goodness, how dreadful! When was this?'

'A couple of weeks back, my lady.'

'But when exactly?' she urged him, suspicion chilling her bones.

Davy rubbed his chin. 'Well, now, let me see. 'Twas nearly three weeks ago and just before the new moon. The night we had the first snow of the winter.'

The same day Gabriel had been left for dead. She put her hands to her cheeks and Davy hurried on.

'I suggested he should leave it 'til another night, my lady, but he *would* go.'

'And you are sure of the day?'

'Certain sure. I remember, 'cos I lent him my muffler to wrap over his own, so bitter it was. Poor soul, not even that could save him, in the end.'

Davy sighed and shook his head while Nancy stood, speechless, as the dreadful doubt hardened into near certainty. At last she put a hand on the groom's shoulder.

'Oh, Davy, how terrible. Did Peter tell you what made it necessary for him to go into Darlton that night?'

'Nay, ma'am. He'd taken to walking in of an evening to drink at the tavern. He didn't seem too happy those last few weeks.' He glanced about him before continuing quietly, 'I think he was afeard for his position here. Since the master invited his lady to stay, most of the old stable hands have left or been turned off. Jones, the old coachman, he went off to live with his sister in Wales. But the Earl told us *we* was safe and I believed him. Why, me and Peter both came here as lads, in your grandfather's time. We're part and parcel o' this place and so I told'n, but Peter got some maggot in his head and wouldn't settle. Said his conscience was troubling him.'

'I am sorry about that, Davy. I hope you do not feel you must leave, too.'

'Me, m'lady? Nay. I just keeps me head down and gets on with anything I'm asked to do.' He grinned. 'Me and Lucas, we rubs along all right, as long as I let him rule the roost. And there ain't half the cattle in the stables that there used to be, his lordship not being so flush as he once was. But I shouldn't be saying that to you, ma'am. Disrespectful.'

She smiled a little. 'You may say what you wish to me, Davy, remember that.'

'Aye, Lady Ann, I will, and if there's anything I can do for 'ee…'

'Well, as a matter of fact there is. I would like to ride out, if we can find me a mount and a saddle.'

The groom's face cleared. 'A mount would be no problem, ma'am, I remembers how you used to ride any of his lordship's horses. And riding astride, too!'

Nancy laughed. 'I think for propriety's sake it should be a lady's saddle, if there is one.'

'As it turns out we still have your old saddle, ma'am. Old Peter wouldn't let us get rid of it and he kept it polished, too. "Just in case my lady comes back to us," he used to say.' Davy blinked and added, his voice a trifle unsteady, 'And you *has* come back to us and looking very well, too, if you'll forgive me saying so. I just wish he was here to see you, ma'am.'

'I wish it, too, Davy.' Nancy felt her own eyes filling up and was obliged to take a deep breath before she could speak again. 'But enough of that. Let us go into the stables and find a suitable mount for me!'

Nancy wanted to go and find Gabriel immediately and tell him what she had learned, but that was impossible. Even if there was a horse for her, to arrive at the Blickers' house at dawn and demand to see their guest would give rise to the liveliest conjecture. It would be all around the neighbourhood before the day was out. Even the most infatuated young lady would baulk at being so forward. Besides, Gabriel had said he would come courting her and it was most likely he would make a morning call this very day. It was important they did not miss one another.

After deciding that the Earl's old bay mare would suit her best and Davy's assurance that he would saddle her up at a word, Nancy went back to the house, praying that Gabriel would not fail her. The morning stretched before her and she knew she should pass the time with ladylike pursuits. That way she would be available, should any visitors be announced. She made her way to the drawing room where she spent an hour practising at the pianoforte before taking her embroidery to the morning room, where she set her stitches with impatient fingers and strained every nerve to listen for the sounds of an arrival.

The clock on the mantelpiece was chiming eleven when Gabriel walked in with all the assurance of one confident of his welcome. He was wearing a dark frock coat and buckskin breeches that disappeared into a pair of highly polished top boots, but he looked every bit as elegant in his riding dress as he had in his ball dress the previous evening. Not that Nancy was going to tell him so, she decided as she put aside her embroidery.

'Good morning, my lord.' She tried not to look or sound too pleased to see him. 'How good of you to come again so soon.'

'My Lady Ann, I cannot stay away.' He added, as the door closed upon them, 'I can see by your look that you have news for me. Quickly, while we are alone, what have you discovered?'

She told him briefly all she had learned about the death of her old groom.

'Gabriel, he died on his way into Darlton, the self-same night you were attacked. That *cannot* be mere chance. I am almost sure he was your informant.'

'And you think someone prevented him from getting to Darlton to meet me?'

'He *was* an old man,' she said cautiously, 'but he had never suffered a day's illness in his life. It was Lady Craster's people who found him. We only have their word for it that he had collapsed.' She shook her head, reminding herself not to jump to conclusions. 'Perhaps I am being too fanciful.'

'And perhaps not.'

She squeezed her hands together and fixed her eyes upon him. 'He lived here all his life, Gabriel, it must have been something serious to unsettle him so much. If he thought my father was in trouble, that would do it, I think.'

He walked over to the fireplace, staring down into the flames for a moment before glancing back at her.

'If the Earl is involved in this smuggling business, it might be safer for you to leave Masserton now.'

'That may be so, but old Peter showed me more kindness than I ever had from my parents. He taught me to ride and I have learned that even after I ran away, he kept my lady's saddle, hoping I would return. Twelve years—' She broke off for a moment to collect herself, then lifted her chin and gazed steadily at Gabriel. 'I am no longer in a tearing hurry to quit Masserton. I want to find out the truth. Hester and I are going to search the house again from top to bottom. If the missing papers are here, we will find them! And if my father is implicated, then so be it.'

'Nancy, be careful. It could be dangerous for you.'

'Perhaps, but I am on my guard now and there are still some of the old servants here. Kindly, honest souls whom I may turn to, if I need help. I am determined to do this, Gabriel.'

'Very well.' He came closer. 'But I pray you will not run any risks.'

Her heart skittered. She had grown accustomed to looking after herself and his concern unnerved her. She felt weak, vulnerable. Afraid for her own safety and that was something new. As if, for the first time in years, she had a reason to live.

'I beg your pardon, my lord, I was still at breakfast.'

Lady Craster's breathless voice sounded from the doorway and Nancy saw something very like a flicker of regret in Gabriel's eyes before he turned away from her.

'Then I must apologise, ma'am, for coming so pre-cipitately.'

He kissed her fingers with practised grace and, ob-serving the way the lady relaxed, Nancy knew he was forgiven. Lady Craster invited him to sit down and flicked a glance at Nancy.

'Lady Ann, have you ordered refreshments for our guest?'

'Not yet, ma'am, no, I was waiting for you.'

Susan shook her head at her and said with a soft laugh, 'But why, my dear? You know you need not stand upon ceremony here, this is your home now.' She walked across to the bell pull and tugged it, smiling at her guest as she did so. 'I am sure Lord Gabriel must be ready for a warming drink, after riding here on such a cold day, is that not so, my lord?'

Nancy sank back in her chair and resumed her sewing while Susan engaged him in conversation. She was thankful she had told him all she knew, for there would be no further opportunity to talk privately now. Refreshments were brought in and then the Earl joined them, staying until Gabriel took his leave an hour later. He accompanied his guest to the door, leaving the ladies alone in the morning room.

'I think, after all, you are wise not to pin your hopes upon Lord Gabriel,' remarked Susan, almost as soon as the door closed. 'He is undoubtedly very attractive, but even on such a short acquaintance it is clear he is a flirt.'

'As you say.' Nancy rose. 'If you will excuse me…'

'Oh, pray do not go yet, my dear, there are one or two little things that you might do for me.'

Nancy listened while Lady Craster outlined numerous menial tasks that could easily have been done by the servants. However, in the main they involved returning the house to order following last night's ball, and as this gave Nancy another opportunity to talk to the staff and roam freely around the house, she made no demur. She went off to her room, found a linen apron to slip over her muslin day gown and set to work.

Hester was searching the servants' rooms at the top of the house and Nancy concentrated on the main bedchambers, armed with a pile of linen which she might use as an excuse if she was discovered. There was nothing in her father's rooms to excite her suspicions, but she knew that any papers were more likely to be in his study, which she dared not search until the Earl was out of the house.

Lady Craster's bedchamber and dressing area were both tidy and after a swift and unproductive search Nancy decided her time would be better spent talking to the servants. She slipped out and was heading for the main staircase when she saw Lady Susan and the Earl disappearing into the Blue Bedroom. She stopped just out of sight of the open door to listen.

Lady Craster's voice floated out to her: 'This is the pattern I have chosen for this room, my lord. What do you think of it? The blue will be perfect with the existing bed hangings and curtains, so that will be a saving, will it not?'

'But I'd swear that is the first paper you showed me.'

'My dear Hugh, I assure you it is *very* different. If you are happy, I mean to order it.'

'Do as you please, Susan, I haven't time for such matters. I want to take the dogs out for some sport while the daylight lasts.'

'Oh, *do* say you like it, my love. I have spent so many hours debating which would be best, but I would dearly love your approval before I order the paper. You *do* like it, do you not, Hugh, dear?'

Nancy's lip curled at the wheedling tone, but her father was clearly won over. She heard him chuckle.

'Bless you, you must do as you think fit, my dear.

After all, you are paying for it. And if you think it is worth it…'

'Of course it is, dear sir. Only think how grand these rooms will look when we have guests to stay.' Susan's voice grew softer, almost a purr as she added, 'After our honeymoon.'

Nancy moved on, there was nothing to be learned there, but at least if her father was going out she could search the offices with little fear of being discovered.

The rest of the day proved equally fruitless. She found an excuse to look in her father's study as well as talking to staff, but she learned little of interest, apart from confirming the night of old Peter's death. No one could tell her anything more about the groom's death and enquiries about Lady Craster were met with a blank stare. The only servants who might be relied upon to know something of the lady's past were her maid, Lucas the groom and her coachman, all of whom had been with her for years, but since they viewed Nancy with suspicion, she dared not approach them.

She was feeling quite dispirited by the time she returned to her room to change for dinner, where Hester was waiting for her and was clearly big with news.

'You have found something hidden in the servants' quarters?'

'No, Miss Nancy, nothing like that, although I searched them thoroughly, I promise you. But I was collecting the clean shifts from the drying rooms when one of the grooms stopped me. A grey-haired man, with a chipped front tooth.'

'Davy?'

'Aye, that's the one. He said your gentleman visitor had a message for you. I presume he means Master Gabriel?'

'Lord Gabriel has been our only visitor today.' Nancy spoke calmly enough, but she could do nothing about the blush stealing into her cheeks.

'Aye, well. Davy said to tell you that his lordship will be riding out on Garmore Hill early tomorrow morning, if you was free to join him. First light, he said. He impressed upon me that it is a great secret and no one else is to know.' One of Hester's rare smiles dawned. 'I think he scents a romance.'

'It is what Lord Gabriel wants him to think.'

'I know that, ma'am, but anyone seeing you together as I have done these past weeks—'

Nancy stopped her. 'It was a pleasant interlude, Hester, but I assure you it is nothing more than that.' She turned to the mirror. She looked more like a scullery maid than a lady, with her hair escaping from its pins and a smudge of dirt on her cheek. She was no consort for a lord, especially not for the son of a marquess. 'It could never be more than that.'

Even the gown that Hester had put out for her to wear that evening, a lilac-coloured sarsenet trimmed with quilled ribbon, did not make her feel more like a lady. It was expensive, but far too dashy for her present low spirits, for which sackcloth and ashes seemed preferable.

She had forfeited her good name and her reputation and there was no way to regain either. Society would always look askance at a woman who had run away from home and lived for more than a decade without the protection of a husband or a father. She straightened her shoulders. When this was over, she would return to Prospect House, to her work and the friends who valued her, but for now she had a role to play and she was determined to do it well. Nancy left her bedchamber with her head held high and went downstairs to join the others for dinner.

When she entered the drawing room her father's resentful glance only made her lift her chin a little higher.

'What, another gown? That husband of yours was surely a warm man to trick you out so finely.'

'If not in the first style of elegance,' remarked Susan with a soft laugh. 'But he was in *trade*, was he not? Money can never make up for good breeding. My own family can trace its line back centuries. We came over with the Conqueror.'

'Camp followers, perhaps,' murmured Nancy sweetly.

'Mind your manners, girl!'

'Why should she, my lord, now you have acknowledged her and she can claim her inheritance?' Nancy looked up, surprised, and Susan's eyes snapped angrily. 'Your father has this morning informed me of your grandmother's legacy. Thirty thousand pounds!' Her lip curled. 'Pray do not tell me you did not know of it.'

Oh, yes, Nancy knew of it. Mary had written to her two years ago with the news of her grandmother's death. Nancy had written back, begging her sister not to mention it again. Later, there had been notices in the newspapers, requesting that Lady Ann Chartell should contact the London solicitors to learn something to her advantage and she guessed the old lady had mentioned her in her will, but Nancy had kept her silence. She had seen very little of Lady Elmstone during her childhood and had no strong affection for her. She had no desire to take anything from the family she had abandoned.

She said calmly, 'I knew Lady Elmstone was dead, that is all.'

'*That is all?*' the Earl mimicked her. 'Confound it, madam, she left a fortune to you, as long as you came forward within seven years of her death. Called you her neglected granddaughter. Pshaw! I could make good use of such a sum!'

Nancy was about to declare that he could have it, with her goodwill, but she stopped herself. Two years ago, she had been settled at Prospect House and wanted nothing more than the modest living she had there. But now she felt a certain restlessness. She might yet decide to live in the world a little more, and thirty thousand pounds would allow her to do that.

'If my grandmother had wanted you to have the money, Father, she would have left it to you.'

'Under the terms of the will, another five years and I could have claimed the money for myself.' He glared at her. 'I should never have acknowledged you!'

Lady Craster put a hand on his sleeve. 'Hush, my dear, how could you have done otherwise? Lady Ann might have sought refuge with friends or neighbours in the area. Just think how that would have looked, to cut your own daughter. Imagine what people would think of you. Of us.'

'Aye, you are right,' he conceded. 'But 'tis damned galling that the ungrateful chit should inherit such a sum.'

He was still muttering when Mickling came in to announce dinner. They moved to the dining room where Nancy, determined not to spend the evening exchanging reproaches or recriminations, did her best to turn the conversation to more cheerful subjects. She succeeded well enough, introducing such innocuous subjects as the weather and the numerous calling cards that had been received from neighbours since the ball.

The Earl soon lost interest and turned his attention to his dinner while Lady Craster's waspish mood was replaced with her usual façade of honeyed sweetness. She deigned to ask Nancy which of the local families she thought would expect a morning call.

'All very tiresome,' she concluded with a sigh, 'but I suppose it must be done. But not tomorrow. I have things to do tomorrow. And Dr Scotton is calling.' She turned to the Earl. 'I hope you have not forgotten, my lord, that the good doctor is coming to examine you?'

'Scotton?' Nancy looked up. 'What has happened to Dr Gough? He was always our family doctor.'

The Earl snorted. 'A country physician and out of touch with modern methods. Scotton has an established practice in Lincoln and more to the point he understands my gout. I hope he comes early, I mean to take the dogs out in the morning.'

'I am *very* anxious that you remain in good health, my dear.' Lady Craster reached out and covered the Earl's hand with her own. She gave a falsely tender smile that made Nancy's skin itch. 'My lord's well-being is very important to me, as I am sure it is to you, Lady Ann. I would be obliged, my dear, if you could look out for Dr Scotton tomorrow and have him shown directly up to your father's room.'

'Of course, Susan.'

'You are very good. Now, another thing. With the weather as it is, we cannot expect the poor man to come all this way for a few hours, so I have decided he should have the rose bedchamber. It is a little small, perhaps, but I am sure it will suffice for one night. In the morning, Lady Ann, I would like you to make sure the bed is aired and that he has everything he needs for his comfort.' She sighed. 'I would have liked to replace the floral wall hangings before anyone slept there again, it is so terribly faded.'

'All in good time my dear,' replied the Earl, helping himself to another slice of beef. 'We can't have all the rooms out of service at once, you know. And the fellow is only a physician, after all. But perhaps, to save time, you should choose a paper from that sample book before Hewitt takes it away.'

'Oh, no, my lord, that room requires a very different treatment.' Susan pursed her lips and continued, her tone disapproving, 'I had instructed Hewitt to call in the morning and receive my order in person, but I have just had word that he will not be coming. He will not venture from Lincoln until he can do so in a carriage! Most infuriating. As if it would hurt him to come on horseback. I am tempted to send Lucas to him with my instructions—'

The Earl put down his knife and fork.

'What! Why should we put a servant to the time and trouble of going all the way to Lincoln when the rascally fellow promised to call here?' he exclaimed. 'I'm damned if I will allow it.'

'But, my lord—'

'My dear Susan, a day or two won't make any difference. Why fly into such a pelter over a trifle?'

Nancy felt a very ignoble glow of pleasure at her father's irritation with his lady love. Under the pretence of deciding between the stewed apple or the lemon curd, she watched Lady Craster fight down her anger at not getting her own way. It was almost a disappointment when at last she regained her calm and said, with a little laugh,

'You are very right, sir, another day is not important. In fact,' she added brightly, 'it will be all for the best, because now we have Dr Scotton staying in the rose room, Hewitt would not be able to see it tomorrow. And he will need to do so, you know, to measure up before he can send over suitable papers.'

'I don't see that room needs to be changed at all,' grumbled his lordship. 'All this shilly-shallying over patterns and wallcoverings. Damned nuisance!'

Nancy concentrated on her food while her father and Lady Craster continued to bicker gently. As soon as the meal was ended Nancy excused herself, pleading fatigue from the previous night's dancing, and took herself off to bed, praying that even if the snow was too bad to allow the wallpaper supplier to drive from

Lincoln, the weather would be fine enough for her to ride out and meet Gabriel.

She desperately wanted to see him, but she was honest enough to know it was not just to discuss the missing documents. Seeing him again at the ball, having him pay court to her, even if it was only a pretence, had brought back all the desire she had tried so hard to suppress. His voice, deep and seductive, those blue eyes with their disturbing gleam, set her body tingling with anticipation. She curled up in her bed, trying to ignore the building excitement at the thought of meeting Gabriel in the morning.

The overnight frost was sparkling in the first rays of the early morning sun when Nancy set out on her father's bay mare. It had not been difficult to leave her bed before dawn for she had slept fitfully again and had been relieved to get up and dress for the coming meeting. Davy had brought her mount out on to the drive some way from the stables, so that they did not disturb the other servants, and she had ridden off, her spirit soaring with a delicious expectation.

The snow still lay in thick drifts where the road was hedged by trees, but the more open ground was clear and she enjoyed a gallop across the fields. Garmore Hill was situated halfway between Masserton and the Blickers' property and when it came in sight, it was just as Nancy remembered it, partly wooded and offering a good view of the surrounding countryside. She trotted up the gently rising track and as she approached the summit a lone rider emerged from the trees. Her heart leapt and a smile tugged at her mouth, but she kept her tone light and friendly.

'Why, Lord Gabriel, this is a pleasant surprise.'

'Yes, isn't it? Quite a coincidence to find you here.'

She laughed. 'I used to ride here often when I was a child. It is a popular picnic spot in the summer, but not used as much in winter. However, it is a good choice. Anyone seeing us might well believe we met by chance.'

'They might also expect me to take the opportunity to flirt with you.'

'And of course that is what you do with every female, is it not?'

He grinned at her. 'Indubitably. Therefore, let me entice you into the cover of the trees, where we may talk unobserved.'

They guided their horses into the small wood, away from prying eyes, and when Gabriel suggested they should dismount and walk a little way, she readily agreed. She waited until he was standing beside her, then kicked her foot free of the stirrup and slid down into his arms. It was the most natural thing in the world to look up into his face and smile. Immediately he lowered his head and captured her mouth. His lips were cold, but his kiss set her body on fire and she responded hungrily. Everything was forgotten, she revelled in the taste of him, the desire that was unfurling as his tongue worked its magic, dancing and teasing, drawing out her very soul.

She gave a little moan when he broke off and she heard his answering sigh.

'I would like to take you, here and now,' he murmured, pressing delicate butterfly kisses over her eyes, her cheeks.

She wanted that, too, so much so that her body ached at the very thought of it. Her breath caught as he began to work his way along her jaw then, with another sigh, he released her. She clung to him for a moment, afraid she would crumple without his support. Dear heaven, she was weak with need. Almost shaking. When had it come to this, that she had allowed a man such power over her?

He gave her a wry smile. 'I suppose we must turn our attention to more pressing matters.'

'Yes, we must.'

She quickly silenced the wanton voice in her head that confessed she would much prefer him to make love to her. This was only ever meant to be a brief liaison, a little flirtation. That was all either of them wanted. All they could have.

She saw the familiar teasing gleam in his eyes. He said, 'Perhaps one day, in another season.'

In another life!

'Perhaps.'

It took every vestige of her willpower to reply with a flirtatious smile, knowing all the while that when this was over, they would go their separate ways. He would soon forget her and she—well, Nancy would always have the memory of his lovemaking.

He pulled her hand on to his arm and they began to walk. Nancy glanced up. Gabriel was looking solemn now and she envied his ability to move so easily from pleasure to business. She must do the same. After all, the suspicions surrounding Masserton Court—her father's involvement with smuggled documents, old Peter's death—they were serious enough to warrant her full attention. The very thought of it sobered her.

He said, 'You have found no trace of the missing papers in the house?'

'No, nothing.' She sighed. 'I *cannot* believe my father would be involved in anything treasonous.'

'Not knowingly, perhaps. And the only carrier from London to call recently was for Lady Craster?'

'Yes.' Small comfort, to think her father might be duped, but Nancy clung to it. 'They delivered her ball-gown. I tried to find the packaging, to see if there was any clue there, but the servants tell me it has all been burned. *If* the documents were delivered on that carrier's wagon, then it is very possible they will be moved on in a similar fashion.'

'Indeed it is. Not only possible, but highly likely. I wish we could wait until I hear something from London about Meldrew and Sons, then we might be more sure of our ground and I could have Captain Graves and his men tear the house apart, but I needs must tread carefully. The problem is that the snow is thawing. Once the documents are moved on, we might never be able to prove the connection. We might also lose track of them, and if they reach the Netherlands there will be hell to pay.'

Nancy stopped. 'Perhaps you should investigate Mr Hewitt, who is supplying the wall hangings for the Court,' she suggested. 'Lady Craster was angry that he would not call this morning to collect the sample book. More dismayed than the situation warrants, I think. And something else that puzzles me. The blue room is always locked when Lady Craster is not in it. Why would anyone want to secure an empty room?'

'If I was Hewitt, I would want those papers in my possession for as little time as possible,' said Gabriel. 'He might be waiting until the roads from Lincoln to the ports are clear.'

Nancy gave a little hiss of exasperation. 'The blue room is the only place that Hester and I have not been able to search. Lady Craster keeps the key.'

'Do you mean to tell me that you do not add lock-picking to your accomplishments?' he asked her, his voice teasing.

'No, of course not. Do you?'

'As a matter of fact, I do,' he murmured. 'It is a very useful attribute for seducing a lady.'

Nancy's cheeks flamed at the message in his laughing eyes. She looked away quickly, reminding herself that such outrageous comments came easily to a hardened flirt. But she had to admit it eased the tension of the situation, just a little.

'You are shameless,' she scolded him. 'And I cannot believe you would stoop to such base tactics.'

'Well, no,' he confessed. 'So far it has not been necessary.'

She choked upon a laugh.

'*Quite* shameless! I pray you will concentrate upon the problem of the missing papers.'

'I beg your pardon,' he said meekly.

She looked up suspiciously, but he appeared to be quite serious now, so she continued.

'There is one other possibility. Lady Craster has summoned a Dr Scotton to call tomorrow and examine my father. A precaution, she says, but this is a new physician. She has persuaded my father to abandon the excellent Dr Gough, who lives in Darlton and has attended our family since I was a baby. I know nothing of the new man, save that he has a practice in Lincoln, but it seems odd to make him travel all that way for no good cause. He is to stay overnight, which I suppose is not unreasonable, with the weather as it is.'

'Then it is possible he could be the courier. I will have John make enquiries about the man.'

She stopped, saying with a little cry, 'Oh, I hate being so suspicious of everything and everybody!'

'I know, my dear.' Gabriel pulled her into his arms. 'I dislike it very much, not being able to trust anyone.'

'Then why do you do it, Gabriel?' She looked up at him, searching his face. 'Is it for the money?'

He grinned. 'I may not be rich as Croesus, but I am not without a feather to fly with! I have a very comfortable fortune of my own, thankfully. No, I needed some sort of occupation, the church did not appeal, I had tried the army, but I found it too confining. What I am doing gives me a way to help my country while providing a chance to use my wits. And there is an element of danger, which stops me getting bored. The life has suited me.' He paused, then added thoughtfully, 'Until now.'

'Are you growing tired of it?'

'I think perhaps I am.'

There was an enigmatic look in his blue eyes as they gazed down at her. She could not read it, but he looked very serious. It unsettled her. Or perhaps it was merely the chill wind that soughed through the trees at that moment. Nancy glanced up at the sky, where the sun was creeping higher.

'Susan—Lady Craster—has asked me to meet the doctor, when he arrives, so I had best get back.'

'Of course.'

They returned to where the horses were tethered and Gabriel pulled her close for one last kiss. She leaned against him for a moment, her head resting on his shoulder.

'When shall I see you again, Gabriel?'

'Tonight.' He grinned when she looked up in surprise. 'Did the Earl not tell you? I, er, bumped into him yesterday and he invited me to shoot with him today. He suggested I come to the Court for dinner, afterwards.'

'He has said nothing of this to me.'

'I think he sees me as a potential suitor.'

'Quite possibly. I know he would be glad to have me gone from the Court.'

'There you are then.'

She gave a rueful chuckle. 'I do not think Susan shares his optimism, she thinks you a rake. Although she did tell me I should do my utmost to secure you.' She added, as he threw her up into the saddle, 'She wants me out of the way, you see.'

'Casting her in the shade, are you?'

Nancy laughed at that. 'A Long Meg like me? I do not think so. She might perhaps fear my influence with my father, although I doubt that, very much.'

'She might be afraid you will discover something they would rather keep hidden.'

'Such as handling stolen documents. That still seems very unlikely to me. I do not like the woman, but what reason would she have for passing on government secrets?'

'That I do not know, but everything I have seen and heard points towards Masserton Court being used as a transfer point.' Gabriel had been holding the horse's head while Nancy settled herself, now he checked the stirrup and saddle girth. 'I think it very likely that the papers are hidden in that locked room and even more likely that they will be leaving the Court tomorrow. If I cannot find an opportunity to search that room when I join you for dinner this evening, then I shall have to come back later in the night. I shall take the precaution of warning the Blickers not to wait up for me, in case that event becomes necessary. And I will need you to leave a door unbolted.'

He rested his hand on her knee and even through the thick folds of her skirts she could feel its warmth, its strength. Her mind wanted to wander off to the memories of that same hand roaming over her naked skin and it was with difficulty she dragged it back to the present.

'I can do that,' she told him. She bit her lip. 'If you *should* find the missing plans at the Court, is there anything we can do to protect my father?'

'I will do what I can. You have my word. I am sorry you had to become mixed up in all this.'

'So, too, am I. But even if your theories are completely wrong, old Peter's death is suspicious.' She gathered up the reins. 'I believe *something* is going on at Masserton and I want to know what it is.'

Chapter Thirteen

Nancy rode quickly back to the Court, where the butler met her at the door. He informed her, a faintly anxious note in his usually imperturbable voice, that breakfast was over and the Earl wished to see her. Immediately.

Nancy nodded and went off to find her father. She was aware of a familiar unease knotting her stomach, as it had done when she was a child and had been summoned to account for some misdemeanour. She pushed it aside. She was a grown woman now and no longer answerable to her father for her actions.

She found him with Lady Craster in the drawing room.

'Where the devil have you been?'

She opened her eyes at his angry demand and spread her hands.

'As you see from my dress, I have been riding. I took your hack up to Garmore Hill. I am sorry if you wanted to use her...'

'But, my dear, you were unaccompanied,' put in

Lady Craster, her voice dripping with spurious concern. 'What if you had taken a tumble and no one to help?'

Nancy gave her a cool glance. 'I have always ridden out alone here.'

'You were always too independent for your own good! Susan was looking for you. I only allowed you to remain here because she put in a good word—'

The lady gave a gentle laugh and laid a hand on his sleeve. 'Pray do not work yourself into a pelter, dear sir. Lady Ann, you must understand that it is natural for your father to be concerned for you. In future you will not ride out without a groom.'

'As you wish. If you think one can be spared, now Peter is no longer here.' She turned to her father. 'What happened to him, Father? Davy told me only that he died.'

'A bad business.' Her father shook his head. 'Very bad. Poor fellow went out one night and didn't come back. They found him in the morning, on the road. Frozen to the spot.'

Her father had never been one to hide his true feelings and she felt sure that his sorrow was genuine. That, at least, was some small comfort.

'But that is not why we wish to speak to you,' declared Susan. 'Your father is about to take his gun out—'

'Oh, has Dr Scotton arrived already? Has he examined you, Father?'

'Bah! I don't have time to wait in for the fellow!'

The flash of anger in Susan's blue eyes confirmed

Nancy's suspicions that the doctor had been summoned at her behest and not the Earl's.

'No, of course the fellow hasn't had time to ride here from Lincoln,' he went on.

'That is why you must be on hand to greet him when he arrives.' Susan gave Nancy one of her steely smiles. 'I am very busy today and the doctor will need to be entertained, given refreshments and so on. He can examine your father before dinner. It should not take long.'

'Then if you excuse me, I shall go and change.'

'Aye, do,' growled her father. 'And one more thing. I expect Lord Gabriel to be joining us this evening. I've invited him to come back here for dinner, ain't that so, Susan?'

With her lips pressed together and the tight set of her jaw, Lady Craster looked less than pleased with the Earl's announcement, but she made efforts to appear complacent.

'We are just giving you the hint,' she purred, like a cat ready to show her claws at any moment. 'That you might be prepared for company.'

'That I might be suitably attired?' Nancy suggested. She had not missed Susan's disapproving look towards her riding habit, tailored to accentuate every curve of her full figure, and she added mischievously, 'Mr Hopwood always liked to see me rigged out in the very best style.'

'*Lord* Gabriel is accustomed to moving in the highest circles.' Susan's eyes flicked over Nancy again, this time fixing on the large buttons and profusion of silver frogging on her mannish jacket. 'Something a little less…exuberant might be in order. There will be no need to dress up, because his lordship is coming to take pot luck with us and even though the good doctor will be here, too, we will be dining informally. But you do not want to give Lord Gabriel a disgust of you.'

'And he mustn't think you would accept anything less than marriage,' growled the Earl. 'Ravenshaw has a reputation as a dangerous flirt.'

Nancy did not wish to be warned about Gabriel's reputation. She responded sharply.

'Thank you for telling me, but I think I had ascertained that for myself. However, I must go, if I am to be fit to receive Dr Scotton.'

With that she whisked herself out of the room and hurried up the stairs, almost shaking with the tumult of emotions swirling around inside. She knew her dress was too extravagant, designed to cause comment, she had been prepared for that, but what shocked and surprised her was her reaction to their disapproval. She felt all the raging emotion of an angry child, trying to provoke some sign of affection from her neglectful parents and instead only drawing their criticism.

When she had decided to return to the Court, she had not imagined she would feel so overwhelmed by the past. She had thought all the hurt and anger and loneliness was gone, but it was still there, reinforced by seeing Lady Craster as the recipient of her father's affection. The only spark of comfort during the past weeks had been Gabriel's company but even that was only temporary, she understood that. When his work here was finished he would move on and she would return to Prospect House to resume her life there.

'And the sooner that happens the better!' she muttered, storming into her bedchamber and throwing her crop and gloves on to a chair.

But somehow, the words did not ring quite true.

Nancy changed into a sober morning gown of green cambric and went to the kitchens to inform the cook that there would be two guests for dinner and to approve several extra dishes. She was on her way back upstairs when she heard the sounds of an arrival. A quick peek into the hall confirmed it. A gentleman was divesting himself of his wide-brimmed hat and heavy greatcoat. The butler had been given his instructions, so she hurried to the morning room to receive Dr Scotton. She was relieved to find Hester already waiting there for her, calmly knitting a pair of socks.

She put her work away when Nancy entered.

'So, our visitor has arrived, has he?'

'Mickling is even now showing him up.' Nancy quickly sat down beside her. 'Have you brought my embroidery? Good, let me have it, if you please. I want to present a picture of calm domesticity!'

She barely had time to ply the first stitch before the visitor was announced. She rose to greet him, holding out her hand.

'Ah.' He came towards her, beaming. 'Lady Ann, your most obedient servant, ma'am. Lady Craster has told me so much about you.'

Nancy was a little surprised to hear this, but she replied calmly enough, 'Good day to you, Doctor. I regret my father is out just now and Lady Craster is engaged. She sends her apologies and will join us presently.'

'Ah, yes, she mentioned that might be the case in her note. Such an industrious lady, I cannot express how much I admire her.'

Nancy kept silent and observed the doctor as he bowed over her fingers. He was a big, grey-haired man, dressed plainly in a brown riding coat, breeches and top boots. He was corpulent, but there was an impression of power about him and behind his genial smile she thought his eyes held a calculating look. She was glad she had Hester with her in the room.

She presented the doctor to her companion and they sat down to wait for Mickling to return with refreshments.

'I believe this is your first visit to Masserton for some time, Lady Ann?' remarked the doctor. 'An absence of several years, I understand.' He added in a confiding way, 'Lady Craster explained the circumstances to me, you see, knowing it is best I am aware of all the facts, if I am to treat the Earl. It must be a comfort to be reconciled with your father.'

'Yes, it is.'

'And you yourself are a widow. My condolences, madam.'

She shrugged off a faint irritation at his familiarity. If Susan had not informed him, then she thought it likely her father would have done so. Doctors were often recipients of their patients' innermost thoughts.

'Yes. My husband died some time ago.'

'I trust his family have been kind to you?'

'Mr Hopwood had no family, Doctor. I was everything to him.' The lies tripped from her tongue much more easily than they had done when telling her father her fictitious history. Or when she had told Gabriel. She wished she had not thought of him, for she felt a strong desire to have him there to support her.

'What, no family at all? And no children.' Dr Scotton shook his head. 'That must be a sadness to you.'

'Since my husband was in trade, I think the Earl considers it a blessing.'

She had had enough of talking of herself and smoothly turned the conversation. She asked him about himself and he was very willing to talk, telling her at length about his practice in Lincoln before moving on to more innocuous subjects, which filled the time until she could send the doctor off to his bedchamber. She suggested he might rest until the dinner hour, but he only laughed at that.

'I never rest during the day, Lady Ann. Once I have changed out of my travelling clothes I shall inspect his lordship's library, if I may?'

'By all means, sir. I will make sure there is a good fire there.'

'And perhaps you would like to join me. I have enjoyed our conversation and we might continue. I am sure there is much we might discuss.'

But this was too much for Nancy. She declined gracefully and when the footman had taken him off to escort him to his room she sank back in her chair with an exaggerated sigh.

'Thank goodness that is over. I am exceeding cross with my future mama-in-law for insisting I should entertain the worthy doctor.'

'I thought you handled him very well,' remarked Hester. 'To my mind he is overly inquisitive.'

'I suppose it fits with his calling to be interested in people.'

'I did not take to him, Miss Nancy.'

'Nor I, but my father seems to approve of him.' She lowered her voice: 'It would suit me very well to discover that he is in league with Lady Craster, but I think that may be just wishful thinking on my part.'

'I think it is, my lady,' replied Hester. 'Just as I can't help thinking Master Gabriel may have it wrong about the missing papers business. We have found no sign of anything odd at Masserton Court.'

'Apart from old Peter's demise.'

Hester shook her head. 'Even that is easily explained with the icy weather.'

'But for it to happen the very same night we came upon Lord Gabriel in the copse?'

'Perhaps there was a band of marauders abroad in Darlton that night, causing mayhem. It doesn't necessarily follow that there is any great conspiracy.' She saw Nancy was not convinced and added, 'I admit I don't feel comfortable here, but that's more to do with the way the Earl and his lady treat you than any sign of wrongdoing. I think 'tis time we packed our bags and left, ma'am, and that's a fact.'

Nancy was more than half inclined to agree with her companion. She decided not to make Hester even more anxious by telling her of Gabriel's plan to search the blue room that evening. If that failed to bring any results, then Gabriel would have to make enquiries elsewhere. And if he should find the missing papers in the blue room—either way it would bring an end to their liaison. It had to come, but she could not prevent a faint sadness at the thought. She pushed it aside, reminding herself that she had already made her plans for the future.

She said, 'You are right, Hester, there is no reason for us to remain here. We shall begin packing this very day. You have my permission to start putting things in the trunks. Tomorrow I shall tell my father that I am quitting Masserton Court.'

The short winter day was fading when Gabriel accompanied Lord Masserton back to the Court for dinner. The Earl's dogs had driven up numerous birds and since Gabriel had allowed his host to bag the majority of them, the Earl was in excellent humour. When they reached the house, Gabriel was shown to an upstairs room where he might wash the dirt from his hands and face while his coat was carried off by a footman to be brushed.

Some time later he presented himself in the drawing room in tolerably good order.

He found his host and hostess already there, together with a large man in a plain suit whom he guessed to be Dr Scotton.

'Lord Gabriel.' Lady Craster came forward, her hand held out and a smile lilting on her lips. 'How delightful that you could join us. Lord Masserton tells me you had good sport today.'

He kissed her fingers. 'We did indeed, ma'am. A most enjoyable day's shooting.'

When he straightened, she continued to cling to his hand for a moment and raised melting blue eyes to his face. An invitation, if ever he saw one. Trying to out-shine Nancy, he thought with an inward smile. She wouldn't do it. His taste now ran to a very different sort of woman. Full figured and dark-haired... He turned obediently when the Earl presented Dr Scotton to him.

'Delighted, my lord.' The doctor made a creditable bow, despite his bulk, and when Gabriel asked him if he was there in an official capacity, he gave a hearty laugh.

'Precautionary, my dear sir, precautionary. As his lordship's physician I like to assure myself that he is going on well.'

'My lady insists the doctor check me over at regular intervals, eh, Scotton?' The Earl gave a bark of laughter and shook his head at Lady Craster, 'It's no use my telling her that I have never had a day's illness in my life, save for a touch of gout.'

'Which makes you very cross.' Lady Craster gave his arm a playful tap with her fan.

Dr Scotton laughed dutifully and looked towards the door as it opened.

'Ah, and here is the Lady Ann. Now our party is complete!'

Nancy came in and paused for a moment in the doorway. Without appearing to stare, Gabriel took in every glorious detail. She looked like some fiery angel in a gown of tawny silk, cut to show her figure to advantage. As befitted a widow, it was trimmed, albeit sparingly, with black lace. She wore no modest fichu around her shoulders and the tiny strip of lace around the low neckline only drew attention to her generous bosom. Her dark hair had been brushed to a deep shine and was dressed in loose curls, piled up on her head, with one glossy ringlet falling to her shoulder. Diamonds winked at her ears, but instead of a costly necklace she had chosen to tie a simple length of black ribbon around her throat. He thought she had never looked more desirable.

As she swept into the room Gabriel moved across to intercept her. She looked at him, her brown eyes sparkling, but not with pleasure. Something, someone, had angered her.

'Lady Ann, you look…magnificent.' As he lifted her hand to his lips he murmured, 'Are you trying to dazzle the good doctor?'

She choked back a laugh, replying for his ears only, 'My father and Susan *gave me the hint* that I should wear something demure this evening.'

'And instead you chose your most ostentatious creation.'

The sparkle was back, this time full of mischief.

'All Mrs Hopwood's gowns are ostentatious! Susan looks as if she would like to rip this one right off my back!' She twinkled up at him. 'Are *you* outraged?'

'Not at all. Although I admit I would like to do the same, but for a very different reason.'

Nancy blushed and laughed at that. She shook her head at him and responded in a louder voice so all the room might hear.

'I fear you are an incorrigible flirt, Lord Gabriel.'

He inclined his head, a smile tugging at his mouth as Nancy walked away from him.

'Lady Ann, do come and sit next to me and tell me what secrets you and Lord Gabriel have been hatching.'

Gabriel was not deceived by Lady Craster's playful tone. Her eyes had been snapping angrily since Nancy's arrival.

'Why, nothing, ma'am. I was merely begging his lordship to forgive me for appearing a trifle...overdressed this evening. I was explaining that I have nothing more suitable for a quiet family dinner.'

Nancy sat down beside her and made a play of arranging her skirts, apparently as oblivious of her father's scowl as she was of Lady Craster's displeasure. Dr Scotton laughed gently and tried to engage his hostess in conversation and thankfully it was not long before dinner was announced.

As Gabriel escorted Lady Craster to the dining room, his own particular devil prompted him to remark how well Lady Ann was looking this evening.

'The lady has such lively spirits,' he added. 'She must be a delightful companion for you.'

'Indeed she is.' There was a semblance of gritted teeth about the lady's response. 'We must hope her liveliness will make up for the fact we are an uneven number at dinner.'

'My dear Lady Craster,' declared the doctor,

overhearing, 'with two such jewels at the dining table, how could we find anything wanting?'

Across the table, Nancy met Gabriel's eyes for a brief moment of shared humour. She was seated beside Dr Scotton and Gabriel observed her as she responded to his questions. She was indeed a jewel, he thought. She rivalled any of the beauties he had seen in town. Her luxuriant hair glowed in the candlelight and her profile, with its straight little nose and determined chin, was quite perfect. True, she was not petite, but he himself was tall and, when she was in his arms, she was the perfect height to rest her head on his shoulder. He remembered the times she had done so, with her curls tickling his chin.

Confound it, if he was not a confirmed bachelor he might even be tempted to—

'…do you not think so, Lord Gabriel?'

Lady Craster's voice dragged him out of his reverie. He was forced to apologise and ask her to repeat the question, but he consoled himself with the fact that his preoccupation should only help to convince her of his interest in Nancy.

Nancy was relieved that the gentlemen did not sit too long over their port that evening. She had thought Susan would upbraid her for wearing the tawny silk, but she chose rather to demonstrate her displeasure by ignoring Nancy. She scooped up a copy of the *Lady's Magazine* and read it by the light of the candles.

However, when the Earl came in with his guests,

Lady Craster quickly jumped up, declaring gaily that she had not expected to see them for an hour yet.

'Damned sawbones wouldn't let me take more than a single glass of port,' grumbled the Earl.

'Now, now, my lord, you know it is for your own good, if you are to avoid a painful recurrence of the gout. I am sure none of us wishes that to happen, do we, Lady Ann?' The doctor lowered his bulk into a chair beside Nancy and gave her an ingratiating smile. 'Besides, Lord Gabriel and I were only too pleased to join the ladies.'

He proceeded to engage her in conversation to the exclusion of everyone else. He questioned her about her marriage and her childhood, but Nancy was loath to add to the story she had already fabricated and answered him cautiously, deftly turning aside his more probing questions. She could only be thankful when the tea tray was brought in and gave her an excuse to move away. She was beginning to feel uneasy. There had been no opportunity for Gabriel to slip away to search the blue room, neither had she been able to speak privately with him, and she must do so if he was to gain access to the Court later.

She hovered near the tea tray and when Susan had filled the cups she carried one first to the doctor, then returned to collect another two, one for herself and one for Gabriel, who had strolled across to the unshuttered window and was gazing soulfully out into the night.

'Tell me, Lady Ann, is there anything more beautiful than a winter landscape by moonlight?'

'It is pretty enough, when viewed from the comfort of a warm room,' she replied, handing him his tea.

'Always so practical,' he murmured, keeping his back to the room. 'Which door can be left unlocked for me tonight?'

Nancy moved to stand beside him, as if contemplating the view.

'There is a garden door, reached from a path at the back of the wash house. Keep your horse to the grass and no one should hear you approach. And you can tether him to the railings. There is nothing to take anyone out that way after dark.'

'Good. Perhaps Mrs Yelland could oil the hinges.'

'I have already taken that precaution,' she told him, smiling slightly. 'I think it best not to involve Hester in this. I told her not to wait up for me. I will be there to let you in.' She saw a movement from the corner of her eye. Dr Scotton was approaching so she raised her voice slightly. 'There is a good moon and a clear sky to light you home tonight, my lord.'

He did not fail her. 'Indeed there is. I shall be at the door no later than two.'

'Two o'clock?' The doctor gave a chuckle. 'Good heavens, my lord, I understood your friends lived no more than a couple of miles from here! You will be in your bed much sooner than two! Ha-ha, you society fellows and your town habits. I am sorry to disappoint you, but the Earl and his lady do not keep such late hours.'

'And Lord Gabriel will not wish to remain very late,' added Lady Craster, coming across to join them.

'The Earl tells me you are leaving for the north in the morning, my lord.'

'Leaving!' Nancy could not help the exclamation. She had known he must go, yet to hear the words from Susan was a bitter blow.

'Why, yes, did I not tell you, Lady Ann?' His innocent tone did nothing to assuage Nancy's anger. 'Now the roads are clear I must be on my way.'

'Of course.' Susan flicked a triumphant glance towards Nancy. 'Lord Gabriel cannot tarry here on a whim, you know, Lady Ann. He has obligations to his family, however much he wants to stay.'

'I certainly do. Have obligations, that is.'

Was that a faint glimmer of apology in his eyes? Was he trying to tell her he must do his duty? Nancy knew that, of course she did. Had she not told herself only that morning that their idyll was over?

'But we are not yet out of time,' declared the doctor, beaming at everyone. 'We must enjoy the rest of our evening together. It is not often that I am privileged to enjoy such company as this.' He turned to Nancy. 'Perhaps, Lady Ann, you would sing for us, before we retire. You might send us off to our slumbers with a lullaby, perhaps.'

The suggestion shook her.

'Oh, but I cannot,' she said, backing away. 'I am so out of practice.'

'You are too modest, madam. My lady says she has heard you singing and playing here, on this fine Broadwood.'

'But that is for my own amusement, sir, and I cannot accompany myself well enough to please an audience.'

'Then let me play for you,' offered Gabriel. 'I am quite proficient, you know, and I should very much like to hear you sing. Let us repair to the pianoforte. I noticed a pile of sheet music on a side table, including songs in a notebook that bears your name.'

'Is that still there?' She gave an uncertain laugh. 'I compiled that collection years ago. Too long ago to remember the songs.'

His eyes gleamed as he countered even that excuse.

'Then you can read the words over my shoulder as I play. Come, I am sure we shall be able to find a piece to suit us both.' He put his hand under her elbow and turned his charming smile upon the doctor. 'If you will excuse us, sir...'

'Gabriel, let me go,' she begged as he escorted her across to the pianoforte. 'I do not want to play. Or sing.'

'Oh, why? I thought all ladies liked the opportunity to shine.'

'Why do you think I only practice here when I am alone? My father is not at all musical and neither is his fiancée,' she said crossly. 'They will find my performance tedious in the extreme.'

'But Dr Scotton wishes to hear you. To...er...send him to sleep.'

She giggled and felt better for it, but was still determined to resist. 'I am sure he will manage to sleep without it.'

'But how can you disappoint the poor man, when he is clearly enamoured?'

'Easily,' she hissed at him. 'The *poor man*, as you call him, has been following me about the house all day, making a nuisance of himself!'

They had reached the side table and she stood, irresolute, as Gabriel sorted through the music sheets. As a child, music had been something she enjoyed, but only in secret, or with her sister. She recalled her mother saying that if they were going to the expense of hiring a music teacher for Mary then he might as well teach her, too. Father had been even less encouraging and had made no secret of his views.

Mary must learn, of course, but Ann—Ann will never amount to much.

She closed her eyes, trying to blot out the cruel words. If only he had continued to think her of such little worth. If only the rich and lascivious Viscount Packington had not shown an interest in her.

'What about this?'

She opened her eyes. Gabriel was holding up the open book.

'You have called it "Laura's Song", but I know it better as "No One Shall Govern Me".'

She glanced at the page. It was the last thing she had written in her book, shortly before she had run away. The song was supposed to be a warning to young ladies, for Laura had ended as 'a pettish, pert old maid'. Nancy had preferred to risk that fate rather than marry the man her father had chosen for her.

'That is a little too close to my own story.' She took the book and flicked back a couple of pages. 'This one would be better, I think, "Sweet Jenny, the Maid of the Moor".' She flushed and thrust the book back at him, suddenly embarrassed. 'I would rather not sing at all tonight.'

'But you will, won't you?' He held her gaze, a smile of encouragement in his blue eyes. 'If I play, you will sing it? For me?'

Nancy hesitated, but she knew she would not refuse. The chance to perform for Gabriel, to make music with him, just once, was far too tempting. He read the answer in her face and smiled at her. Without a word he sat down at the pianoforte, placed the open notebook before him and began to run his fingers over the keys.

'The lasses of Scotland are bonnie and free...' Nancy began, barely glancing at the words, which readily came back to her. Her voice strengthened as her confidence grew and by the time the song had ended she was happy to sing again. This time it was 'The Lily in the Vale', then 'Robin Adair' and when Gabriel suggested a duet she agreed. It did not matter to her that her father was dozing in his chair or that Susan was looking bored. As the song progressed she forgot her audience, forgot everything save the pleasure of singing, her voice blending with Gabriel's fine tenor as the music dipped and soared in the tale of two lovers, parted then reunited. Without thinking, she put her hand on his shoulder as the song reached its final chorus and as the last notes died away she found herself smiling, most foolishly.

'Oh, *brava*, Lady Ann. *Bravo*, my lord! As fine a performance as I have ever heard!' Dr Scotton applauded enthusiastically and, at a nudge from Susan, the Earl jerked awake with a snort.

'Eh, what? Oh, aye. Very good, very good.'

Gabriel was laughing up at her and Nancy beamed back, feeling inordinately pleased that they had performed so well together.

'I am impressed, my lord,' she murmured. 'Is there no end to your talents?'

'Thank you. I am considered very good with my hands.'

She almost choked at the innuendo and had the greatest difficulty keeping her countenance as she moved away from the pianoforte.

'Heavens, 'tis nigh on midnight,' exclaimed Susan. 'How the time has flown!' She rose, clearly signalling the end of the evening.

'It has, indeed, and I must go.' Gabriel dutifully nodded towards the doctor, then turned to Nancy. 'Lady Ann.'

She gave him her hand. Her spirits were still bubbling with happiness from the singing and she said impulsively, 'Thank you. I had not expected to enjoy myself so much this evening.'

He kissed her fingers, mouthed the words *two o'clock* at her and turned to take his leave of his host and hostess. Then he was gone and it was all Nancy could do not to sigh.

'What a delightful evening,' declared Lady Craster, when the door had closed behind him. 'It is a shame that Lord Gabriel will not be calling here again.' She gave Nancy a condescending smile. 'I did warn you, my dear, not to build up your hopes about the gentleman.'

'A very pleasant fellow,' remarked the doctor, 'but not one to be relied upon, I fear.' He gave a laugh. 'These rich men are all the same, Lady Ann. They make very charming companions, but they never settle.'

'That is exactly what I have been telling her.' Susan walked across to Nancy and took her arm. 'I think it time we retired, my dear.'

They left the room together, but as soon as they were outside the door, Nancy gently released herself.

Susan gave a little tut. 'I hope you do not take the doctor's warning amiss, or mine,' she said. 'You have been away from good society for a long time and as a widow I fear you may be susceptible to the charms of such a plausible rake.'

'Thank you, but your advice is unnecessary,' replied Nancy, her chin up. 'Although I question if Lord Gabriel is so very bad.'

'Oh, he is, my dear, believe me, I have met his sort before.' Susan laughed softly. 'And even if he were in earnest, you are the relict of a tradesman. The Baxendens would never countenance the union, be you ever so rich.'

'I am well aware of that.'

Susan was perfectly right, Nancy recalled how she had been shunned by the *ton* when she was masquerading in London as a wealthy widow. Society thought she was tainted by trade, but the truth was far, far worse. If society considered any connection with trade polluted the blood, what would they think of a woman

who had been earning her living as a cook? Her grandmother's legacy might make her acceptable to an impoverished gentleman, but as a wife for the son of a
marquess, a man who had a comfortable fortune of
his own? Unthinkable. She had never aspired to that,
she told herself. She had never asked more of Gabriel
than to spend a short time as his lover. Suddenly tears
felt very close. Bidding Lady Craster a goodnight, she
hurried away to her room.

Chapter Fourteen

Nancy lay in her bed, waiting for the house to fall silent. By the light of her bedroom candle she watched the hands of her little clock move around. One o'clock. One thirty. She strained to listen for any sounds of movement in the house, but there was nothing, even the creaking timbers had settled for the night.

Silently she slipped out of bed, pushed her feet into her soft kid slippers and threw a silk wrap over her nightgown. She opened the door and peeped out into the empty, silent stillness of the passage. She knew the house well enough to avoid the creaking boards and the moonlight through the lantern roof over the stairs was sufficient for her to creep down without a candle. When she reached the garden door she carefully slid back the bolts and waited.

From somewhere above stairs she heard a clock strike the hour and almost before the chime had died away the handle turned. Silently the door opened and Nancy breathed a small sigh of relief as Gabriel came in.

* * *

In the dark shadows of the hall Gabriel could just make out a pale, wraith-like shape at the bottom of the stairs. Nancy. As his eyes grew accustomed to the gloom, he saw that her glorious hair hung loose about her shoulders and she wore little more than a thin silk robe with the belt knotted tightly about her waist. He could not stop himself reaching for her. After the briefest hesitation she came willingly into his arms, her lips tasting so sweet he was sorely tempted to carry her off to bed. It was less than two weeks since she had left Dell House but she was constantly in his thoughts. Impossible, of course. He had his orders. But later, perhaps, when this was over, he would come and find her.

It was Nancy who broke off the kiss, but he heard her soft sigh and could not stop himself from teasing her.

'Have you missed me?' he whispered.

Even in the darkness he knew she was blushing, but she pushed herself out of his arms and beckoned him to follow her. Without a word she picked up a bedroom candle and tinderbox from the console table and led the way up the stairs and through a labyrinth of passages to the locked room.

'Do you need me to light the candle?'

She was so close that he felt her soft breath on his cheek.

'No.' He reached into his pocket for the bundle of bent picks. It was the work of a moment to find the correct one, ease it past the wards and twist it to lift the locking lever. The bolt released with a faint click and they slipped inside. Nancy closed the door and leaned her back against it.

'So, you add housebreaking to your accomplishments,' she murmured. 'What a varied career you have had, my lord.'

He grinned. 'During my short spell in the military I was in charge of one or two…er…irregular soldiers.'

She gave a tut as she set to work lighting the candle. It added only marginally to the moonlight, barely enough to register to anyone who should happen to be out of doors. He glanced about the room. It had been stripped of most of its furniture and large expanses of wall gleamed pale and barren. From the strong smell of fresh paint, he guessed that the wood around the doors and windows and the panelling below the chair rail had been repainted.

Nancy pointed to a bow-fronted chest of drawers draped with holland covers. A large parcel rested on the top.

'The pattern book,' she whispered. 'Packaged and ready to be taken back to Lincoln.'

Tucked under the string was Lady Craster's letter of instructions to Hewitt and Sons. Gabriel picked it up and weighed in his hands.

'Hmm. It is too light and too thin to contain the missing documents. They are more likely to be hidden in the pattern book itself. Bring the candle a little closer.'

With extreme care he unfastened the string and removed the oilcloth wrapping to reveal a large book with board covers and curling letters proudly proclaiming the name: *Hewitt's Paper Hanging and Papier Mâché Manufactory*. Gabriel ran his fingers over the edges of the rag-paper samples that had been bound into the book and gave a small nod of satisfaction. From between the pages he pulled out a stiff sheaf of papers, folded and bound with a red ribbon.

'Success.'

Nancy stared at the embossed seal securing the ribbon. Until that moment she had not truly believed the missing documents could be at Masserton Court and she felt a chill run down her spine. How could her father be involved in this? Surely he would not knowingly risk dishonour, disgrace and execution. And yet here was the proof. She put one hand to her mouth, feeling a little sick.

'Nancy?' Gabriel was looking closely at her. 'Are you going to faint on me?'

The gentle taunt had its effect.

'No, of course not.' She drew a breath and held the candle a little higher. 'Go on.'

He drew out his penknife, heated the blade on the candle and gently eased the seal from one length of the ribbon. The outer paper was blank, no more than a protective covering. Gabriel took the inner sheets and opened them. Nancy peered over his shoulder, but the closely written lines danced before her eyes and she could not read them.

'Is that what you are looking for?' she breathed. 'Is that the plans?'

'Oh, yes.' His voice was grim. She fought down another wave of nausea and Gabriel said softly, 'I should not have dragged you into this. Oh, Nancy, you must wish you had never met me.'

She shook her head. 'I wish this was not happening, but my not knowing of it would make no difference. What will happen now?'

'I will take these papers to London and the sample book must continue on its journey, hopefully with no one the wiser about its contents. Captain Graves can then apprehend the carrier and everyone else involved.'

'Including my father.'

'Yes. I am so very sorry.'

For one wild moment she considered begging Gabriel to destroy the papers, to forget everything and run away with her. He wouldn't do it, of course. Those betraying England must be stopped, she knew that, it was what had to be done. But she still could not believe her father was a traitor. Perhaps Gabriel would give her time to warn him, so that he might flee the country...

Gabriel was refolding the closely written papers. 'We need to replace them with something,' he said, slipping them into his coat. 'In case anyone decides to check the documents are still there.'

Nancy went over to the small table by the window, where Susan's notes and papers were spread in disorder. She sifted through the sheets, scanning them quickly by the light of the candle and selecting several which she carried back to Gabriel.

'Here. Use these.' She added, unable to keep a faint tremor of relief from her voice, 'They are all addressed to Lady Craster, there is no mention of my father.'

'Nancy, I will do my best, but I cannot promise to keep him out of this.'

'I understand that. The best he can do is to plead ignorance. Better that he is thought a crass fool than a traitor.'

She pushed the papers into his hands. They were slightly smaller than the originals, but once they were folded and placed inside the plain outer sheet, she could see no discernible difference. Gabriel retied the ribbon, then carefully warmed the bottom of the wax seal and fixed it in position before putting the documents back between the pages.

Somewhere in the house a board creaked and Nancy jumped.

She touched his arm. 'You should go. It is vital you get those plans away. Let me finish off here.'

'No, I'll do it. I memorised how it was packaged and tied.' He gave her a reassuring smile. 'There is no hurry, I cannot set out for London before dawn and I need to brief Captain Graves.'

To Nancy's stretched nerves it felt like a lifetime before the oilcloth was once more wrapped and tied. She snuffed the candle before they left the room and waited nervously while Gabriel relocked the door. She tried to steady her breathing, but knew she would not relax until he was clear of the Court. Her knees felt decidedly weak as she led him back down the stairs, remembering to deposit the candle and tinderbox on the table as they passed it. At the garden door, Gabriel stopped.

'Thank you,' he said softly. 'I owe you more than I can say.'

'I did what had to be done. I would be happier if my father was found not to be involved.'

'I will do what I can for him, you have my word.'

She nodded silently, beyond speech. He pulled her into his arms and kissed her, hard. She could not help herself responding, taking what comfort she could from their kiss, knowing it would be the last. When the kiss had ended and he raised his head, she pushed herself free.

'Go now. Take those papers back to London with all speed.'

He caught her hands, saying urgently, 'Come with me. It is not safe for you here. I could pick you up at first light and take you to London.' He squeezed her fingers. 'I want you with me, Nancy. We are good together.'

She fought down the sudden lump in her throat. She wanted so badly to go with him, but as what, his mistress? One of the dozens he had spoken of. When he grew tired of her she did not doubt he would pay her off handsomely, but she did not want that. She had enjoyed his company, the memories of the days—and nights—they had shared were squirrelled away, ready to be conjured up whenever she was feeling low, but it was better that they end this now, while she could walk away with her head held high, even if her heart was not quite unscathed. She summoned up a laugh and forced a cheerful note into her voice.

'We *were* good together, weren't we? But we both agreed it could only ever be a short liaison, while the snow lasted.'

She looked past him. The fields were still mostly white, but there were darker patches now, where the snow had disappeared. Time to end this.

She said, 'You need not worry about me, Gabriel, I am in no danger. I intend to set out for Prospect House today, this very morning, and as neither my father nor Lady Craster wants me here, they are hardly likely to object to my leaving.'

Gabriel was watching her and she was very afraid that if he did not go soon, her resolve would crumble. She would cast off the last vestiges of pride and throw herself into his arms. She gave him a little push, saying sharply, 'Be off with you, my lord, and do your duty for King and country!'

He hesitated a moment, as if he would speak, then he was gone, striding away into the darkness.

Nancy watched him go, his image burning itself into her memory: the broad shoulders, confident step, the glint of moonlight on his dark hair and his breath like smoke in the night air. Silently she cried out to him to turn back, to give her one last smile, but he kept walking. He was going back to his world and, in the morning, she would return to hers. She was suddenly aware of the icy night air penetrating her flimsy wrap and she shivered. Closing the door, she quietly slid the bolts in place. There was no reason they should ever meet again.

Gabriel rode away from Masserton Court, his horse's hoofs beating a rhythmic tattoo on the hard ground. He had achieved his objective, to retrieve the stolen plans and discover how they were getting out of the country. He had already informed his people in London about Meldrew, the London carrier, and he could now pass on his information about the wallpaper supplier to Captain Graves. The captain would be able to intercept Hewitt's wagons on their next trip to the coast and he had no doubt that the sample book from Masserton would be among the packages, together with the papers incriminating Lady Craster.

He should be congratulating himself on a job well done, but the thought of Nancy nagged at him, like unfinished business. He recalled his last sight of her, standing in the doorway, pale and insubstantial as a ghost. A laugh shook him. There was nothing insubstantial about Nancy. Their nights together had been hot, despite the icy weather. He recalled the feel of her in his arms, warm and passionate, the way their bodies melded, two parts of one glorious whole. How could one ever have enough of that?

'I wish—'

He pressed his lips together before more words escaped into the cold night. Confound it, he was growing maudlin! He never regretted the ending of his flirtations. Ever. At five-and-thirty he was too set in his ways to change now. Nancy was right, their affair had been a pleasant interlude, designed to while away the snowy days. If she did not regret their parting, then neither should he. Spring was coming, the *ton* would be returning to London for the Season and there would be any number of young beauties there to tempt him.

A few months in town and this whole episode—and Nancy—would be no more than a faint memory.

He settled his hat more firmly on his head and cantered on into the night.

Gabriel was admitted to Hollybank by a sleepy footman and he made his way swiftly and silently to his room, where he found his man dozing in a chair.

'Why the devil did you sit up for me, John?' Gabriel roused him with a hand on his shoulder. 'You know full well I can put myself to bed.'

'Aye, my lord, I do.' Thoresby yawned widely and got up. He went over to the hearth and used the poker to stir the coals into life. 'Did you find what you were looking for?'

'I did.' He patted his coat pocket. It felt like a hollow victory. For once he felt none of the satisfaction that usually accompanied the conclusion of a mission. But he suspected that was because he was exhausted. 'A few hours' sleep and we will be on our way to London.'

'You might like to know what I've learned in Lincoln today—'

Gabriel rubbed a hand across his eyes. Suddenly he was sick of this whole business.

'Leave it 'til morning, man,' he snapped. 'I'm dog-tired and need my bed.' John's stoic acceptance of his outburst cut him and he put out his hand. 'Forgive me, my friend. That was uncalled for. You had best tell me now.' He waved John back into his chair and perched himself on the edge of the bed.

'I doubt it's anything important, my lord, it just adds

a little more to what we already know. I have discovered that Lady Craster lived for several years in Lincoln, before she was married. Seems she had family here at one time. And I learned that she made a visit to the city in the late spring, just before she went off to Brighton.'

'Where she met Lord Masserton,' added Gabriel. 'So that would suggest she set out to ensnare him.'

'Just what I was thinking, my lord, Masserton Court being ideally placed for her contacts in Lincoln.'

'No one would question a lady sending to London for her gowns and she then passes on the stolen papers, which make their way to the coast and on to the Netherlands.'

Thoresby shook his head. 'And all the while our people have been watching the southern ports. Threw us neatly off the scent, didn't they?'

'What about Dr Scotton?' Gabriel asked him. 'Did you find any connection there?'

'No, nothing. He's had a practice in Lincoln for many years and is pretty well respected there. He and his partner run a private madhouse on the outskirts of the city, which also houses pauper lunatics, paid for by the parish.'

Gabriel snorted. 'That is no guarantee of his abilities or his character! However, it is unlikely he'd want to jeopardise that lucrative income by running foul of the law. And it's likely Lady Craster knew the doctor when she lived in Lincoln, so she would feel confident recommending him to Masserton. No, my money is on the carrier, Hewitt. Captain Graves can follow that up tomorrow.' He stood up and stretched. 'Thank you, John. If that's all, I'll bid you goodnight. We have a long journey tomorrow and we both need some sleep.'

'And after London, my lord, are we travelling back to the north?'

'Why the devil should we do that?' exclaimed Gabriel, conscious of the warmth creeping into his cheeks. How could his man know he'd been thinking of following Nancy to this Prospect House she had talked of? Even though it was over between them, he wanted to see where she lived. To assure himself that she was safe.

John looked at him innocently. 'To visit your father, sir. At Alkborough.'

'Oh.' Gabriel did not for one moment believe this was what he had meant, but he could hardly challenge him. He said, 'No. We'll stay in town for the rest of the winter. I have had enough of the north!'

Nancy double-checked the bolts before making her way back to her room. She had left orders for Hester to wake her at first light, so she must try to get some sleep. They planned to leave Masserton Court in the morning and take the first coach north. The moon was full overhead now, shining all the way down to the lower stairs and Nancy, lost in her own thoughts, did not notice the candlelight on the landing as she began her ascent. Her father's angry voice startled her so much she almost missed her step.

'What the devil are you about, madam?'

She stopped and clung to the handrail, her heart hammering so hard she thought she might faint.

'Come up here this minute!'

Keeping one hand on the rail, Nancy climbed the last few stairs until she reached the landing. Three figures awaited her: her father, Susan and Dr Scotton, who was holding aloft a bedroom candle. Nancy leaned against the banister and stood before them, arms folded. Not by the flicker of an eyelid did she show her unease when she observed that they were all fully clothed.

She said, 'I thought you had all gone to bed.'

'We were in the drawing room,' snapped her father. 'We were about to retire when a sudden draught alerted us to the fact that a door was open somewhere in the house. Unluckily for you, madam!'

'Lady Ann!' The doctor addressed her with measured disapproval. 'One must ask what *you* are doing abroad at this hour?

'Is it not obvious?' Susan's voice was scathing. 'She was seeing her lover off the premises.'

Nancy looked back at her defiantly. She had to give Gabriel time to get away and convincing them she had taken him to her bed was much less likely to result in his being pursued than if they knew he had taken the documents. She pulled her silk wrap about her a little more securely, thus drawing attention to her state of undress.

'And what if I was? It is none of your concern.'

'Ravenshaw!' The Earl spat out the word. 'Impudent dog!'

'I am of age and a widow, too.' She added softly, 'As is Lady Craster.'

'Susan and I are betrothed. You are a fool if you think giving yourself to Ravenshaw like a common whore will persuade him to marry you.'

'I do not think it! I was merely amusing myself.'

'Oh, shameless, brazen woman,' cried Dr Scotton. 'What a way to repay your father's kindness.'

'Kindness! Since I arrived at Masserton I have been treated more as a servant than a daughter.'

'But a disgraced daughter,' Susan reminded her silkily.

'Aye,' growled the Earl. 'And a damned ungrateful one, too.'

Nancy put up her chin. The longer they remained arguing here, the safer Gabriel would be.

'Ungrateful? How so?'

Susan's voice snapped back at her. 'Your father took you in, showed you he was willing to forgive your past behaviour, even your demeaning yourself by marrying a man in trade.'

'Aye, confound it. Does the family honour mean so little to you?' demanded the Earl.

'Perhaps you would have preferred me to take up some menial employment,' she suggested. 'In someone's kitchens, perhaps.'

'I would have preferred to learn that you were dead!' he roared. 'At least then I would have been spared this. You continue to shame me.'

'You are not my keeper!'

'I am while you are under my roof, madam.'

'But that will not be for much longer,' she retorted, perilously close to losing her temper. 'It is clear my returning here has not been a success. I shall pack up and leave in the morning.'

She had thought the announcement would come as a relief to Lady Craster and was surprised that the lady did not look more pleased.

Dr Scotton put up his hand. He said pacifically, 'I fear we are all a little overwrought, Lady Ann. Perhaps it would be best to resume this discussion at breakfast.'

'There is nothing more to discuss,' declared Nancy, 'but I do agree it is time to retire.'

With that she swept past the little party and hurried off to her bedchamber, praying that Gabriel was safe and impatient for dawn so that she, too, might leave this place for good.

Nancy left Hester packing up the remainder of her belongings and went down to breakfast wearing the bronze-velvet travelling dress in which she had arrived. She was determined to leave with all speed and if her father would not allow her to use one of his carriages, she would send Davy out to hire a vehicle to carry them to Tuxford.

Susan and her father were already at the breakfast table, but she was relieved that there was no sign of Dr Scotton. The Earl was clearly not in a good mood and did not break off from grumbling to his fiancée as Nancy went in.

'I do not see why you had to send a man all the way

to Lincoln with that pattern book. Surely it could have waited for Hewitt to come and collect it.'

'I told you, my dear lord, the sooner the order is placed the sooner we can have the blue room straight again.'

So, the sample book had been returned and Susan's complacent manner suggested she had no suspicion that the documents had been removed. That at least was good news, thought Nancy as she took her seat at the table. Susan eyed her coldly.

'Good morning, Lady Ann.' She pushed the coffee pot towards her. 'I am glad you have deigned to join us.'

Nancy waited for her father to greet her, but he merely regarded her with frowning, resentful eyes. She drank her coffee and helped herself to a Bath cake, trying to ignore his ill humour.

'May I have the carriage, Father, to take Hester and me to Tuxford this morning?'

Her father continued to watch her in silence and it was Lady Craster who responded.

'I am sure that can be arranged. What time do you wish to depart?'

'As soon as possible. Hester is packing the final bags now.'

'Shall we say noon?'

'I would rather it was earlier.' Nancy refilled her cup. The events of the night had left her feeling tired and dull. She hoped more coffee would revive her.

'I am afraid that is not possible,' murmured Susan. 'Lucas is ridden to Lincoln and will not be back much before twelve.'

'There are other hands in the stable who could pre-pare the carriage,' Nancy argued. 'Davy, for example.'

'We shall see. My dear Lady Ann, you are looking very pale, this morning. And you have eaten very little. Do have another Bath cake. Or a little bread and butter.'

'Thank you, no.' She was definitely not hungry, but she did feel excessively tired. 'I think I shall go…'

She placed her hands on the table, but did not have the strength to push herself to her feet. Her mind felt cloudy, it was too much effort even to speak. She sank back in her chair, her eyes closing.

The few hours' sleep Gabriel managed to snatch felt nowhere near long enough, but he made his way downstairs to break his fast with his hosts and to take his leave of them. Lord and Lady Blicker were both at the breakfast table and anxious to know about his dinner at Masserton Court. He described the evening, avoiding more than one mention of Nancy, although she was foremost in his mind. He tried not to think of her coming into the drawing room, her silk gown glow-ing in the candlelight, accentuating every curve and movement of her body. Tried not to recall her ethereal appearance in that flowing nightgown, her loose curls cascading over her shoulders, tempting him to drive his hands into her hair and pull her closer, to lose himself in her. No, he must not think of Nancy.

His wandering thoughts were recalled by Lady Blicker and he was obliged to beg her pardon and ask her to repeat herself.

Her kindly eyes twinkled. 'I was saying we shall

not be offended if you elect to stay at Masserton Court on your next visit, rather than Hollybank.'

Gabriel smiled politely and was about to change the subject, but his host got in before him.

'Aye, Lady Ann has grown into a fine young woman. Accomplished, too, and a capital rider, as I recall. A good match for any man.'

'Especially now she has her grandmother's fortune,' added his lady.

'Oh?' Gabriel could not help himself. He had heard nothing of this, but was glad if it was true. For Nancy's sake.

'Did you not know?' his hostess looked at him, surprised. 'Lady Elmstone left her well provided for, when she died, although at that time no one knew quite where the poor girl might be, or even if she was still alive.'

'Thirty thousand pounds!' Lord Blicker chuckled. 'Must be a blow for the Earl, Lady Ann coming back like she has, after all these years. I've no doubt he thought the money was his.'

Gabriel's breakfast had turned to ashes in his mouth as the implications of this news hit him. An unscrupulous widow, an impoverished earl who had never shown any affection for his daughter and a doctor with links to an asylum. He could be wrong. Gabriel prayed he was wrong, but he knew at that moment there was no way he could ride off and leave Nancy to her fate.

Chapter Fifteen

Nancy woke up slowly. Her head was aching and her mouth felt unpleasantly dry. When she opened her eyes, the daylight made her wince and she closed them again quickly. She tried again and looked about her, trying to order her sluggish thoughts. It was clearly late morning. Had she overslept? No, she was wearing her velvet travelling dress. Slowly, painfully, her memory returned, and with it the conviction that she had been drugged. Something in the coffee, perhaps. She forced her mind to think back. Had Susan taken any coffee from the pot? She thought not.

The door opened and Nancy managed a single word.

'Hester?'

'Mrs Yelland is gone.' Susan came into view, Dr Scotton at her shoulder. 'She has left. Stobbs shall attend you for the remainder of your stay here.'

'Gone?' Nancy stared uncomprehending at the dresser, who curtsied to her.

'When she heard of your disgraceful behaviour she decided she could no longer remain in your service,' Susan told her. 'Now, Dr Scotton has prepared a draught for you.'

'I do not want any medicine,' declared Nancy. 'He is not my doctor.'

'Your father has instructed me to attend you, Lady Ann,' he said, in a voice of authority. 'You are clearly distraught.'

'Then let me rest!'

The doctor came closer, a small glass in his hand and Nancy could smell cloves and cinnamon in the concoction he held out to her.

'Now, now, madam, this will do you good—'

'I do not want it!' She slid off the bed, struggling to make her limbs obey her will. 'Where is Hester? I demand to see her. This minute.'

'Lady Craster has told you, she is gone.' The doctor came around the bed towards her.

'What have you done with her? She would never leave me!'

She tried to push past him, but immediately the maid grabbed her arm. When Nancy protested Dr Scotton handed the glass to Susan and caught Nancy in a vice-like grip, pinning her arms at her sides. Panic made Nancy fight violently, but she was no match for the three of them and she choked as Susan tipped the laudanum down her throat.

'I am sorry to say Lady Ann is clearly hysterical,' declared the doctor, as she was helped, coughing, back to the bed. 'This accords with the observations I made yesterday, at his lordship's request. A spell under my care is best for her, I am sure.'

Exhausted by her efforts, Nancy lay curled up on the bed while the three of them stood around, keeping watch. She had no idea how much of the drug she had actually ingested, but they were obviously waiting for her to sleep, so she dutifully closed her eyes. She could feel the drowsiness stealing over her again, but she fought it. She must try to understand what they were saying, before she lapsed back into unconsciousness.

'The Earl and I agree with you, of course, but…the legal situation?' Susan posed the question delicately.

'The Earl's lawyers will advise you, of course, but I think you may be easy on that point, Lady Craster. You have ascertained that the lady has no relatives on her husband's side and, having returned to her father's house, she has put herself into his care. As to her mental state, we need not rely solely upon my judgement. My partner will also examine her. I am confident his opinion will be very much the same as my own, in this case. We need to keep her safe until she is fully recovered.' There was the briefest hesitation before he continued. 'If she ever does recover.'

'Thank you, Doctor. I am sure the Earl will be only too pleased to reimburse you for your trouble.'

There was silence. Nancy opened one eye a fraction to see that they were all standing around the bed, looking at her. She kept very still, breathing slowly, as if asleep.

The doctor murmured, 'Perhaps you would ask the Earl to send for the carriage now, ma'am.'

'I would prefer to wait a little longer.' Lady Craster's voice was very soft and Nancy knew there would be a cold smile on her face. 'Lucas will be returning from Lincoln at any time and I would like him to accompany you. Just in case you need any, er, assistance. He is completely to be trusted, whereas some of my lord's other servants have been too long in the service of the family.'

'I quite understand, madam.'

'Good. Let us repair to the drawing room. The Earl will wish to know your diagnosis. My maid can keep watch here…'

They were leaving her. Nancy thought, if she was alone with just the maid, she might be able to overpower her. She must keep still and listen for the sounds of their withdrawal. But even before they had reached the door she had slipped back into oblivion.

It was very quiet when Nancy woke again and the light was fading. It must be late afternoon and the short winter day was coming to an end. Carefully she looked about her. She was alone. Fighting against the sluggishness of her mind and body, she heaved herself off the bed and staggered across to the washstand.

There was some clean water left in the jug and she drank as much of it as she could, then poured the rest into the bowl and washed her face. It helped, but her thinking was painfully slow and laboured. She went to the door and tried the handle, but it was locked. She knew her window was too far from the ground to allow her to escape that way. Perhaps she might pick the lock, as Gabriel had done. Gabriel, who would be in London by now. Too far away to save her.

'That sort of thinking will not help you,' she told herself crossly. 'Think, Nancy!'

She found a hat pin on the dressing table and bent it, but after several fruitless minutes twisting it this way and that she gave up and went to sit on the bed. What had happened to Hester—had they really convinced her to leave? She was a friend and companion rather than a servant and Nancy could not believe she could be persuaded to go willingly. Although perhaps, if Hester was suspicious, she might have gone to fetch help. The idea gave Nancy some hope, but it was only conjecture and she dare not rely upon it. She rubbed her arms. She was on her own. If she was to survive, she would have to save herself.

Nancy put her hands to her throbbing temples. What did they plan to do to her? Susan was ordering the carriage. The doctor had said she would be in his care. His practice was in Lincoln. Was he taking her to his house, perhaps? What had he called her? Hysterical. And Susan had mentioned reimbursing him. It made no sense, but the fog in her brain would not allow her to think it out.

She heard voices and quickly scrambled back on the bed. If she could convince them she was still asleep they would not force any more laudanum upon her. She closed her eyes and forced herself to keep still. The lock clicked and footsteps came into the room. She heard her father's gruff voice.

'She sleeps still. How much have you given her?'

'Enough,' murmured the doctor. 'In cases such as

these, my lord, sometimes it is unavoidable, when a patient turns violent.'

'I would not have the servants think I am compelling her to go against her will.'

'Which is why the carriage is waiting for us in the stables and we are taking her there ourselves,' the doctor explained patiently. 'Sometimes these old family retainers can be quite distressed by this sort of thing. It will be best if you tell them about it afterwards.'

A female voice replied. Lady Craster's hatchet-faced maid.

'You'll have to help the doctor, my lord. She's a strapping piece and too much for me.'

'Oh, very well, Stobbs. But she'll have to walk,' the Earl replied. 'None of us is strong enough to carry her.' He shook her roughly. 'Ann, Ann. Come along, girl, get up.'

She stirred and groaned, made a show of blinking owlishly at them and pretending she wished to go back to sleep.

'Hester,' she muttered. 'Where is Hester? What have you done with her?'

'She is safe enough,' growled the Earl. 'She will be released once we have you put away.'

The doctor coughed. 'If you will take one arm, my lord, we will walk her down the back stairs.'

Nancy groaned softly and leaned heavily upon her escorts as they guided her out of the room while she tried to make her muddled brain think of what to do. All she could think of was Gabriel. Gabriel would help her, if he knew. Perhaps someone—some servant who

had known her as a girl—would send word to him, if
they realised what was happening to her. But they met
no one on the stairs, and the passages were similarly
deserted. There was no one she might call upon for
help. She sagged even more heavily upon her father
and the doctor. If nothing else, she would make them
work hard to take her away!

They half-carried her to a back door and out on to
the secluded path that led to the stables. She kept her
head down, but the fresh air was beginning to clear the
fog from her mind and she breathed in deeply.

'Nearly there, thank heaven,' gasped the Earl.
'Susan has given Lucas instructions to have the car-
riage ready. The sooner you have her safely locked up,
Doctor, the better.'

Locked up! They were putting her away, somewhere.
A cold chill ran through Nancy. Susan had mentioned
reimbursement…now, at last, she understood. They
were paying the doctor to pronounce her insane. Once
that happened, she would be beyond all help.

They had reached the stable yard and she could
see the waiting carriage with Lucas standing by the
open door. Bedside him was Lady Craster, dressed
in a pale blue redingote trimmed with white fur, her
hands pushed deep into a swansdown muff. She looked
around when Nancy was brought into the yard.

'Ah, there you are, Lady Ann. I thought I would
come and see you off.' Her smile was as wintry and
chill as the weather. 'To say goodbye, my dear. We
shall not meet again.'

Any lingering doubts were swept away and Nancy was filled with blazing fury.

'No!' Anger gave her strength for one final, desperate struggle and she tried to wrench herself free of her captors. The Earl was caught unawares and he released her, staggering back. The maid rushed forward, but a blow from Nancy's free hand sent her reeling away, clutching her bloody nose.

'Help! Someone help me!' She fought harder, trying to shake off the doctor's iron grip. The Earl made no attempt to close with her again and she cried out to him, 'Father, for pity's sake tell him to let me go!'

He shook his head at her. 'You brought this on yourself, girl, with your licentiousness and wicked disobedience!'

'Enough of this,' declared Susan, impatiently. 'Lucas, help the doctor get her into the carriage.'

The groom grabbed Nancy's flailing arm and the doctor shifted his own grip, panting, 'Come along now, my lady, you had best come quietly.'

'I'm damned if I will!'

They were dragging her closer to the carriage door and she was tiring. She made one last, desperate cry.

'Help me! Davy, *Davy!*'

Lucas gave a savage laugh. 'Call Davy all you want, my lady. I've laid him out cold. *He* won't help you.'

'No, but I will.'

Chapter Sixteen

Gabriel's voice rang out like a clarion call, bringing everyone to a stand. Nancy looked up to see him striding into the yard, followed by a dozen red-coated soldiers. Relief flooded through her, although she was struggling to think clearly.

'You were on your way to London,' she said. 'What about—?'

She fell silent as he gave her a warning glance and the slightest shake of his head.

The Earl marched forward, blustering. 'This is no business of yours, my lord.'

'Is it not?' replied Gabriel, unperturbed. 'It appears to me Lady Ann is being coerced into something she does not wish to do.'

'She is my daughter, sirrah. Allow me to know what is best for her.'

'They plan to lock me away,' cried Nancy, trying to shake off the hands that still held her prisoner. 'They are bribing the doctor to say I am insane.'

Scotton began to protest until Gabriel raised his hand and silenced him.

'Let us hear the lady out, shall we? And I think you should release her, too.'

Lucas and the doctor fell back and left Nancy struggling to stand unaided. She swayed alarmingly, but in two strides Gabriel was at her side.

'It's all right,' he said, putting one arm about her. 'I have you now.'

She clung to him, suddenly weak with relief. She was afraid she might faint and it was imperative she told everything and quickly.

'They drugged me,' she explained. 'At breakfast this morning. Laudanum in my coffee, I think.' The faintness was passing and she glared at the Earl. 'I could not work out why you should want to do such a thing to your own daughter. Then I realised it is because you want the thirty thousand pounds I have inherited from my grandmother. You would have me incarcerated in an asylum so that you can contest the will.'

'What nonsense, girl,' the Earl blustered. 'This is no more than wild raving. She is out of her mind.'

'On the contrary, my wits are clearing now, after your attempts to poison me!' With Gabriel beside her, Nancy's strength and her courage were returning. 'My sister sent me a copy of the will. I read it only once, but I remember very clearly what it said. In the event of my being unable or unwilling to take the inheritance, it would pass to my nearest living relative.'

Her father's face had reddened angrily. He scowled

at her. 'And why shouldn't I have the money? *You* have done nothing to deserve it!'

'My dear Hugh, we are wasting time,' put in Lady Craster. 'All this talk about wills is sheer nonsense. My Lord Gabriel, there is nothing amiss here, I assure you. Dr Scotton merely believes Lady Ann would benefit from a spell away from Masserton, to rest. Do you consider you know more about these matters than a medical man, my lord?' She gave a soft laugh. 'I think you have overstepped yourself, my lord.'

'We shall see.' His arm tightened reassuringly around Nancy. 'I shall have my own doctors examine the lady, if necessary, although I really do not think it will come to that. We shall see what the magistrate says about it. I am sure there will be witnesses who will vouch for Lady Ann.'

'Oh, goodness, Hester!' Nancy put a hand on his chest. 'They said she was not here, but she would not have left me. Then later, my father said... They have imprisoned her, Gabriel! She must be locked away somewhere.'

'Very well, we shall find her. Captain?'

He glanced at the officer, who immediately despatched two of his men to search the house.

'This is too much,' snapped Susan. 'Surely there is no need to involve the militia in our domestic affairs?'

'Captain Graves and his men are here on quite another matter,' Gabriel replied. 'One that concerns you more nearly, madam. Not content with encouraging the Earl to steal his daughter's inheritance, you have made him a dupe for your traitorous schemes.'

The Earl looked up. 'Eh? What's that?'

'She has been using you, Masserton. Her accomplices in London have been sending government documents here to be smuggled out of the country.'

Lady Craster laughed. 'Lord Gabriel is air-dreaming. He has no proof.' She smiled at the captain. 'You may search Masserton Court from top to bottom with my blessing. You will find nothing there to incriminate me.'

'She is right,' put in Nancy. 'The sample book was returned to Lincoln this morning.'

Gabriel nodded. 'And doubtless by now is on its way to the coast.'

'What of it?' Lady Craster shrugged. 'I am not responsible for what the supplier does in the line of business.'

'But instead of the naval plans you secreted between the pages, it now holds several of your own bills. The original documents are now on their way back to London.' Gabriel felt Nancy's anxiously enquiring gaze and gave a slight smile. 'John Thoresby has taken them, with a military escort.'

Lucas gave a small growl. 'We've been rumbled, my lady.'

'Hold your tongue,' snapped Lady Craster. 'There is no proof I had anything to do with it.'

'It pains me to contradict you, my lady, but I learned this morning from Captain Graves that they have arrested a clerk in Whitehall,' said Gabriel. 'A greedy little man who was prepared to coerce the minister into giving him the plans. His cousin is one Samuel Meldrew, a carrier who has the contract to deliver gowns for any number of London businesses, including Mrs Wells. Your dressmaker, my lady. She has confirmed she has despatched several gowns to you here at Masserton and the dates of your orders coincide very neatly with government papers going missing. It was a simple matter for Meldrew to secrete the stolen documents in the dress boxes. You then passed them to Hewitt.'

'What is all this?' demanded the Earl. 'I don't understand.'

'Hewitt's brother-in-law is a Brussels merchant, trading in luxury goods and selling Hewitt's wallpapers in the Netherlands,' Gabriel told him. 'He is also vehemently opposed to William I and the new regime. There are those who would pay well for papers that discredit our government and threaten the fragile peace in Europe. I also know that Lady Craster's fortunes have improved considerably this year, with several large payments. Is that not so, madam?'

'A traitor,' exclaimed the Earl, bemused, *'Susan?'*

'Yes, Lord Masserton.' Gabriel nodded. 'Your fiancée has been spending the last few months supposedly deciding between wallpapers, but every time she returned a book of samples to Hewitt there were government papers hidden between the leaves. And she has been paid very well for her troubles.'

The lady gave a derisive laugh. 'What nonsense! Surely, Hugh, you do not believe such lies?'

'You allowed her to replace many of your old servants and to put her own men in charge of the stables,' added Nancy. 'It was they who killed old Peter. They attacked him and deliberately left him to die out in the cold.'

The Earl shook his head at her. 'Nonsense, girl, no one would do that.'

'Hysteria,' declared Susan. 'For heaven's sake, my lord, let the doctor take Lady Ann to the asylum, where she can be properly cared for. Only a deranged mind would think of such a monstrous act.'

'I agree,' replied Gabriel, 'but in this instance the deranged mind was not Lady Ann's. Your creatures tried to do the same with me, Lady Craster, when I was making enquiries in Darlton.'

'*You* was the cove asking the questions!' cried Lucas.

He took a step back, staring in horror at Gabriel. Lady Craster shot him a warning glance, then turned to the Earl.

'My dear lord, this is all nonsense,' she cried. 'Concocted by your daughter and her lover, to discredit me. She has fabricated this whole tale out of jealousy.'

Nancy gave a little choke of anger. She said, 'Peter had arranged to meet Lord Gabriel on the night they were both attacked. He was unhappy with what was going on here at Masserton.' From the corner of her eye she noticed that a figure had staggered from the stable. 'Ask Davy, if you do not believe me.'

'You be quiet!' Lucas barked at the old groom, who was leaning heavily against the doorpost, his pale face bloodied. 'I knew we should have finished you, when we did for the others.'

The Earl had been standing by in silence, but now he suddenly came to life.

'Murdered? Old Peter? And *you* a traitor, Susan. Damme, madam, you have deceived me mightily!' He started towards the lady, who whipped a small, silver-mounted pistol from her muff.

The Earl stopped. 'Are you out of your wits, Susan? You—you *love* me. We are to be married.'

'Married!' She laughed, the sharp sound echoing off the frosty walls. 'That was never in my plans.'

'But…but we are betrothed! Everyone knows of it.'

'Your neighbours know of it, certainly, since you insisted upon having a ball to celebrate!'

'But what of our plans?' he demanded, bewildered. 'You wanted to be a countess. And children. You promised me an heir.'

'Children!' Susan's face twisted in distaste. 'There was never any question of my carrying your child.'

'But there must be! By God, madam, you have been in my bed enough times and you told me you could give me a son. Do you think I would have allowed you to make free with my house if you could not?'

'You gullible fool, there are ways to prevent a baby.' Susan's glance flickered towards the doctor, who was looking more and more uncomfortable. She turned back to the Earl, her lips curling contemptuously. 'You were the means to an end, Hugh, dear. I just needed a house near Lincoln and you were…convenient.'

The Earl had been growling and shifting from one foot to the other like an angry bear, but he suddenly let forth a bellow of rage. Nancy gave a little cry of fright as Susan raised her arm, the pistol pointing directly at his heart.

'Another step and I will shoot you!' she cried. 'And I know how to use this.'

Captain Graves took a couple of paces forward, but Gabriel waved him back. Gently putting Nancy to one side, he walked towards Susan.

'Don't be a fool, Lady Craster, there are a dozen armed men here. You will gain nothing by spilling more blood.' Nancy pressed her hands to her heart as he moved closer to the deadly weapon.

He put out his hand. 'Give that to me.'

Time had stopped. No one moved. Nancy held her breath and kept her eyes on Susan's face as Gabriel stood before her, cool and resolute. He might look invincible, but he was only flesh and blood, and she was very much afraid Susan would shoot him out of pure spite.

Finally, after a tense silence that stretched for ever, Susan gave a little shrug and handed him the pistol. Nancy felt the relief to her very bones and she fancied a collective sigh ran around the stable yard.

'Thank you, my lord.' Captain Graves stepped up. 'Sergeant, get these people into the carriage and you, Corporal, you will sit up on the box and make sure that coachman doesn't pull any tricks. We'll take them all to the castle.'

Susan looked up at Gabriel.

'I take it you are working for the Crown? I guessed as much, seeing you here today. It would go ill with me to kill you, I suppose.' She added contemptuously, 'And poor Hugh is not worth a bullet.'

The Earl turned on her angrily. 'Am I not? Why, you damned—'

Captain Graves took his arm. 'Come along my lord, into the carriage, if you please.'

'What? You can't want me. I know nothing of all this!'

'The magistrate will decide that in Lincoln, my lord,' said the captain, polite but unmoved.

The Earl was marched off, pausing only to complain when he realised he was expected to travel in the same vehicle as his groom and Lady Craster's maid. Only when the Sergeant brandished his rifle did he climb, grumbling, into the coach.

Captain Graves turned to Lady Craster. 'My lady?'

'Yes, yes, I am coming.' She cast a last look at Gabriel. 'With hindsight, I should have threatened to shoot Lady Ann. You would do anything to save her, isn't that so, my lord?' She laughed. 'She swept you off your feet at the first glance, did she not? And it is clear the feeling is mutual. Pity, I might have made a play for you myself, if it hadn't been obvious you are head over heels in love.'

Lady Craster walked away to the carriage and Gabriel stood frozen in shock. He felt winded, as if he had been punched in the gut. *Was* he in love with Nancy? Was this what it felt like, this unsettling feeling that he was not complete when they were apart? But they were friends. Good friends. That was the reason for going against orders when he realised she might need help.

That does not mean I am in love with her, he thought. *I would do as much for any friend.*

He looked across to where Nancy was standing. She could not have failed to hear Lady Craster's words and he saw she was staring at him, her face pale. In fact, she looked quite horrified. That delivered another blow, this time like a vicious kick in the ribs. She thought he was suffering from unrequited love!

'We have everyone in the coach now, Lord Gabriel.' Captain Graves was at his shoulder. 'My Sergeant will remain here with a couple of men to secure the house, pending a thorough search. The rest of us will escort the prisoners to Lincoln.'

'Yes, yes, of course, Captain. Thank you. I will follow in a few moments.' Somehow, he managed to respond calmly while his mind was in turmoil. Love. He was too old for such emotion. It could not be true. Lady Craster had been fooled by his play-acting.

The small cavalcade had rattled away and Davy had gone off to the house to have his wounds dressed. Gabriel and Nancy were alone in the yard. She was smoothing her sleeves, as if to remove all traces of the rough hands that had held her, but she looked distracted, troubled. He longed to take her in his arms and kiss away that worried frown, but as he moved closer she tensed. His embrace would not be welcome.

He said, 'Are you well enough to go to Lincoln today? You will need to give evidence about what they tried to do to you.'

'Must I?' She wrapped her arms about herself. 'I would rather not bring charges against my own father.'

'After what he has done I think you owe him no allegiance, but I understand.' He shrugged. 'Let him stew in the cells with the others for a while. Captain Graves will be questioning them about the more serious crimes of murder and treason. You might be required as a witness, although if we can persuade the lady's accomplices to confess, that may not be necessary.'

'If I am called, then I shall do my duty.' She shivered. 'I know it must come to trial and I am afraid my father's circumstances may go against him, his lack of funds...'

'There is no evidence that your father knew anything about Lady Craster's activities. Indeed, she as good as said so before us all today, so there is every chance he may escape any severe penalties.'

She touched his arm. 'You will do your best for him, won't you, Gabriel?'

'You have my word on it. And I am hopeful of the outcome. He is not the first man to have lost his head over a pretty woman.'

If she noticed the self-mockery in his final words she gave no sign.

'Thank you.' She turned away. 'Excuse me, I must find Hester.'

'Nancy!' He could not let it go. He had to speak. 'What Lady Craster said, about us—'

She stopped, her back to him, and said lightly, 'Oh,

heavens, I took no note of *that*. Susan delights in making trouble. Pray do not think I shall be wearing the willow for you, Gabriel.'

He tried to smile, but his habitual insouciance had deserted him.

'I would like to think you will miss me a little.'

She turned her head, presenting him with a view of her lovely profile.

'Well, of course I shall,' she answered, a little impatiently. 'We enjoyed ourselves, did we not? But it was never going to last and there is much to be done now. You have your work to finish and I must go back to Compton Parva.'

'You will return to Prospect House?'

'For a while, but once I have my grandmother's legacy I think I shall set up my own establishment. Buy a little house, perhaps. And I shall write a book on household management.' She laughed. 'I have always wanted to do so, you know, and being back at Masserton has convinced me that it would be well received. The meals here were not as good as I remember. Why, the cook does not even have a recipe for Bath cakes, I had to show him! And many of the newer staff did not know how to go on at all, but that is no doubt because Mrs Crauford is too old now to manage them properly—'

'Damnation, woman, stop it!' She turned to look at him then, eyes wide with alarm, and he put out his hand to her. 'Nancy, it doesn't have to end like this. I want to—'

'There you are, Miss Nancy. Thank the Lord!'

Nancy turned away with relief as Hester came hurrying into the yard and ran up to hug her. Whatever Gabriel had been about to say she did not want to hear it. She had been trying to marshal her thoughts ever since Susan's parting shot. She had known her own heart for some time, but that Gabriel could be in love with her—it was unthinkable. Impossible. And yet...

If it *were* so, if he did think himself in love with her, then it made everything a hundred times worse. But whether or not that were so, she was very much afraid Susan's words had convinced Gabriel he should propose. She would have had to refuse him, even though it would break her heart. It was one thing to masquerade for a short time as a respectable widow, but as Lord Gabriel's bride the truth would have to be told. How she had lived and worked and although she was not ashamed of what she had done to survive, the *ton* would have a very different opinion. They would laugh up their sleeves at Gabriel, think him a lovesick fool to take a wife who had been no better than a servant for the past dozen years.

'Oh, my dear ma'am,' cried Hester, clinging tightly to her, 'I have been kicking myself for allowing them to deceive me so. I was lured away to the attics in the east wing and locked in a room up there, where no one could hear me! Not that I was afraid for myself, for that uppity piece that calls herself Lady Craster's maid told me I should be set free as soon as you was securely locked up in the doctor's asylum.'

Hester rattled on, but Nancy barely heard her. Still

hugging the older woman, she peeped at Gabriel. He had told her his father wanted him to take a wife and settle down, but the Marquess of Baxenden was hardly likely to think the prodigal daughter of a disgraced earl a good match for his son. She would be shunned, ostracized and Gabriel would be humiliated.

She squeezed her eyes shut, pushing back the tears that burned her throat. Even if, by some miracle, she was accepted as his wife, they had known each other only a matter of weeks. His affection for her would not last and she could not bear to see it die, to have him make excuses for spending days, weeks away from her. To become the society wife who turned a blind eye to her husband's infidelity.

She murmured a few soothing words to Hester, then drew herself upright, taking in a long, steadying breath so that she might address Gabriel.

'Thank you, my lord, I shall do very well now that I have Hester with me. You had best follow the captain to Lincoln and make your report.'

Her face and throat ached with the effort of looking and sounding cheerful. She forced herself to return his searching look with a smile and prayed he would go before the leaden weight inside her grew too oppressive and she gave way to the tears that must surely follow.

At last he bowed.

'Very well, my lady. I will bid you good day.'

With that he turned and walked away. The glinting smile she knew so well had quite disappeared from his eyes, but it would return. The memory of their snowy idyll would fade and more quickly from his mind than hers, once he had found himself another mistress. A searing pain welled up inside and as soon as he was out of sight she buried her face into Hester's shoulder and let the tears fall.

Chapter Seventeen

The view from Nancy's room at Prospect House was generally pleasing, but on this drear spring morning, the Yorkshire landscape looked bleak and unappealing. A blanket of grey cloud hung low over the fields and trees and there was the steady drip, drip of rain from the eaves.

With a sigh Nancy turned away from the window. It was four months since she had last seen Gabriel and the longing for him was as strong as ever. Some days she regretted that she had not gone to London for the trials, even though she had not been called as a witness. She might have seen him then, although she would not have wanted him to see *her*.

She suspected he had used his influence on her behalf and she was certain he had done so for her father, who had been lampooned in the news sheets, but had been acquitted of anything more serious than being a gullible fool. The Earl had retired to Masserton Court to lick his wounds, but Nancy's letter to him had received a scathing reply, proving he was not at all grateful to Gabriel for his efforts. She knew she would have to thank him on her father's behalf, when she wrote. And she would do so, she thought, her hands going instinctively to her belly. She *must* do so, but not yet. Not yet. Not while the pain was still so raw.

Gabriel was her first thought on waking every morning and her last before sleeping. She missed his smile, his teasing remarks. She missed his lovemaking. In an effort to forget, Nancy busied herself with the concerns of the house, but in her long absence things had changed. She had returned to find her replacement in the kitchens was a very competent cook and, knowing she no longer wished to live the rest of her life at Prospect House, Nancy had declined to resume her position there. Instead she pottered around, helping out with whatever was required. Thankfully there was always plenty to do. Everyone at the house welcomed her return, but she soon saw that although they enjoyed her company, asked her advice and welcomed her help, Prospect House had gone on very well without her. In truth, they did not *need* her.

Neither did Hester, who was lodging with a widow in Compton Parva. The two older ladies had become firm friends and although they were always happy to see Nancy, they had their own concerns to occupy them. Nancy thought with sadness that she was not really needed anywhere now.

'I fear I have grown very conceited,' she muttered to herself. 'How very foolish to feel so low merely because I am not essential to anyone's happiness.'

What made it worse was everyone's kindness.

They treated her as if she were convalescing and in need of cossetting. Nancy had told only her friend Mrs Russington about her adventure in Lincolnshire and in the strictest confidence, but although Molly had not breathed a word, everyone at Prospect House was aware that *something* had happened during her months away.

And being females they all think it must have been a romance, she thought bitterly as she made her way downstairs. *The sooner I find myself a house of my own the better. Somewhere I can be miserable in peace!*

She sighed. That plan must wait. Molly had counselled her against moving out of Prospect House, at least for a while, and Nancy knew it was sage advice. In the next few months she would need her friends around her. Pinning on a cheerful smile, Nancy went into the kitchen where Martha, the new cook, was already at work preparing food for breakfast.

'Ah, good morning to 'ee, ma'am.'

Martha greeted her with a smile and a wave of her porridge spoon. She had been an upper servant for a wealthy baronet until she succumbed to the advances of his son and heir and had been thrown out on the street. She was a little in awe of Nancy and today, as always, she asked her if there was anything she would like to do. And as always Nancy replied that she was at her disposal.

'Well, there's not much cake left and you have such a light way with your hands, Miss Nancy, I'd be obliged if you'd make up another. And perhaps a couple more, to sell at market tomorrow, if you have time.'

'All the time in the world,' said Nancy, trying not to make it sound like a penance.

She slipped an apron over her plain gown and began to gather together the ingredients. An almond cake, she decided. And perhaps some rout cakes for the market. Prospect House supported itself with its farm produce and anything they could make for the weekly market, and heaven knew there was little enough to sell at this time of the year. Reaching for the jar of dried fruit, she remembered Gabriel stealing a handful of currants at Dell House. She realised how she had loved him even then. Even though they had known each other only a few days.

Where was he now? She wondered. Was he in town, flirting with the pretty debutantes arriving for the Season? Or perhaps he had already found a mistress and installed her in some discreet little house. A mistress who would spend her days making love to Gabriel, not making cakes to sell at market.

The latest addition to Prospect House's residents, a diminutive young maid in the last months of pregnancy, came into the kitchen, one hand protectively resting over her extended stomach.

'Excuse me, Miss Nancy, there's a gennelman askin' t'see you.'

Nancy stopped rubbing the butter into the flour. Her heart began to thud painfully against her ribs and she could *feel* the blood draining from her cheeks.

Turning from the stove, Martha took one look at her and said to the maid, 'Thank you, Dolly. Did he give you his name?'

The girl's hands flew to her mouth. 'Oh, lawks, I forgot to ask.'

Martha tutted, but she gave Nancy a reassuring smile. 'It'll be someone we know, Miss Nancy. Moses wouldn't have let him in, otherwise.'

'No. No, of course.' Nancy picked up a blunt knife and began to scrape the flour mixture from her shaking fingers. 'I will go up. Is he in the morning room?'

'N-no, Miss Nancy. I left'n in t'hall.'

'Then run back up now, Dolly, and show him into the morning room,' said Martha, patiently. 'Then come down here and I will have a tray of refreshments ready for you to carry up.

'Bless the child,' she said, when the maid had gone, 'she has such a lot to learn.' She went over to Nancy and put a hand on her shoulder. 'Are you all right, my dear? You've gone as white as a sheet. Shall I go up and see your visitor? It's most likely to be some sort of house business. It might even be old Jem Cayton, come to see if we're ready to take those piglets from him yet. Although I can't see how even Dolly would call *him* a gentleman!'

'No more do I.' Nancy managed a smile. 'Do not fret, I shall go and see, as soon as I have washed my hands.'

Martha was right, it was most likely a neighbour, nothing for her to worry about at all. Yet the tiny flame of hope she had kept buried for the past four months would not quite be extinguished.

Trying not to hurry, she washed her hands and re-

moved her apron, then put a hand up to her hair. She
caught the cook's knowing look and flushed rosily.

'You are as pretty as a picture, my dear,' said Martha, ushering her out of the kitchen. 'Now stop daw-
dling and go!'

Dolly was on the stairs, returning for the refreshment tray and Nancy stopped her.

'Well, did you find out the gentleman's name?'

'No, Miss Nancy. Was I supposed to?'

Hiding her frustration, Nancy carried on to the
morning room. At the door she paused, squaring her
shoulders before going in, her head held high. The
room seemed darker than usual, for someone was
standing by the window, blocking much of the light.
The man had his back to her, but there was no mistak-
ing that tall figure, or the broad shoulders. Or the long,
powerful legs thrust into top boots that were today lib-
erally splashed with mud.

'Lord Gabriel.'

How many times had she dreamt of this meeting?
How often had she imagined what she would say? A
calm, friendly greeting, assurances that she was very
well, thank you, that she required nothing from him
and, no, she had not missed him at all. But now, when
he was only yards away, all the practised phrases deserted her. She felt flustered and not a little cross.

'How did you get in here?' she managed to say at
last. 'We do not allow strange gentlemen to enter this
house.'

'Strange gentlemen? I should think not!'

He turned from the window and came towards her.

She thought idly that she had been right when she had said that the mischievous glint would soon return to his eyes. It was there now, causing her heart to beat erratically and sending those deliciously familiar chills running up and down her spine. However, it did nothing to improve her temper. How dare he walk in, looking so cool and collected, while her own thoughts were in such disorder?

'I called upon Mr and Mrs Russington yesterday,' he said, coming closer. 'I was very circumspect, but they already knew about your—ah—adventure last winter.' The glint deepened. 'Mrs Russington was extremely helpful and provided me with a note to give to that man mountain you have guarding the gate, granting me safe passage.'

'She had no right to do that,' said Nancy crossly. 'She should have written to ask my permission first.'

'And would her missive have received more response than any of mine? Oh, yes,' he continued, when her eyes flew to his face, 'it is useless to deny knowledge of them, I paid the messengers handsomely to make sure my letters reached this house and every one of them assured me that they had handed it to a member of this household. Unless your friends here are singularly deceitful, then I am confident at least some of my notes got through.'

Her eyes slid away from him. 'Yes, my lord, I received them.'

'Did you read them?'

'Only the first one.' They were all bundled up and hidden in the bottom of a drawer. She had intended to burn them, but somehow, such a final act had been beyond her. 'It was barely three weeks from our first meeting to saying goodbye. A brief incandescence, like a firework. It could never last.'

'Do you not think we should at least put it to the test?'

She put up her hand, as if to ward off a blow. 'Please, Gabriel.'

He moved away and for one searing, heart-stopping moment she thought he was leaving. Instead, he began to pace the room.

'It wasn't until Lady Craster said it that I realised how much I love you.' He spoke as if they were discussing something as mundane as the weather. 'I have never felt this way before, you see, so I did not recognise what it was, at first. Oh, I have been attracted to many women, but it has never lasted. They have never haunted my dreams and never before has their absence made me feel that I had lost a part of myself.' His perambulations brought him back to Nancy and he reached for her hands. 'I have gone through the last few months like an automaton, doing my duty during the day, but the nights! Oh, Nancy, the nights have been so cold and lonely without you.'

'Ah, don't!' She did not have the strength to remove her hands from that warm, sustaining grasp, but she turned her face away.

'Have you not missed me?' he asked her. 'Just a little bit? Perhaps you have been happy with your friends here, living this very useful life.'

'I have been *wretched*,' she admitted at last.

With a sigh he pulled her close. His long fingers

caught her chin and gently pushed it up so that she was ready to receive his kiss, long and lingering and every bit as arousing as she remembered.

'Oh, my darling,' he whispered. 'I was so afraid that you had forgotten me.'

'No, no, but I *must*.' It was an effort to break free of him and walk to the window. The rain had stopped and she could see the drift of daffodils by the far wall. Their cheery brightness taunted her. 'Don't you see, Gabriel? We live in such very different worlds, there can be no future for us. We can never have more than those few snowy weeks at Dell House.'

'Why not? Unless you do not love me?' When she did not reply he went on, 'I wrote to explain, Nancy, I want you for my wife. To live the rest of our lives together.'

Her clasped hands writhed, the knuckles showing white. 'That is not possible. I am disgraced. You know my story.'

'You ran away from your home to save yourself and survived by taking honest work. I see no disgrace in that.'

'Do you not? Society will disagree with you.'

'Then society may go hang!'

She blinked rapidly, fixing her eyes on the grey horizon.

'You are very kind, Gabriel, but it is not just my past that will condemn me. My father—the family name— is now a source of ridicule and…and scandal.'

'Scandals quickly fade, my dear, believe me.' She heard his hasty stride as he came up behind her. He took her shoulders. 'If you are worrying about what my family will say, I pray you will not. They will be delighted to see me leg shackled at last and to the daughter of an earl.' He continued, a laugh in his voice, 'A woman with thirty thousand pounds to her name, no less.'

'Not quite,' she said, momentarily distracted. 'I have given half of it to the charity, to build another Prospect House.'

'So much the better,' he said promptly. 'I have more than enough for the both of us.' He turned her towards him and grasped her hands, tucking them against his chest, where she could feel the beating of his heart, steady and sure. 'I do not need your money, my love. I do not *want* it, but I think you will feel happier to have something. It will guarantee a modicum of independence for you. We can put it in trust in case you ever wish to leave me.' She made a half-hearted protest and he tightened his grip. 'If you think I am offering you a life of unalloyed leisure, madam, let me disabuse you. I have several properties that I have rarely used. They would all benefit from your good management. And if you are determined to write your book, I will not stop you.'

'Oh, Gabriel.' She pushed him away, half-laughing, half-crying, and hunted for her handkerchief.

'What I am trying to say,' he continued, looking at her with a slight, hesitant smile playing around his mouth, 'is that I want you, on any terms I can get you, Nancy, my darling. Preferably as my wife, but I will take you as my housekeeper, or my cook, if I must. And if you are determined upon your independence, upon setting yourself up in your own establishment, which

Molly Russington tells me is your intention, then perhaps you will let me visit you. As your friend,' he said humbly. 'If you will not allow me to be your lover.'

'Oh, can you not see how impossible that is? Please, Gabriel, stop!' She mopped her eyes and looked up to find him regarding her, his face so grave and anxious that she went to him, holding out her hands. 'Oh, my darling, I could not bear to meet with you, knowing that I could not take you in my arms. Or to my bed. That would be the greatest torment possible.'

'Then marry me, Nancy. Throw in your lot with mine. We will roam the world, share adventures and grow old most disgracefully. Or not, if you prefer a quiet life,' he added, pulling her close and gently tucking a stray curl behind her ear. 'What do you say, my love? My father despairs of me making a respectable alliance. You would be the answer to his prayers. He would ensure there is no scandal attached to us. We might live at one of my properties—even Dell House, if you want to be close to the Earl.'

When she shuddered he laughed. 'No, perhaps not. Well, if you don't like any of my present houses we will buy something you *do* like where we can live, raise our beautiful children—'

'Children!'

'Yes.' He grinned down at her. 'Did I not tell you I want children? Dozens of 'em! And they will run free, causing mayhem in the house, climbing trees and careering over the park on their ponies.' His eyes softened and he ran the back of his fingers gently over her cheek. 'They will *not* be ignored by their parents and left to the care of servants. Nor will they need to amuse themselves in the kitchens. They will join us in our adventures—or, if you prefer, we will stay at home and be models of decorum and respectability.'

Some devil prompted her to say, 'I prefer the idea of embarking upon a life of adventure.'

'Then that is what we shall do, my dearest love, just as soon as we are married. Are you set upon a lavish wedding, or would a special licence and a ceremony here, among your friends, suffice? I want to make an honest woman of you. No,' he said, covering her face in kisses, 'what I *want* is to take you to the Continent, to Paris, Rome, Naples, and in every city I want to make love to you. I want to strip every piece of clothing from your body and have you naked in my bed the whole of the night. The day, too, if you wish.'

'I think it must be a special licence,' she told him, pulling his hand down and pressing it against the front of her gown.

There was no doubting the delight that shone in his eyes when he realised what she was telling him.

'A baby! You are sure?'

She nodded, blushing and laughing. 'Yes, I am sure. One of your wishes is already coming true. But that is not the only reason we should be married quickly,' she murmured, reaching up to guide his mouth back to hers, 'for I want all those other things, too, and as soon as possible!'

Epilogue

September 1817

Nancy was reclining on a daybed in the morning room. She had just returned from the nursery where she had fed young Master Gabriel and left him sleeping peacefully under the watchful eye of his nurse.

She was reading a periodical, which she waved at Gabriel when he walked into the room.

'My love, have you seen what is published in *La Belle Assemblée*?'

He leaned down to kiss her then sat by her feet. 'What does it say?'

Nancy began to read.

'"*Births: At Ravenshaw Lodge, Hampshire, to Lady Ann Ravenshaw, a son. This follows the announcement earlier this year in the* Compton Parva Courier, *reprinted here for the benefit of our Readers, of the marriage of Sir Gabriel Ravenshaw, Bart., recently elevated to his present rank for his services to the Crown, to Lady Ann Chartell, daughter of the Ninth Earl of Masserton, at All Souls' Church, Compton Parva.*

"In the absence of the lady's father, the bride was given away by Mr Charles Russington before a packed congregation, which included the groom's parents, the Marquess and Marchioness of Baxenden, and Lord Stanford, Sir Gabriel's elder brother. Among other guests of note were Lady Aspern, sister of the new Lady Ravenshaw, and her husband Lord Aspern."'

She gave a sigh.

'I cannot say I like our business being broadcast quite so publicly. The mention of our wedding makes it clear to everyone that I was with child when you married me.'

'But the mention of my parents and brother makes it equally clear that the match met with approval. A nine-day wonder, my dear. It will be forgotten quickly enough.' Gabriel took the paper from her. 'But you may have to get used to being in the public eye, especially when your book on Household Management is published in the spring.'

'But Mr Murray promised I would not be named.'

'And you will not be. It will merely read, "By a Lady" and Murray will only tell one or two people, in the strictest confidence, of course.'

'And within days it will be all over town! How tiresome!'

'Not at all.' He dropped the paper on the floor and pulled her towards him. 'I shall be very proud to be married to a celebrated author.'

For the next few minutes Nancy forgot everything

but the pleasure of being thoroughly kissed by an expert. When the kiss ended, he settled her more comfortably against him and they sat in silence for a while, listening to the birdsong outside the window.

At last she said, in a small voice, 'It might be a disaster. Cooks will dislike my recipes and housewives take offence at my advice.'

'Or it may be so successful that Murray demands another book. However, I have a solution. We can begin our tour of the Continent a little sooner that we planned. We shall set off in the spring. Baby Gabriel and his nurse can travel with us. In fact, he may have a whole entourage of his own, if you wish it. I confess I am impatient to take you to Paris and Rome, as I promised.' He pulled her on to his lap, murmuring into her ear, 'And to do all those other things I mentioned at the time.'

Nancy shivered with delight. She slipped her arms about his neck and said, with wicked innocence, 'I have forgotten just what you promised me, Gabriel. Something about removing all my clothes…'

With a growl, he tightened his hold on her.

'Then let me remind you,' he muttered. 'My wilful, wanton wife!'

* * * * *

*If you enjoyed this story
read the other books in the
Saved from Disgrace miniseries*

The Ton's Most Notorious Rake
Beauty and the Brooding Lord

*And be sure to check out these
other great reads
by Sarah Mallory*

The Duke's Secret Heir
Pursued for the Viscount's Vengeance